All she saw were the man's eyes in her rear-view mirror, but it was enough. She froze, her hand still on the gear shift lever, her mind paralyzed with fear as the wagon jerked to a stop and the engine sputtered and died. Recognition was instant, and the intent in those eyes obvious, especially to her. She opened her mouth to scream, not even thinking of using the horn; but even that was cut off as his arm came suddenly around her throat, the pain sharp and her vision blurring.

Her fingers, reaching back, knotted desperately in his long greasy hair. It was the last thing she was conscious of besides the excruciating pain . . .

Fawcett Gold Medal Books
by Richard Harper:

DEATH TO THE DANCING MASTERS

THE KILL FACTOR

RICHARD HARPER

FAWCETT GOLD MEDAL • NEW YORK

AUTHOR'S NOTE

The Kill Factor is a work of fiction. There is no Mimbres County in Arizona. There *are* illegal aliens, ranches, homicides, and sheriff's departments. Though I have attempted to recreate accurately police procedures in general, any resemblance to real departments, persons, or events is purely coincidental.

PROLOGUE

EXPLODING with murderous intent, he beat the guy with a mindless fury, his arms working like pistons, his thick-balled fists hooking and pummeling belly and ribs, jabbing and crossing to jaw and cheeks, nose and eyes—venting his anger in grunting, gasping, wordless noises.

With his rapid, hammerlike blows driving into his smaller, already stunned opponent, it was already no contest. Then he picked up a length of chain to finish the job.

"Shit," Virgil "Dutch" Masters grumbled and ground out the butt of his cigar in an ashtray made from a World War II artillery shell. He was standing beside his desk, in a small cinder-block building set in a clearing in the midst of a citrus grove near the main irrigation canal, and he continued to ignore the man standing silently by the grimy front window that overlooked the darkened yard outside.

Sighing heavily at last, Dutch settled himself into the leather-cushioned chair behind the desk and turned on an old goose-neck lamp. A window air conditioner purred contentedly near-by, and an adding machine at his elbow trailed a coil of tape into a wastebasket as he stared for a moment at the wall. The dusty head of a javalina, complete with tusks, stared back at him with glassy eyes while he collected his wits.

"I don't want any more of 'em buried on my land, Jesse,"

he said, looking again at his foreman with hard, glass-blue eyes. "It's too risky."

"They're buried deep, Dutch, those others," the foreman answered, turning around. "They'll never be found. Never even missed. Not here. The last two were up from Zacatecas, both of 'em, deep in Mexico. Came north to work like thousands of others and just disappeared. Who's to care?"

"And this last one?" Dutch asked, pushing back a blue baseball cap and scratching his receding gray crew cut. "What's his name and where's he from?"

"Enrique Vasquez. From Jalisco, down near Guadalajara. Came here alone."

"Well." Dutch got up, and his chair, relieved of his weight, squeaked sharply. "I don't want any more planted in the groves. Not anywhere on my land." He scowled, thinking, then looked at his foreman again. "Pour some booze down him and dump him in the canal."

Jesse Peralta took off his own cap and uncertainly smoothed his fingers through his thick black hair. "I don't know, Dutch—he'll be found for sure."

"So? Another wet got drunk, got in a fight, and fell in the canal—or was pushed. What difference does it make? Who's going to worry one way or the other about a dead wetback, for Christ's sake, much less trace him back here. Do it, Jesse—" He met the foreman's brooding gray gunmetal eyes. "Do it now."

Outside, the night was still and dark, with only the chirping of crickets in the surrounding citrus groves and long clouds scudding across the moon. Jesse Peralta's hulking five-ten, 190 pounds easily lifted the body of the 150-pound Mexican and carried it over to his truck, where he dumped it unceremoniously onto a canvas tarp in the back. Then he folded the tarp over the dead man, climbed into the cab, and started the engine.

Bumping over the rutted dirt trace that led toward the main irrigation canal, he still wasn't sure it was the thing to do. It was too much like a movie he had seen once—dumping a body into the water on a moonlit night. Buried, they were gone, out of sight forever. But it was Dutch's land, he reasoned, and his laborers.

The trace gave out and he turned the truck down a lane between the trees until the grove itself ended. He doused the lights as he drove out onto the cleared shoulder that edged the canal. Getting out, he drew back the edge of the tarp and lifted out the body. He carried it to the edge of the bank, laid it down, and with his boot nudged it over the steep incline into the sluggish, moonlit water. It didn't even make much of a splash.

As he was walking back to the truck, he realized he'd forgotten all about pouring a little booze into him.

A mile and a quarter downstream, a paved road crossed the same irrigation canal. And when Al Moulder hit the brakes on his ancient pickup, they grabbed, almost throwing him into a skid. But he managed to correct the sway and ground to a halt in the gravel along the shoulder, still not sure of what he had seen in his rearview mirror.

Tossing the bottle he had been nipping from into the weeds, he got out and stared back down the empty road, trying to separate things from the deep shadows and remember what he had seen. It was after midnight, but the nearly full moon was bright where it shone between the clouds, and the bridge over the canal he had just crossed stood out plainly; the bridge and a few tall cottonwoods growing along both banks, and the dark open desert on either side. That was all there was.

Yet there had been the lights of a car, traveling behind him and closing fast. Then suddenly, just as the car's headlights illuminated the bridge rails, they had swerved and disappeared, leaving the bridge as empty in the moonlight as if the car had never existed.

But he swore that it had. He just hadn't heard anything, because the radio had been blaring in his pickup, but something—and he began walking back down the road, still not absolutely certain he had seen anything at all. It was getting like that lately, after he'd been drinking. God knew he never drank much; never enough to get really drunk. Just steady. Seemed like he just drank steady these days, since Millie died.

At the bridge he found stark evidence that he hadn't been hallucinating. The old wooden guardrail on one side was broken through—splintered wide open by a sudden impact. Hustling over to the opening, he stared down at the wide canal where the water flowed, serenely undisturbed, beneath the bridge. The moonlight reflecting off the shimmering surface showed him nothing.

Hurrying now, he scurried off one end of the bridge and down the weed-grown bank. Tall reeds grew close to the canal edge here, and he began slipping and sliding in the damp earth as he worked his way around to where he could see clearly. And there it was—a car under the water, tilted kind of crazy-like, with the lights still burning, diffused and dim. Then suddenly they went out.

But the faint outline of the car was still there, and a few bubbles still disturbed the smooth flow of the water. Jesus, old Al Moulder thought, the driver! He stared around him in the darkness, as if help would suddenly appear out of no-where simply because it was needed. But there wasn't even another car in sight on the road. *He* was the only help avail-able. And he had emphysema, and he'd been drinking; and he could barely swim, anyway. What could *he* do? He decided he could try.

The canal wasn't deep. Eight, maybe ten feet; and the current wasn't that strong. Without further thought he plunged into the tepid water, only then remembering he had forgotten to take off his shoes. Straining and floundering around, he fought for the near side of the car, the driver's side. He could barely see as he caught hold of the door handle and tried to open it. No use. But he realized the window was open and the driver was slumped over the wheel; he even managed to catch hold of a handful of shirt. But that was all he could do, and he was nearly out of breath. Panicky now, he turned to fight his way back to the surface, his mind registering something else he had seen—or thought he saw: the billowing white skirt of a woman at the edge of the seat next to the driver; like she was down on the floor.

Surfacing with his tight, diseased lungs straining for air, he knew he couldn't do it. How long had they been down there now anyway—how long before an oxygen-starved brain was useless?

He clung to the rough cement siding of the canal a moment, half in and half out of the water and wheezing heavily, wondering if he even had enough strength to pull himself out of the water. Maybe he would drown, too. The sudden clutch of fear and adrenalin moved him. Clawing up the slanted bank back into the weeds, he rolled over and sat up, still breathing with difficulty, and stared down at the barely visible outline of the car. Even the bubbles had stopped now.

They were dead, he thought grimly. There was nothing he could do. Nothing anyone could do now. But he staggered up and hurried wearily along the muddy bank back to the road anyway, heading for his truck. He had to report it. But he had no CB, and the nearest phone he knew of was three miles away, in Mimbres Junction.

In a Mexican border town eighty miles to the south, Arturo Vasquez, aged fourteen, waited in the shadows beneath a battered palm that stood outside a squat adobe bar with a faded sign over the door: CANTINA ROJA. He was there to meet a "coyote" who, for a hundred American dollars, would smuggle him into the United States and guarantee him work on a farm near a place called Mimbres Junction.

A revolving red light mounted above the door of the bar lit the surrounding darkness with an eerie red glow as cars came and went from the dusty parking area. Arturo wondered how long he would have to wait. The coyote had said eleven o'clock, but Arturo knew it was now after midnight, and nothing like the truck that had been described to him had pulled up outside the bar.

Squatting down again beside a plastic water jug and a multicolored fiber bolsa that held all his belongings, he wondered what he would do if the smuggler did not come. He did not know if he would have the courage to attempt the illegal crossing into the United States alone.

But the truck came at last, a scarred old U.S. Army vehicle

with a big white star still emblazoned on the door, its slatted sides loosely stacked with mesquite firewood. The truck had only one headlight, and even it winked out as the machine lumbered onto the dirt parking lot and shuddered to a halt. There were two men in the cab, and one remained behind the wheel while the other got out and urinated beside the front wheel. Then he sauntered over to Arturo. "You bring your money?" he asked.

Arturo nodded.

"All of it?" The man's breath was rank with whisky. "A hundred American?"

"Sí." The boy started to dig the bills out of his pocket, but the coyote waved him off.

"Wait here, muchacho. I've got to go inside." And he disappeared into the cantina.

Minutes later he came out again with two more men who were also carrying fiber bolsas and plastic jugs, and he waved Arturo over to the truck. There he collected the payments from all of them and led them around to the back. Dropping the tailgate, he exposed several long coffinlike spaces framed out beneath the firewood, some of them already occupied by people. Arturo couldn't tell if they were men or women, but the coyote hissed for them to hurry and climb in, "Vamos, hombres—ándale!"

Picking one of the empty spaces and pushing his jug and bolsa ahead of him, he crawled into the tight close darkness beneath the wood. Lying on his side against the outer edge of the truck, he found he could see through the narrow cracks between the slats as the truck started up, its engine coughing. Then it lurched heavily on bad shocks as it pulled out of the parking lot and turned east on the blacktop road that paralleled the border, headed away from the town and into the desert.

Twenty minutes later the truck pulled over at a small roadside shack where a lantern burned on a pole outside. Arturo recognized it as an agricultural check station for Mexican produce, and the truck engine rumbled roughly in idle while the driver talked to a man who had come out of the shack.

Then the gears grated and the truck moved forward again, continuing on down the road through the darkness for nearly an hour before suddenly turning north, off the pavement, jolting easily across the soft sand on its dual rear tires, then onto rocky hard-pan desert covered with the shadowy forms of cacti and greasewood and scattered mesquites, the vegetation lighted now by a nearly full moon that had emerged from behind a cloud.

When they passed a tall, pointed cement column that rose starkly against the moonlit sky, Arturo remembered it was the national boundary marker he had been told to watch for, since the wire-mesh border fence had extended only a few miles beyond the port of entry. Somehow he had thought he would feel differently once he had crossed the line, but it certainly didn't look any different; the same scrubby desert growth, the same moon hovering in a sky now sparkling with stars as the clouds cleared.

The old truck jolted and jerked along without even its one eye now, traveling only by moonlight and working its way across sandy washes and following winding arroyos, and even climbing over small rocky hills. Arturo's muscles soon tired of the constant bracing with his fingers and toes as he was bounced and slammed along with the others in the tight confines under the wood. He was wedged in too tightly to change his cramped position, or even to maneuver his water bottle around so he could drink.

He had no idea how much time had passed. He was beginning to think the jarring, jolting ride would never end when suddenly the truck stopped. The engine shut down. Its innards gurgled and growled in the still desert night. Then he heard the door squeak open. Boots crunched on the rocky earth outside, and the tailgate rattled and banged down. "Everybody out," a voice commanded. *"Vamos, pobrecitos— dese prisa!"*

Stiffly, they emerged from the crawl spaces beneath the load of firewood and stood beside the truck, stretching and stamping some life back into cramped muscles as they looked warily around. There was nothing to be seen except the dark, endless desert. Even the moon had set. Arturo, glancing at his traveling companions, noticed now that four were men, two were boys not much older than himself, and one was a young woman.

Two of the men had turned aside and were relieving themselves when the driver of the truck suddenly drew a revolver from his belt and pointed it at them all. "End of the line, my children," he said. "You're on your own now."

His companion had taken the woman by the arm and was pulling her away from the truck. She struggled briefly, then walked slowly with him behind a bush. The others stared in shocked silence.

Then one of the men said to the coyote, "You're supposed to take us to a farm—a town—it was agreed. There was to be work there. You were to get us past the Migra checkpoints. You took our money—"

"*Cállate, cabrón!*" the coyote snapped. They could all hear the rutting sounds behind the bush, and the woman's sobbing. But no one dared even look in that direction as the coyote shrugged. "A change of plans, that's all. The Migra patrols are putting too much pressure on us— we can't chance going any farther." Then he waved the gun menacingly. "Now move out, all of you. If I'm caught going back, I'm just a poor woodcutter who strayed across the line by mistake." And turning, he stepped behind the bush to take his turn with the woman while his companion came out and held the gun.

"How do we know which way to go?" one of the men asked.

The man who held the gun now pointed it overhead at the starry outline of the Big Dipper. "North," he said gruffly. "Go north. You will find something. Just watch out for the rattlesnakes."

As if to emphasize his warning, a real coyote's mournful wail rolled out of the darkness as the group picked up their bolsas and jugs and started out, and Arturo fell in with the rest. They walked north through the vastness of a desert night, except one of the men who straggled, looking back, as if waiting for the woman.

*   *   *

A murder; an apparent accident; and another batch of illegal Mexican workers crossing the border. Three incidents that took place on the same warm September night, a little after midnight; all within an eighty-mile radius of Mimbres Junction, Arizona; and all within the jurisdiction of Detective-Sergeant Douglas Elgin Roberts, homicide specialist with the Mimbres County Sheriff's Department.

ONE

DOUG ROBERTS' footsteps echoed through the long empty corridor of the county morgue. Pushing through the glass-windowed double doors at the end of the hall, he glanced around, found no one there, and sat down in an old captain's chair that he tilted back against the wall. He stared up at the big round face of the clock on the opposite wall. It was ten past six in the morning. He waited, dozing.

At eighteen past, a young thin-lipped white-coated attendant came in, trailing a faint odor of formaldehyde. Nodding, he went wordlessly to the bright rows of glistening steel drawers that banked one wall.

"Good morning to you, too," Roberts said quietly, tilting his chair back.

"Sorry," the attendant answered, "haven't had my coffee yet. What are you doing here, anyway—wasn't it an accident?"

"That's what I'm supposed to find out."

"Well, this is one of them." The attendant pulled open the heavy drawer, which rolled easily on its casters. "Brought in a couple of hours ago. Still damp, still fully clothed, just like they found 'em. Sheriff's deputies pulled 'em out. The car was still in the canal, but they probably hauled it out by now. Autopsy's scheduled for later this morning." He dragged open a second drawer. "Interesting though," he added, a smirk beneath his pencil-thin mustache. "The girl's not wearing any underpants."

11

Roberts looked at the attendent. "You naughty boy—you peeked." The sonofabitch is actually blushing, he thought, and took out his notebook. He looked down at the body of the man. Fortyish; thinning brown hair; a mole near his chin; about twenty pounds overweight. He lifted the dead man's right hand, studied it, turned it over. Manicured nails. He looked at the attendant. "Office worker, businessman?"

"Close. Banker. Don't you recognize him?"

"No. Should I?"

"Hell, that's Edwin Winters, a prominent man down in Mimbres Junction. President of the Rotary, head of the United Fund drive, Citizen of the Year three years running. He even ran for county supervisor last year and almost won. A hell of a guy."

"No shit. I guess I oughta get down that way more often. Or maybe I just don't step out in the right circles." He moved to the girl. Twentyish; platinum-blond hair worn shoulder length, though tangled and matted now. An odd twist to a once-pretty face, as if she'd been shocked by her own death. "Who's she? And don't tell me another pillar of the community."

"Oh no, just a teller at his bank—a new one, Kathleen Cole, age twenty-three." The simpering smile was there again. "I suppose they were lovers."

Roberts ignored him, picking up the girl's hand; slender, light, and lifeless. Long fingernails—he looked more closely—phony fingernails; two were broken off, and the real ones were bitten down to the quick. He laid the hand down gently. It had never set easy with him, no matter how often he faced it—a wasted human life.

"I really don't understand it," the attendant was saying. "He was a strong family man, a deacon in the church!"

"I know—a hell of a guy. A real homebody."

"He was!"

Roberts looked at the attendant. "Don't take it personally. Did they say which one was driving?"

"He was. A witness saw the car go off the bridge in his rearview mirror. He dove in and tried to get them out, but the guy was an old man, and sick. He called the deputies and they pulled 'em out. Dead, of course. The banker was behind the wheel, the girl opposite but down on the floor. Her neck's broken.''

The double swing doors burst open at that moment and a young Mexican-American came in: thick black hair, black eyes, a bushy black mustache. When he stuck out his hand and flashed a smile, his perfect teeth lit up the already bright room. Roberts couldn't help looking behind him for the trail of broken hearts.

"Hi, I'm Gomez. Transfer from Robbery. Inocencio Gomez. What have we got?"

"What the hell are you doing here?" Roberts shook his hand woodenly.

"I'm your new partner—supposed to get some Homicide experience.''

"Well, get it someplace else. I told 'em I'd work without a partner. And I'll be damned if I'll work with anybody named Innocence."

Gomez's ingenuous smile refused to go away. "Then call me Rabbit. That's my nickname. I'll explain it sometime over coffee."

"Our relationship's not gonna last that long." He turned back to the two corpses and continued with his notes.

"These the victims?" Gomez persisted, stepping up beside him.

"Yeah—the car went off a bridge into the main canal last night, just outside Mimbres Junction."

"But not an accident?"

Roberts shrugged.

"Hey, the gent's fly is unzipped," Gomez commented, looking over his shoulder. "Does that mean something?"

Roberts looked at him. "You're very observant. They teach you that in Robbery? The lady is without benefit of panties too—our friend here has already checked. So I suppose you can put the two together and come up with the same reasonable conclusion he has."

"Sure." Gomez grinned. "They were friends."

In the awkward silence that followed, Inocencio Gomez

finally took a good look at the two victims. As he crossed himself, his dark lean features grew increasingly sober.

"*Jesucristo,*" he whispered, "death is always so goddamned final, isn't it, man?"

"If you can look at it that way, maybe there's hope for you in Homicide after all." Roberts closed his notebook and looked over at the attendant. "The autopsy report?"

"As soon as . . ." the attendant answered lamely, and shrugged.

"This week would be nice—since it's only Monday." Roberts turned to Gomez. "C'mon, Gomez. If you insist on working Homicide, let's go have a look at the car and the scene."

In the large L-shaped building that housed the Mimbres County Jail and Sheriff's Department, they climbed the wide marble stairs to the second floor, and Roberts halted in front of a door marked: LIEUTENANT—HOMICIDE DIVISION. "I've gotta stop in here. You check out a car and I'll meet you in front in fifteen minutes."

When he opened the door, Lt. Walter Lang and one of the newer secretaries in the pool sprang apart. "Jesus H. Christ, Roberts." The lieutenant spun around in his chair as the girl blushed and straightened her skirt. "Don't you know how to knock?"

"I never knock, Chief," he smiled. "Miss too much that way."

"Okay, Lucy." The lieutenant motioned the girl away. "I'll have more dictation later."

Roberts waited until the girl had gone and the lieutenant's stormy features had settled into their normal scowl. The chief was a hypocritical prude, and Roberts never missed a chance to rub it in. "Dictation, Chief?" he quipped. "C'mon, your hand was halfway to Paradise when I walked in."

"Shut up, Roberts." With his shaved dome and ever-present sunglasses, the chief affected a kind of half-assed Kojak look, but with a perpetually stinking cigar stuck in his petulant lips instead of a lollipop. He didn't offer a cigar to the detective-sergeant as he clipped a new one for himself and growled, "I

know what you want, and you can forget it. You're stuck
with him." He fired his desk lighter and sucked heavily,
loosing great clouds of blue smoke toward the ceiling.

"You should have given him to Vice, Chief. He's too
pretty for homicide."

"You don't have to marry him, you just have to work with
him. You think it was my idea? It's this damned Affirmative
Action shit—spics and niggers—the Department's starting to
crawl with 'em."

"I'm not complaining about his race, I just don't need a
new, inexperienced partner. I've broken in three of them this
year. Give me a break."

"Give *you* a break? Jesus Christ, Roberts, you're the
biggest pain in the butt I've got! Anyway, it's decided. They
want him to get some homicide experience, probably gonna
kick him upstairs. He's bright enough. Street-wise and college, too. And a good record in Robbery—two citations and a
lot of busts."

"So what's he gonna learn from me?"

"Nothing good, Roberts, nothing good. But like I said, it
wasn't my idea. You want to know the truth, it was the
captain's. He figures Gomez will go so far wrong with you
guidin' him, he'll never be able to get the fuck straightened
out. Either that or you'll drive him goddamned bananas and
he'll quit. Now is that straight enough for you?"

Detective-Sgt. Douglas Elgin Roberts smiled wryly. "So
the chief of detectives doesn't like Mexicans."

Lt. Lang leaned forward, growling around his cigar,
"Goddammit, Roberts, you didn't hear anything like that
from me—now get the fuck out on that Winters case."

Roberts headed for the door. His hand was on the knob
when the lieutenant's voice rang sweetly once more. "And
send Gomez in here before you go—I want to talk to him."

Roberts turned. "He's already checking out a car. By the
time we get to Mimbres—"

"*Now*, goddammit, Roberts, I want to see him *now*—that's
an A-number-one-official-fucking order, so if you don't want
a charge of—" But the door closed on the lieutenant's final
words.

*   *   *

Detective Inocencio Gomez knocked lightly on the lieutenant's door and entered. "You wanted to see me, sir?"

Lt. Lang eyed him speculatively before laying aside his cigar. "I'll make this short and sweet, Gomez. I didn't ask for your transfer here, and I don't know what they told you in Robbery about your new partner, but if it was anything good they were lying in their teeth. You're to work with him, learn from him, but don't get involved in any of his funny ways—he's a loser."

Gomez flashed his winning smile. "That's not the word around the Department, sir."

"So what's the word around the Department?"

"That he's the best damned homicide specialist you've got, and you've got some good ones."

"That's bullshit," Lang scoffed.

"If you say so, sir."

"And don't smart-mouth me, Gomez. I get enough of that from Roberts."

"No, sir." The detective's winning smile had faded.

"Just do your job. He's had some success, I'll admit. But I'll just warn you this once—you start copying his unorthodox methods and you'll get burned right along with him. He's had as many suspensions as he's had citations. Now get lost."

Checked out in an unmarked Sheriff's Department car, they drove the forty miles to Mimbres Junction through irrigated farmlands laid out in quarter-mile rows between barren mountain ranges that had shaped a broad fertile valley eons ago.

It was late September, but the long hot summer still hung on. At least it was cool in the air-conditioned car. Roberts, letting Gomez drive, slouched beside him and chewed on the stem of an unlit pipe. He seldom lit it anymore; it was too much trouble. He wondered if that was a sign of mid-life crisis.

The morning sun was slanting through the car's glass at an angle that showed him a partial reflection of his face, and he thought about the birthday he had coming up—his forty-seventh. His tousled, graying hair seemed to recede at the temples a little more each day, and his rugged features looked walked on by a hundred winters.

It just wasn't worth it, he decided. His ex was right; he'd never amounted to a tinker's dam, because all he ever really wanted to do was solve murders. And the killing went on and on. There was never any end to it.

But the deliberate taking of a human life had always disturbed him deeply. He could never understand it. There was always a motive of course; at least a reason, an excuse. And most murderers knew their victims; they were usually related. But the actual why of it, the point at which one human's brain clicked in some strange way and he became a god with the right to deprive another human of his life—that was what always eluded him. No one had that right. Life was too precious. It was too short a time from here to there for any man. There were too many natural and unnatural forces working against his making it, without another man taking it from him before his time. He thought it was the same with the stupidity called war, but at least the risk there was usually deliberate and known to both sides.

"Roberts," Gomez's voice startled him out of his reverie, "—that Scotch?"

"What—?" Roberts looked at him. "Scotch? No, Scots. Scotch is the whisky."

"Oh, sorry." Gomez flashed his teeth again. "I'm Mexican."

"I'd 've never guessed." His words were stroked with sarcasm.

But Gomez was unabashed. "I'm part Indian too—Opata. And I guess even part Negro, if you go back far enough. Some of my ancestors were black slaves brought over by the Spaniards—before they discovered how to enslave los Indios."

"Terrific—a history lesson. Now I'll give you one. My ancestors ran around the wilds of Britain naked and painted themselves blue—if you go back far enough."

"Jesus, man, no kidding?"

"Just drive, Gomez."

Gomez started to light up a slim black cigarillo.

"Those cancer sticks'll kill you. Don't smoke 'em around me—unless my pipe's lit, too."

The younger detective shrugged and put the cigarillo away. "You married, man?" he asked.

"No. Divorced."

"Tough. Any kids?"

"One—a boy thirteen. He lives with her, and she's getting remarried. Gonna try a lawyer this time. Any more questions?"

Gomez flashed his smile all over the car. "Married, I'm not. No one woman could handle all this."

"And modest, too."

"I said I'd tell you why they call me Rabbit."

"I don't think I want to hear."

"It's not just for my exceptional abilities on the football field."

"Football?" Roberts stared at him, remembering now. "Yeah, Rabbit Gomez, a running back at the university—that was you, huh? How come you never turned pro?"

"Because I wanted to be a cop."

"Jesus," Roberts shook his head.

"I was too small for the pros anyway, and actually I was tagged Rabbit a long time ago, in high school, but not for football. I played there, too, a real Saturday hero. In those days Mexicans still lived in one special part of town, and I was never allowed to date an Anglo. But I got even. I managed to knock up three of them by my senior year."

"No shit," Roberts stared at him again. "Well, you sure as hell weren't 'chicken' Gomez, but I'm surprised you ever find time for any detective work. And to think your mother named you Innocence—turn here." He pointed down a dusty side road, and the car made the turn on squealing tires, the dust boiling up over the hood as it lurched in the ruts. "And slow down for Christ's sake. I'm not immortal."

"So you never did tell me what we've got, man," Gomez said, easing up on the gas. "Suicide? A double murder?"

"That's lesson number one, Gomez. Don't jump to any conclusions. What we've got remains to be seen."

Citrus groves lined both sides of the road, which paralleled a broad irrigation canal, with more orchards on the far side.

The long motionless blades of wind machines showed here and there above the trees. "How much farther?" Gomez asked.

"We're almost there. We took a back road so we don't have to go through the town." He pointed. A short distance ahead, the canal flowed under a bridge that supported a paved road. Several vehicles were parked around the bridge on both sides of the canal. Even at this distance they could see the shattered rail.

Two sheriff's cars, with flashing red lights and stars on their doors, were parked beside a lime-green carryall with wire mesh over the windows and the round logo of the U.S. Border Patrol emblazoned on its side. The whole area had been blocked off with rope linked to sawhorses, and inside the perimeter a fourth car had been pulled out of the canal. Hooked by the front to a tow truck, it was still dripping water, and everyone was grouped around it.

Pulling up alongside the barrier, the two detectives got out and stepped over the rope. Since Roberts knew one of the deputies, he introduced Gomez as his new partner. The deputy introduced them to the others, then pushed back his stiff-brim hat and scratched his head. "I don't know what you're gonna make out of this one, Sergeant. We just now got the car hauled out, and by the time it cleared the water the trunk was hanging open—and look what we found."

The others parted to reveal a tarp-covered, oblong shape lying on the ground at the rear of the car. When the two detectives walked over, the Border Patrolman stooped and drew the tarp aside.

"A third body," the deputy explained. "It was caught on the rear bumper. A Mexican."

TWO

"WHO laid him out like this?" Roberts asked. "If he was caught on the rear bumper?"

"He fell off as the car was hauled out," a deputy said. "We had to fish him out."

"Terrific." Roberts had pushed the tarp out of the way and was kneeling—not touching, just looking. Gomez stood a little behind him, and the others had gathered around, stretching their necks to watch. "Hasn't been in the water long," Roberts observed quietly. "A few hours maybe—could have gone in the same time as the others, I suppose. God, but he's taken a beating." He stared at the puffy, lacerated face, the raw cuts and bruises that immersion in the canal had only partially softened.

"Maybe he's got ID," someone said. "Looks like a farm worker."

"Probably a wetback," the Border Patrol agent said, looking up. "No pun intended. When they get his prints I can check it out. We'll have a record if he's ever been picked up—his name, Social Security number if he used one, home state in Mexico or wherever. That's about all—unless he's got a criminal record."

"Thanks," Roberts said. "Every little bit helps."

They all looked around as the county coroner's station wagon wheeled in off the road and stopped in a boil of dust.

"Here's the forensics team," someone said, moving the barrier to let them in.

"And here come the newshounds," the Border Patrolman added.

A TV news van was trying to pull in behind the station wagon as Roberts turned to the deputy-in-charge. "Keep the area secured, Sergeant. Nobody gets near anything but the lab boys. Let the tow truck go on back. They can pick it up when we're through."

"What are we gonna tell the reporters, Sergeant?" Gomez asked Roberts. "They'll be all over us in a minute."

Doug Roberts smiled shrewdly. "Gomez, I'm putting you in charge of that department. *You* give 'em the story."

"Me?" The detective's own easy smile was suddenly gone. "What the hell am *I* gonna tell 'em, man? We don't *know* anything yet!"

"That's why I'm letting you handle the interview."

While forensics went over the car from front to back slowly, carefully, noting everything, sampling everything, a police photographer took pictures and Roberts spent most of his time measuring and sketching the scene. Then he stood there studying that open trunk.

It was empty except for the spare tire, a jack, and a long-angled bar that served as lug wrench and jack handle, all of which rested on water-soaked burlap bags that were spotted with a black substance that looked like tar.

"Water's kind of messed everything up," he told the head lab man, "but get everything you can, especially inside."

"Looks like a pretty clean wash job to me, Sergeant," the lab man said, shaking his head.

"All the more reason to be extra thorough, so humor me—vacuum everything. There probably aren't any prints either, but try. And sample any dirt inside the car, including the trunk. I want to try and match it with any dirt left in the Mexican's clothes. I need to know if he was actually stuffed in the trunk, or riding inside the car. And I want dirt samples from both banks of the canal and both shoulders of the road.

There don't seem to be any tracks around. No footprints, no tire—''

The head lab man was giving him a gap-toothed grin. "How about we just solve the fucking case for you, Sergeant, and you can go have a beer?''

"That would be fine, too.''

"Hey, Sergeant Roberts!'' the second lab man called him around to the other side of the car. The rear doors were standing open and the lab man was pointing inside. A butcher knife lay on the floor, just under the back seat.

Picking it up deftly with his handkerchief, Roberts looked at it closely. "If it had any stains, they probably washed off,'' he said, dropping it in the plastic bag the lab man held open, "but check it anyway.'' And he marked it as evidence.

Besides the knife, they found the usual clutter under the seats: six pennies, a couple of soda straws, gum wrappers, a set of unused tools. And in the glove compartment a flashlight, a box of Kleenex, and the car's registration in a plastic case. "It was the banker's car,'' the lab man noted. They also found a state road map, a tire gauge, and a pair of women's black panties. The lab man grinned lecherously, holding them up. "We'll check these, too.'' A small red rose and the word "Sunday'' were embroidered delicately on one corner.

"At least she had the day right,'' Roberts said, watching everything go into the plastic bags.

They saved the body of the Mexican for last. Roberts watched them bag his hands and then check him out. "How long in the water?'' the detective asked.

"A few hours, give or take.''

"Give or take what?''

The head lab man looked up and smiled again. The gap between his front teeth was really impressive. "C'mon, Sergeant, you'll get the report.''

Roberts glanced over toward the TV news van where the guy was shooting film and Gomez appeared to be charming the young female reporter. When he looked back, the other lab man was placing the contents of the dead man's pockets into plastic bags too: a key that looked like it might fit a footlocker; a rusty pocketknife; a wet slip of paper that looked like a cash-register receipt; a single, soggy dollar bill; a soaked leather wallet, hand-tooled but empty; a soggy pack of Marlboros; and a wet and wrinkled matchbook from a bar in Mimbres Junction called the Watering Hole.

"And this." With his gloved hand the lab man held out a tightly folded letter, written in Spanish. "Looks like the ink ran a little, but maybe it'll be legible when it dries."

"Nothing else to indicate he might be from Mexico," Roberts noted almost to himself. "No pesos or lottery tickets, or Mexican cigarettes." He looked over at the Border Patrolman who had walked up beside him.

"If he's a wetback," the agent said, "he's not a recent arrival—look at his feet, a decent pair of boots. Most of 'em arrive in sandals."

"You think he drowned?" Roberts asked the head lab man. "He sure took a savage beating."

Again the gap-toothed grin. "You're pushing, Sergeant. I'd say the beating had a lot to do with his death, but who knows? The autopsy may find a bullet in him. You'll just have to read the report."

"I'd rather wait for the movie," Roberts said.

When the lab men were done, and the coroner's wagon had left with the body, Roberts told the sheriff's deputy he could send the tow truck back for the car. Then he watched them all leave, including the Border Patrolman in his green carryall and the TV news van.

Gomez walked back over, smiling.

"I guess you didn't find public relations too bad a chore, huh?" Roberts asked him.

"*Híjola*—man, did you dig that chick? I made this case sound like the biggest thing since *Helter-Skelter*. And I got her phone number!"

"Terrific. I hope she gives you the crabs." He turned around and stared again at the wrecked car, its trunk and doors still hanging open like a ravaged insect's wings, its grill and front bumper nearly torn off.

"So what happened here, man?" Gomez was still smiling. "Have you solved the case without me?"

Roberts looked at his new partner. "We have not yet begun to fight. We've got three bodies now, and a wrecked car, and they found a butcher knife on the floor of the back seat. And none of it fits."

"You mean the knife's not the murder weapon."

"Not unless the autopsy finds something that wasn't obvious. We don't even know there *was* a murder."

"Come on—with a body in the trunk?"

"We also don't know the body was *in* the trunk. It was caught on the rear bumper when the car was brought up, and the trunk happened to be open. But the windows were open, too. Maybe the body washed out of the car itself and lodged on the bumper."

"Jesus, man." Gomez cupped a light to a slim, brown cigarillo. "Do you always complicate your cases like this?"

"Okay, Sherlock, what do *you* think happened?"

"Easy, man, with your kind of logic it wasn't murder at all. The banker and the girl were smuggling a wetback in the trunk and they stopped off somewhere for a quickie, maybe had a little too much to drink, and accidentally drove off the bridge. The *mojado* wasn't beaten, he got banged up with that jack and tire iron flying around inside the trunk and he drowned just like them. It's as simple as that."

"It is, huh? If it's as simple as that, they wouldn't need us. And what makes you think he's a wetback, anyway?"

"Shit, man, I could tell *that* by looking at him. I'll bet you a steak dinner."

"He did have a letter written in Spanish, which you can translate later if it's legible, but nothing identified as Mexican was found in his pockets. And he wasn't wearing sandals. You still want to bet?"

"A bet's a bet, Sergeant." He watched Roberts turn and walk out onto the bridge and stand there, studying the opening in the rail. And then he followed him. "Do we really have to sample everything—look at everything?"

"That's right, everything. You never know with a homicide what's going to be evidence and what isn't, so you look at everything. The sorting out comes later." Roberts was stepping off the path the vehicle must have taken. "He was clipping right along," he seemed to be talking mostly to himself now, "and then just whipped the wheel over and went through the rail."

"No skid marks," Gomez commented, coming behind him. "He didn't even hit the brakes."

Roberts looked around and smiled. "An astute observation, Watson."

"So—suicide? A double suicide?"

"There you go, jumping to conclusions again. Suicide, with a Mexican in the trunk?"

"You said he wasn't in the trunk. Maybe he was just swimming in the canal and the car landed on top of him."

"With his boots on? And I said *maybe* he wasn't in the trunk. Maybe he was. But you've got a point. Maybe he was trying to swim *across* the canal—even with his boots on. Who knows?"

"Jesus," Gomez shook his head, dropping the butt of his smoke and grinding it into the pavement. "How do you ever decide about anything on a case, Sergeant?"

"I just let the evidence accumulate. I let the evidence decide. And it does, eventually. So let's wait for the autopsy."

"Meanwhile it can drive us bananas."

"Welcome to Homicide. Now c'mon, till we find out if you owe me that steak, I'll let you buy me a beer."

Gomez glanced at his watch. "It's nearly noon, Sergeant, let's go find a taco joint."

"Okay, but then we'll have to hunt up that witness—old man Moulder—see if he can't remember something."

But back at their car Roberts paused once more, staring around them at the scene; at the bridge with its shattered railing; at the smooth-flowing canal; and at the wrecked car. It all just didn't quite compute.

The detective-sergeant got behind the wheel himself, and as the tow truck came back down the road toward them, he started the engine. "You know," he said, as if still thinking out loud, "all the car windows were open. So it filled quickly and sank. Otherwise, it might have floated long enough for them to get out—at least the driver." He looked over at his partner. "It was a warm, muggy night; and the car had air conditioning. So why do you suppose the windows were rolled down?"

"Jesus," Rabbit Gomez muttered incredulously.

THREE

DAWN that morning found Arturo Vasquez twenty-six miles inside the U.S. border and still traveling north.

The woman had caught up with the others after she was freed by the smugglers. But an argument had ensued as to what to do and where to go, and the group had split up. The woman and one man had turned back toward Mexico, giving up their plan to work in the North. Two boys had gone with them. But two of the men had a map; and after consulting it with the lighted stub of a candle, they had decided to turn east, heading across the desert toward a railroad where they might catch a freight bound for El Paso.

Miguel Ramirez, the oldest of the group, had argued vehemently against all of this; and Arturo, fearful but still full of his own plans, had sided with him. So the two of them continued to follow the Big Dipper north, certain they could still find Mimbres Junction, their original destination.

Unknown to both of them, they had made the only fortunate choice of the group. A U.S. Border Patrol jeep, cruising the dark desert behind them and cutting for sign with its headlights and a spotlight mounted on the windshield frame, had found the group's tracks shortly after the smugglers had abandoned them.

The agents had already picked up the woman's group and handcuffed them in the back of the jeep. But after following the tracks of the two that went east for over an hour, they lost them on hardpan and gravel, and near dawn they gave up and turned back. A Border Patrol plane would sight their bodies three days later, a mile from the railroad, where they had died of thirst in the near 100-degree heat.

For Miguel Ramirez and his fourteen-year-old companion, dawn had also brought the fierce desert heat, and the thirst, too. But by eleven o'clock they had reached a creaking windmill, rising out of the desert scrub; and beneath it was a stone cistern used for watering cattle.

Pushing aside the scum of green algae, they drank and filled their water jugs, and then sat down in a thin ribbon of shade to rest, their backs against the cool stone of the cistern. "*Ay, qué buena suerte, chamaco,*" the old man said, "we are safe now." He had tugged a tobacco sack from his shirt pocket by the string, and separating a thin sheaf of brown paper he began to build a smoke. "I remember this place from a long time ago. When I was a *vaquero*."

"You have been here before?" Arturo had removed his straw hat and was wiping out the sweat band with his bandana.

The old man grunted. "I have jumped the line many times, *chamaco*." He tugged the string of his tobacco sack tight with his teeth and returned it to his pocket. "Mostly in Texas or California. I usually cross alone, but it had been so long since I was in Arizona I didn't trust my memory, and I foolishly paid those coyotes to guide me." He moistened the seam of the cigarette with his tongue and twisted one end of it tight. "But I remember this windmill. I worked cattle near here—five, six years ago. We are less than a day's walk now from Mimbres Junction." He had placed the brown cigarette between his lips, and he offered the sack to Arturo. "Smoke?"

Arturo nodded, fumbling awkwardly with the makings but trying not to show he was as much a novice at smoking as at illegal entries. He spilled a lot of tobacco, but he got it rolled as the old man smiled, exposing yellowed and missing teeth framed by the white stubble of his beard. Scratching a match against the rough stone of the cistern, Miguel lit first his own and then Arturo's cigarette. "There should be plenty of work around Mimbres Junction, *chamaco*," he said, shaking out the match.

Arturo coughed as the rank smoke hit the membranes of his nose and throat, but he managed to smile manfully. "I'm looking for my uncle. Enrique Vasquez. He's working somewhere around Mimbres Junction. He picks up his mail at the post office there."

"There are many farms and ranches in that area," the old man said. "Cotton, cattle, citrus—why do you need to find him?"

"My father—his brother—is sick and cannot work our farm. The family needs him at home now, and since I am the oldest, I am to take his place in the North."

"Well, *chamaco*," the old man grunted, "you are a small one to take the place of a man."

"I can work hard," Arturo argued indignantly, puffing at the cigarette even while hating the foul taste. "I have always worked hard—understand?"

Miguel Ramirez understood only too well. And reaching into his bolsa he shared an onion wrapped in a tortilla with the boy who was almost a reflection of himself—many years ago. He too had been the oldest in a large family, yanked early and suddenly into manhood, almost without ever having tasted childhood. Raised amid the grinding poverty of the slums around Mexico City, he had been apprenticed to an upholsterer. But he had had many trades in his lifetime since then. And of all of them he had liked farming best; the smell of fresh-turned fields, the closeness to the earth. But it had always been on other men's farms, never his own. For him there had been no agrarian revolution. The *ricos* still ruled the land.

"You will have to work hard here in the North, too," he told the boy, rising stiffly and stretching. "I can guarantee when you work for the gringos, you always work hard. But at least there is work to be found. Not like in Mexico, eh?"

"I always found work," Arturo answered proudly. He had finished eating but was still struggling with the cigarette. "But the pay is so small—seventy or eighty pesos a day— maybe four dollars American. I have heard that four dollars can be made in an hour here in the North."

Miguel laughed. "Perhaps—if you are very lucky—and in

the big cities like Phoenix or Los Angeles. But not on the ranches around Mimbres Junction.''

"Then why are you going there?'' Arturo had got to his feet too, wetting his fingers and pinching out his cigarette before tucking the butt in his pocket for later.

Miguel shrugged expressively. "It's a place to start again. I'll only stay a little while and then move on. Where do you come from, you and your uncle?''

"From Jalisco. My village is near Guadalajara. I made trinkets out of leather and wood and peddled them to the *turistas* in the city. I will have my own shop one day.''

"Yes,'' the old man mused, "perhaps that too, if you have luck.'' He too had dreamed, and he pinched a last drag from his own cigarette. "You are young and strong, and so is your dream, my friend. Maybe you will make enough here in the North to help your family and buy your shop, too.'' But he didn't believe it. "Now we'd better go, *chamaco*, before we take root here.''

As they continued north through the blaze of afternoon, the boy noticed that there was less desert and more cultivated land. They crossed two dirt roads, and for several hours followed a power line where the only sound was the wind singing in the wires overhead. They avoided several isolated ranch houses, though Miguel said they could probably get work there and not even go into Mimbres Junction. "The more people,'' he explained, "the greater the risk of being picked up by a Migra patrol.''

"Then stay,'' the boy answered. "I can find my own way now.''

"No,'' the old man smiled, "together we will find a place where we will not get caught.''

"The place where my uncle works is well hidden,'' Arturo suggested. "He wrote us about it. The Migra officers seldom bother them, and when they do there are many places to hide. It is a large citrus farm.''

"But your uncle neglected to tell you the name of this marvelous place—eh, *chamaco?*''

"We wrote him that I was coming to replace him, but got

no answer before I left. I didn't think he would be too hard to find.''

"Perhaps—but if the Migra couldn't find him, how can you?''

It was a good question, but one that remained unanswered as the sun finally dipped below a distant mountain range, and the daylight slowly faded into long purple shadows that gave way suddenly to night. And they continued walking north through the warm September darkness.

FOUR

AL MOULDER had nothing to add to the original police report. The old man's story had been simple and straightforward when Detective-Sgt. Doug Roberts interviewed him Monday afternoon at his run-down rooming house on a side street of Mimbres Junction.

Moulder admitted being a little drunk the previous night, but insisted he had seen what he had seen—the car suddenly swerved and plunged from the bridge into the canal for no apparent reason. And he had tried to get the people out. He was sorry, but he had really tried.

Roberts closed his notebook and rested a hand gently on the old man's shoulder. "You did as much as you could, Mr. Moulder. More than a lot would have. Don't let it trouble you. But try to remember—was there a third body? In the car? The back seat maybe—or somewhere around it?"

Al Moulder had looked genuinely puzzled. "A third body?" His rheumy eyes searched the sergeant's face. "No, sir. The water was dark and murky. I didn't even really see the girl, just the white dress billowing. No chance to look in the back seat, neither. I had to get out of the canal myself or drown."

"And there was no one else around the scene? On the bank maybe, or up by the bridge? Someone on foot, or maybe another vehicle?"

"No, I told you, Sergeant." Moulder shook his head insistently. The man, like his room, was rank with the smells of

32

stale wine, tobacco, and old age. He reached for the bottle of Thunderbird on the stand beside his bed. "Nary a soul, I swear." He took a long pull at the bottle and wiped his lips on his sleeve. "Sergeant, that was what was so awful about it. I was alone out there. If there only *had* been somebody else . . ." his voice trailed off as he took solace again in another nip from the bottle.

"Here," Roberts left his card on the table. "If you should remember anything else, anything at all, call me—day or night. There's two numbers."

As he opened the screen door to leave, he paused and turned. "Oh, Mr. Moulder, in the police report you fixed the time as definitely just after midnight—how could you be so sure?

Moulder looked up, surprised that a detective couldn't have figured that out. "The radio, Sergeant—in my truck—it had just announced the time."

The Mimbres Junction sheriff's substation was in the old courts building on Center Street, a native rock sepulcher with a huge cornerstone carved with the date it was dedicated: 1928. It consisted now of a long drafty hallway that had an unkept hardwood floor and opened into mostly empty offices.

The wooden stairs all had worn depressions in their centers, and the holding cells were in the basement along with the rats. But the few offices still in use had window refrigeration units that were whirring softly. Roberts picked one whose frosted-glass door read CHIEF DEPUTY, and went inside.

Rabbit Gomez was standing by the water cooler, talking to Louise, the switchboard operator. There was no one else in the place. Even the door to the chief's private office was standing open, the room empty.

"Where's the chief deputy?" Roberts asked.

Gomez turned. "In the hospital—his appendix." He crumpled a paper cup and dropped it in the wire basket next to the cooler.

"And his deputy?"

"Out on patrol. Everybody's out. What's happening?"

Roberts moved to the coffee urn and filled himself a Styrofoam cup. "Why aren't you out, too?" he asked over the rim. "Didn't I give you some things to check on?"

"Hey, man, I haven't been idle." He pulled his notebook from his pocket and began leafing through it as Roberts asked Louise, "Okay if we use the chief's office for a few minutes?"

Louise, fat and fiftyish and heavily rouged and mascaraed, nodded languidly and went back to sipping a tall glass of iced tea. The detectives moved into the inner office and closed the door. Roberts, settling with his coffee into the old swivel chair with its thick foam cushion, propped up his feet, while Gomez rested an elbow on a corner of the desk and consulted his notes.

"I talked to the banker's wife," he said. "She was still pretty shook about everything, but I found out why the car windows were rolled down—the AC wasn't working. She'd been nagging him to fix it for a week. And she knew about the girl. Not this one specifically, but extramarital dallying in general. He's fallen off the girl wagon before. He was supposed to be at a poker game last night, but I checked that too and there was no poker game."

"And the girl herself? Kathleen Cole?"

Gomez glanced at his notes. "Kathy. I.D.'d by a coworker. She'd only been at the bank a couple of months—a transfer from Phoenix. Lived alone. Nearest relative notified—a mother in L.A. Hasn't seen her since Christmas. No close contact." He looked up and shrugged.

"And?" Roberts persisted.

"And what?"

"Ever married? Divorced? Any enemies? Jealous boyfriends?"

"Oh shit, I never—"

"You're slipping already, Gomez. It's just like burglary, only more so—keep digging, keep asking questions, turning over rocks. When were they last seen?"

"They worked late and the guard saw them leave together about 6:30. From then on it's a blank. I checked the two bars in town, the Star-Lite Motel, the Steakhouse Restaurant, the movie theater and bowling alley. Zip. So where were they from 6:30 on?"

"Maybe they were at her place," Roberts mused, dropping

his empty cup in the wastebasket, "or maybe they went into the city. And coming back just after midnight, they went off the bridge. But why? Drinking? The autopsy will give us that. What the autopsy won't give us is why there was a Mexican with them—or in their trunk."

"Maybe he was put there by someone else," Gomez suggested.

Douglas Elgin Roberts smiled. "Goddammit, Gomez, you're starting to think like a homicide detective."

Gomez smiled back. "So what did the witness have to say?"

"Nothing new." Roberts took his feet off the desk and got up. "Except that the time was right—just after midnight. The old guy had his radio on. Now I guess we better check in." He walked over to the door and called to Louise, "Think you can get me Lieutenant Lang on that thing, hon?"

While she put the call through he got another cup of coffee from the urn and returned to the chief's office. Then he picked up the receiver and told Lang what they had. "That's right, Lieutenant, a third body. . . . I don't know, Lieutenant. It doesn't make any sense yet. No autopsy report on the other two yet? . . . That figures. . . . Any messages? . . . What? What in hell's a Patricia Lane? . . . All right, I'll take care of it. What else? . . . Where? . . . Okay, we'll be back in the city in an hour, grab a meal, and start the paperwork, then follow up on your lead first thing in the morning. But what we need is hard, physical evidence, and what we've got you could put on the head of a pin and still have room for the Gettysburg Address." He hung up and looked over at Gomez. "Autopsy report's not ready yet."

Gomez smiled. "But Patricia Lane is."

"I don't even know any Patricia Lane. But the lieutenant did have something else. Winters and Kathy Cole did go into the city last night. They were seen in a strip joint out on Redondo Boulevard about ten o'clock."

FIVE

"THEY found the goddamned wet's body already," Jesse Peralta said. "I knew they would." Nervously, he lit another cigarette off the butt of his last one and handed the evening paper to his boss.

"Well," Dutch Masters said, "it was still better than planting any more of 'em around here." His own cigar belched plumes of blue smoke toward the ceiling of the cinder-block office as he folded the paper to the small article at the bottom of the front page underneath a picture of the banker, Edwin Winters.

Reading it, Dutch grunted and threw the paper aside. "It's the banker and his sweetmeat they'll be concerned about, Jesse, not the Mex. And it says that appeared to be an accident. They're just puzzled by the third body. That's natural. It must have drifted down and tangled on the car. Shit, that bridge is what—eight, nine miles away from here? They'll never connect it to this ranch."

But Dutch admitted to himself that it worried him. Not that it was found so soon—it was bound to surface anyway—but that it now involved the damn banker's death. Otherwise he was sure it would have been judged a simple fight and drowning—damn!

Opening the office door, Dutch stepped outside into the yard, which was surrounded by his citrus groves, endless rows of trees heavy with ripening fruit. And the sun, sliding below the horizon now, glinted off the blades of the wind machines that soared above the green leaves; blades that wouldn't turn until the desert winter frosts.

Shaking his head in sudden frustration and muttering profanities, Dutch walked around the side of the building. His foreman followed a few steps behind. It was getting to be too much, all of it, and Dutch finally turned on the source of his latest trouble. "Goddammit, Jesse," he hurled his words like knives, "as if I ain't got enough fucking problems with equipment, gasoline, fertilizer, government interference, and the goddamned taxes! Labor—labor is the only fucking thing I've got any control over!"

They were standing by the tractor shed attached to the building. Its open front revealed a cluttered maintenance shop and a hoist that held the front end of a John Deere suspended over a grease pit. Shelves along the back wall held miscellaneous tools and equipment, and the fading daylight falling through a dusty back window illuminated the cobwebs in one corner.

Pulling off his baseball cap, Dutch mopped the sweat from his brow with his sleeve and stared hard at his foreman. "Killing the goddamned wets is just gonna have to stop, Jesse. It's too risky. I know they're tougher than boot leather, most of 'em, but find a way to discipline 'em short of killing. We can't dump 'em all in the fucking canal."

Jesse Peralta's scowl matched his own, but the man's brooding gunmetal eyes were noncommittal, almost without expression. "It was accidental, Dutch," he shrugged, "like the others. Sometimes I just get carried away. And he was a troublemaker—a fucking Commie—always stirring up the rest of 'em. I know these people, Dutch. I talk their lingo. Believe me, he was trouble—just like the others. He couldn't take discipline."

Dutch Masters continued to stare at him, as if to drive home his point now by sheer willpower. "I mean it, Jesse— no more 'accidents.' I wish to Christ I'd never let you get away with the first one—that made me an accessory."

Jesse Peralta scratched his black-bearded jaw thoughtfully. "Maybe if we could have got him to a doctor—"

Dutch glared at him angrily. "Are you crazy? After you beat the shit out of him? What would we have told a doctor—that he slipped on some grease? And worse, what would *he* have told him? Not only about the beating but that most of 'em haven't been paid in three months? And that even when they are paid, they only net about a dollar an hour? Wise up, for Christ's sake, and just ease off on the beatings. Chain 'em up for a few days instead. They're scared to death of you, anyway." Turning, he walked back to his truck, leaving his foreman standing beside the tractor. Climbing in and slamming the truck door, Dutch leaned an arm on the edge of the open window as he started the engine. "We're gonna have to work the crews till dark this week," he called back, "if we're gonna fill these last two orders."

Jesse Peralta nodded. "No sweat, Dutch, I'll take care of it."

"Yeah, you do that. And you just remember what I said: no more 'accidents,' I mean it."

Jesse Peralta watched his employer grind the gears and drive off down the dirt road to disappear among the citrus trees. Dropping the butt of his cigarette onto the gravel, he mashed it under his boot. He still felt he should have buried the last body, like the others. They'd never be found. Now, as if the goddamned Border Patrol nosing around all the time wasn't aggravation enough, the cops might come butting in, too. Yet why should they, he wondered. Dutch was probably right about that—the body had been found miles away from here, with the banker and that girl. And he had nothing to do with that.

Anyway, he wasn't about to leave this place. He had it made here. In fact, this job with Dutch was the only one he'd ever had that really satisfied him. And he'd had a lot of jobs over the years.

After a bad-conduct discharge from the army for slugging a noncom, he'd bummed around, working oilfields in Texas, farms and ranches in California, and logging camps in Oregon, never able to hold any job for long. He'd nearly killed a fellow worker who accidentally shoveled dirt in his face. His burning, resentful, restless anger was always with him, surfacing more and more frequently, until he finally wound up doing time in the joint in Arizona for armed robbery and assault.

Released, he worked the citrus ranches in Yuma and Mesa and finally Mimbres Junction. But he was only headed for more trouble when Dutch Masters had given him his break. Masters had taken him on as a foreman—and gotten a government tax credit for hiring an ex-con.

But the cheap old bastard was his kind of man, and Jesse found he could get along with him when he couldn't with most others. And he felt born to the job. The sense of power he held over the laborers was exhilarating, literally life and death. If he sometimes got carried away with his discipline, what difference did it make? They were only Mexicans.

Mexicans. He spat into the dust at his feet. His own father had been Mexican. And he had hated his father, and hated the half of himself that was Mexican. But most of all he had hated Carlos, his older half-brother, who was *puro Mexicano* and had been his father's favorite.

On a ranch near Las Cruces, New Mexico, Juan Peralta had married a woman from across the line in Ciudád Juárez, and they'd had Carlos. Three years later she had died, just as World War II was starting, and Juan Peralta soon moved into town with an Anglo woman who was collecting an allotment from her GI husband while he was overseas. And Jesse was the result of that union.

After the war, the woman had returned to her husband and left Jesse with his father and his older half-brother. He was raised by whatever woman happened to be living with Juan Peralta. Part of the time they'd lived in El Paso and the rest across the line in the slums of Juárez; but always the three of them—overbearing father, the favored older half-brother, and Jesse. They'd lived out their hate-filled, brutal lives together. And Jesse knew it was the root of his endless rage.

Carlos had been the cause of his joining the goddamned army. He couldn't take the beatings anymore. Four years older and sixty pounds heavier, Carlos had beat him mercilessly just for the hell of it. And the old man had smiled.

Well, Jesse smiled to himself now, thinking about it and stroking his full dark beard. He had finally fixed Carlos. When he got back from the army, full grown himself, he had beaten the hell out of Carlos and then fixed the brakes on his car on a mountain road. How his father had wept at the funeral. Jesse hadn't seen him since.

No, he was thinking now, he had finally found himself here on old Dutch Master's place. He was a kind of king. And there were seven of them buried out there in the groves. The last one was the only one anybody but he and old Dutch knew about. But like Dutch had said, they'd never trace Enrique Vasquez back to the Masters place; or if they did, what could they prove?

And Jesse knew one thing more: he couldn't guarantee there would be no more 'accidents.' He took too much pleasure in beating the little brown bastards. So when it happened again, he would just have to go back to burying the bodies in the groves. But from now on, even old Dutch Masters wouldn't have to know.

SIX

THEY approached Mimbres Junction in darkness, walking single file along a dry irrigation ditch that led between freshly plowed fields. Miguel Ramirez was leading the way, and already they could see the lights of the town in the distance.

When the old man suddenly slowed, seeking his bearings by the starlight, Arturo Vasquez almost stepped on his heels. "What's wrong," the boy whispered. "You said that is Mimbres Junction up ahead, the place we seek."

Miguel stopped altogether then and Arturo stood motionless behind him, waiting. "We do not want to go directly into the town," the old man said. He seemed to spot something he was looking for, and suddenly climbed out of the ditch, slithered under a barbed-wire fence, and started walking across a field, angling west of the lights of the town. Arturo hesitated only a moment before following. He trusted the old man, but he feared a meeting with the American Migra—the Immigration authorities.

Twenty minutes later they crossed under another fence and jumped another dry ditch, then plunged into the deeper darkness of a citrus grove. Arturo could smell the sharp tangy scent of the unseen fruit as they stumbled over the rough clods between the rows, and he wondered if Miguel really knew where he was going. Then he caught a faint odor of smoke on the infrequent gusts of wind.

"We're almost there," Miguel said.

"Where are we going, *viejo?*"

"You smell that cooking fire? It's an old meeting place. They must still use it. It's safer than the town until we can find where there is work. There—" he stopped and pointed into a clearing among the trees ahead of them.

Rising tall and stark against the starlit sky was a silo, apparently long abandoned. And as they approached it, Arturo could see pale patches of sky through great gaping holes in the curved sides. Again he smelled the smoke, and as they drew nearer he could see the pale flickering light of a fire inside.

Miguel didn't even hesitate. He walked right up to the old silo and ducked through the sagging doorway. When Arturo caught up with him he was already inside and exchanging silent glances with the four men who were gathered around the fire.

Arturo felt a rush of relief when he saw that the four were Mexicans, and obviously *campesinos*—men of the soil—like themselves. They were all in their late twenties at most, and they nodded silently in greeting. One of them stood up and invited the newcomers over to the fire, where an old iron disk had been propped over the flames and another of the men was turning several tortillas.

The others were eating green onions, and one of them offered an open bag to Miguel. *"Mil gracias, hombres,"* the old man muttered, squatting down. He took two and handed one to the boy. "Have you been here long?" he asked them.

"Two days," one answered. "We jumped the line near Naco."

"We've been waiting for someone who was to contact us here about work," the man turning the tortillas said. "What about you?"

"We crossed last night just after midnight," Miguel told him. He was still on his haunches, chewing hungrily on the onion. "A coyote brought us across the border and then abandoned us. He was to have work for us somewhere near here."

"Ay, chingados cabrones—los coyotes!" a man with a flaring mustache spoke up. "We never use them." He reached

for a brand from the fire to light his cigarette. "They will cut off your balls and serve them to you for breakfast."

As they all hunkered down again, sharing the fire and food, Arturo whispered to Miguel, "Would they know of my Uncle Enrique?"

The old man shook his head. "Not these—they are newly arrived, too. We will go into town later and ask around." He rolled a smoke and passed his tobacco and paper around the fire, and they all smoked and talked in low voices while the flames crackled and gusts of wind swept through the holes around them and sent showers of sparks spiraling upward to disappear high in the darkness of the old silo.

"Have you been into town?" Miguel asked at last, looking from one to the other, but they all shook their heads.

"Too many Migra patrols," one said. "It is best to stay clear of the towns. The lemon harvest is starting and someone is to meet us here."

"The boy and I are going into town," Miguel told them. "We are looking for his uncle, Enrique Vasquez. He's supposed to be working near here."

The others shook their heads. "You'd better wait here with us," one said. "There's supposed to be plenty of work and good pay where we're going."

For a moment Miguel was tempted. But finally he shook his head. "No, we will try to find the boy's uncle first. And you'd better put out that fire soon. We could smell your smoke, and the Migra have noses, too."

Minutes later Miguel and Arturo left the others and headed across the fields again, toward the town. They still avoided the roads, even at the town limits, and entered through the back alleys, setting all the dogs to barking.

It was nearly eleven o'clock and most of the houses were dark, but there were lights on the main street. When they came to an intersection, Miguel paused. A corner gas station was closed, but there was a street lamp, and a bar across the street where a fluorescent beer sign flickered feebly in the window. "What are we looking for?" Arturo whispered, still worried about the barking dogs.

"There—" Miguel pointed down the line of mostly darkened buildings to a single storefront, brightly lit, where a sign across the top proclaimed in large letters in Spanish: LA TIENDA SANDOVAL—ABARROTES—CARNE—ROPA. *"Vamos,"* the old man said, and they started down the street, pausing only once in the shadows as a pickup rattled by, its occupants singing boisterously.

Crossing the street with hurried steps, Miguel walked boldly through the front door of the store, Arturo close behind him. The boy winced as a bell jangled loudly over their heads.

The store was filled with warm, familiar aromas. Strings of red and green peppers hung along one wall, and there were huge bins of beans and flour, and sacks of onions and potatoes, and shelves neatly stacked with a variety of canned goods alongside neat piles of new khaki shirts and socks and work pants. There was even a small, neon-lighted meat counter off to one side, with a full-color calendar above it picturing an ancient Aztec warrior and a beautiful native princess.

Arturo began to feel even more at ease when a middle-aged Mexican grocer came out of the back, wiping his thick fingers on a blood-flecked apron as he greeted them in Spanish, *"Buenas noches, señores.* We are about to close, but you are in time—how can I serve you?" The grocer had a big gold tooth right in the center of his jovial smile.

"You don't remember me, do you?" Miguel Ramirez asked him. "I used to have work near here, several years ago."

The grocer squinted, but without recognition. "No, I'm sorry, but there are so many *campesinos* here—" he shrugged.

"No matter," Miguel said, "but I thought you might know this boy's uncle." He nodded at Arturo. "Enrique Vasquez. The boy is looking for him, and he's supposed to be working on one of the citrus ranches around here."

"Ah—Enrique." The grocer's face brightened. "Sure, I know him. He has been here many times—but not lately. Maybe the *chinga* Migra picked him up."

"Do you know where he worked?" Miguel persisted.

"No, he never said."

"Well, we'd like some beans and flour, anyway," Miguel said, "and a sack of that tobacco." He had removed a folded fifty-peso bill from his pocket and smoothed it out on the counter.

As the grocer bagged their purchase, a girl came through the curtained doorway at the back. "My daughter here will finish helping you. I still have some cleaning up to do," the grocer told them. And to her, "Two twenty-five, Rita, out of fifty pesos."

Arturo Vasquez felt as if the Aztec princess in the calendar on the wall had come to life in modern dress, with shimmering long black hair and smoldering eyes. Finding himself suddenly full of mixed and embarrassing emotions, Arturo averted his eyes as she took Miguel's money and rang up the sale.

She smiled pleasantly as she gave the old man a single American coin in change, but her smile suddenly collapsed in a concerned frown as tires crunched on the gravel outside and she stared beyond them out the front window.

Both Arturo and Miguel turned in time to see a long, pale-green bus pull to a halt in the lighted area out front. The boy's warm glow was gone, replaced by a surge of weakness in his legs and a pounding heart as he recognized the round blue logo of the U.S. Border Patrol and saw a dozen stricken brown faces of his countrymen peering from behind the bus's screened windows.

Miguel did not move, and neither did Arturo and the girl. Two Migra officers, dressed in green uniforms and wearing tan Stetsons and black leather gunbelts, got out of the bus. One of them stood by the open door of the bus, cupping a light to his pipe and waiting, while the other began walking slowly toward the front door of the store.

SEVEN

BY the time Roberts and Gomez got back to the city and checked into the detectives' squad room on the second floor of the Sheriff's Department it was almost dark. The squad room was a small, open rectangle with the desks arranged down one wall, and a large topographic map of the county on the wall opposite. At the rear were two interrogation enclosures with one-way glass windows. Beside the map, a green chalk board listed who was where. At the moment everyone was out and the place was empty. The other detective teams were either off duty or grabbing an evening meal, and the calls were being intercepted on the switchboard downstairs.

While Gomez checked them in on the chalk board, Roberts went over to the corner desk, which he would now share with his new partner. It was sparsely equipped with the bare essentials: a telephone, lamp and typewriter, a calendar pad and a stack of blank Crime Reports sheets. There were several messages stuck on a spike next to the phone.

Switching on the lamp, Roberts sat down and began leafing through the messages.

"This our little corner of the world, Sergeant?" Gomez asked, moving to join Roberts.

"This is it." He handed him one of the messages. "Looks like I owe you a steak."

Gomez read the note from the Border Patrol agent they had talked to at the scene. It was a make on the body of the

Mexican found with the car: Enrique Vasquez de Jauregui; a farm worker from the state of Jalisco in Mexico; age thirty-six; picked up eight months ago near Yuma and voluntarily deported through San Luis, Sonora. No criminal warrants.

"Looks like he came back," Roberts said, "like most of 'em. Only this time his string ran out."

"Well, at least we've got I.D.'s now on all three victims. That's a start."

"Yeah." He handed Gomez a second message. "From the lab. No autopsies yet, but reports on the other stuff—nothing spectacular. No traces of blood or semen on the panties, and the knife was clean too, as was the trunk and car tools. Burlap bags did have smears of tar, but nothing else. No blood, no nothing. A nice clean wash job. And only two latent prints left anywhere on the car—both smudged."

"Shit," Gomez muttered.

"Then of course there was the letter." He handed Gomez the sheet that had been unfolded and dried out, but the ink had run and many of the Spanish words were illegible. "Written on common stock, made in the U.S. and sold in Mexico," he quoted from the report, then looked up. "That'll be your job for the next hour or so. See what you can translate."

"Hey, man," Gomez protested, glancing at the wall clock, "I've got a heavy date tonight. I barely got time to shower and shave now—"

"Break it." Roberts smiled unsympathetically. "I'm pulling rank on you, Gomez. You've also got the first Crime Report to type up on this case. There are old cases in the file over there—just grab one and follow the format. And the lieutenant likes 'em tidy, so use plenty of correction fluid for mistakes. The lieutenant budgets big for correction fluid." He smiled sympathetically now. "Relax. Send out for a taco. You're on overtime so enjoy it."

"You're all heart, hombre," Gomez grumbled.

"You got it, pal." Roberts was still smiling as he held up the third message. "You see, this last one's personal, so I'm gonna check out and go see what the hell a Patricia Lane is."

It was nearly 7:30. He didn't really think he could reach anyone, and he was mildly surprised when the phone was answered on the second ring by a pleasing female voice. "Desert Glow Realty, Mrs. Lane speaking."

Ah, he thought, the light dawning. "Patricia Lane? This is Sergeant Roberts, Sheriff's Department—you left a message for me to call."

"Oh yes, Sergeant. You don't know me, but I've been assigned the listing on your wife—your ex-wife's home, and I think I've sold it. But there are some papers that still need your signature. Will there be any problems?"

Douglas Elgin Roberts sighed. "No—no problems. I don't like problems. You want me to stop by in the morning?"

"Fine. Unless it's more convenient tonight. I'll be in the office another half-hour or so—paperwork to catch up on."

"You, too?"

"Pardon?"

"Nothing. What's the address?" He wrote it down. "Okay, I'll be there in a few minutes. It's on my way home. See you, Mrs. Lane." He hung up and glanced back at Gomez, who had rolled a fresh Crime Report into the typewriter and dug out an old file. "Got to go sign my life away," he explained. "My ex remarried and she's selling the house. Or did I tell you that? Anyway, she's moving to a trilevel in the foothills with a hot tub *and* a swimming pool. And he's good to the kid." Roberts was wondering why he felt he had to explain all this. "And hell," he added, "I might just need a good lawyer myself sometime."

Gomez waved indifferently. "Have fun, hombre."

In the parking lot behind the L-shaped concrete building, Roberts found his vintage '49 slant-back Plymouth, its gleaming black paint job reflecting the lights like the day it left the showroom floor. Restored, it was far more durable than most of the new aluminum-and-plastic heaps rolling down the streets around him, and had a lot fewer mechanical problems.

Twenty minutes later Roberts pulled into a small lot where a lighted sign proclaimed DESERT GLOW REALTY—a member of the NATIONAL ASSOC. OF REALTORS and parked between two tall date palms. The place was still ablaze with lights but as he mounted the porch he could see only two women still inside, and the door was locked.

He rattled the knob and waited as one of them, an older woman rotund of figure and sour of face, shuffled out from behind a wooden barrier. Just my luck, he thought, and called, "Mrs. Lane? I'm Roberts!"

The lady lowered her glasses, which were slung on a black ribbon and hung across her ample bosom, as she leaned to unlock the door. "Who?" she asked.

"Sergeant Roberts. I called—"

The door opened and he stepped inside. "Mrs. Lane? I—"

"That's Mrs. Lane over there," she said, pointing.

A tall, shapely, thirtyish woman, whose dark hair was worn long and loose about her shoulders, rose from her desk and greeted him with an extended hand. "Sergeant Roberts—nice to meet you." Her eyes said she really meant it, and her smile was even better.

He shook her hand, feeling oddly ill at ease. He hadn't felt exactly that way about meeting a woman since his divorce, and it scared him. "Maybe tomorrow would be better," he said, "if you're busy."

"No, not at all." She seemed a little uneasy, too, for a moment, but it passed as she led him over to her desk, where she began looking through stacks of papers. "I had everything right here—" She had turned and was bending slightly, her skirt tight across her hips. Her legs were nice too. "Here they are," she said. "I just need your signature in two places—here and here." She pointed, and then looked up at him. "You're sure you don't want an attorney's advice? Your ex-wife can dispose of everything as she chooses—"

"No," Roberts answered, trying to decide if her eyes were green or hazel. "It's all been settled. I just didn't get around to signing these before."

"I see," she said softly.

He picked up a pen and signed hurriedly, wondering if maybe she did see. It had all been very complicated and not much fun, but he knew it was best this way—for everyone. He laid the pen down and looked at her. "That's all?"

"Yes. Thank you—and I'm sorry."

"Sorry about what?" He decided her eyes were hazel.

"Your divorce. It can be very painful. I know."

"Yeah . . . I noticed you're not wearing a ring. Does that mean you're not involved?"

She looked startled, glancing around to see if the other woman had overheard. But the woman had cleared her desk and was already heading for the back door and calling, "Good night, Pat. Don't forget to turn out the lights and lock up."

"Good night." She looked back at the detective. "I'm sorry, what did you say?"

"I was wondering if you were seriously involved—engaged, going steady—whatever it is they call it nowadays."

"Why, yes—no—" She was actually blushing. "No, not really. How did we get into this conversation?"

"You said divorce can be painful—you said you knew."

"I've been divorced for over a year," she answered. "It *was* painful."

"I'm sorry. But mine wasn't, not really. I guess because it was a long time coming. Fourteen years. How long were you married?"

"Three years. Really, Sergeant—"

"So you want to get involved again?" he persisted.

She laughed lightly—too lightly. "With you?"

She suddenly busied herself, putting everything away, and tidying a desk that was already tidy. But he could see her smile and he said, "I haven't had dinner yet. So if you haven't either, maybe we could stop somewhere together."

She straightened, suddenly all business again, "I'm sorry but I've got a date tonight, Sergeant."

"Well," he charged stubbornly ahead, undaunted, "later this week maybe? You wouldn't want me to eat alone *every* night." He walked with her to the front door while she turned out all the office lights except one in the foyer that shone on a large full-color wall map of Mimbres County.

"I really don't know when I'll be free, Sergeant. My hours are a little erratic, real estate being what it is—" She turned and looked at him. "Are you sure you don't want a lawyer to take a second look at those papers before I turn them in? You're giving away an awful lot."

Roberts paused before the wall map and traced the road that led from the city down to the main irrigation canal just outside Mimbres Junction. "I want her to have it," he said. "She deserves it. She put up with me for fourteen years. Homicide detectives aren't all that easy to live with." The map was color-coded to show real properties—commercial, residential, farms and ranches—and his finger drew a circle around Mimbres Junction. "You do much business in this farming area around Mimbres Junction, Mrs. Lane?"

EIGHT

INOCENCIO GOMEZ had taken only twenty minutes to do the Crime Report. There wasn't that much to put in it—yet. It was the damned letter that had taken up his time. His knowledge of written Spanish wasn't all that great, but he wasn't about to admit it. Still, by struggling with it, he managed to make sense of it in spite of the water-streaked words.

Whether it counted for anything would be up to Roberts. He was the homicide expert. Gomez couldn't figure out what the three deaths were all about, or how they could be connected, but he sensed they had a real bear by the tail. He expected that the sergeant would somehow simply piece it all together and show him how it was done.

Gomez felt a growing respect for his new partner. He had even decided he actually liked the fucking gringo, and it was going to be a ball working Homicide with him. It wasn't all that different from Robbery, anyway. They were still running down bad guys, except that solving a murder was a hell of a lot more important than investigating liquor store holdups.

A little after nine, he zipped out of the parking lot in his metallic-silver Trans-Am— still four years of payments ahead of him and it was breaking his ass, but he loved the car. The girls loved it, too. Especially Anita Carrillo. He glanced at the luminous dial of his watch. If he gunned it a little, there was still time for a shower and shave and a little disco.

* * *

Anita Carrillo, Gomez mused, back in his Trans-Am and smelling like a fresh spring rose as he headed away from his apartment toward the Mexican barrio in the old part of town. His own family lived in a small town on the California border, so he saw his parents only occasionally now, and it hurt. But being home wasn't the same anymore, and he'd settled here where he had relatives and taken the police exams for City and County. The County had called him first—four years ago—and he'd only been home twice. *Híjola,* but family ties were strong. Maybe this Christmas—

He smiled to himself, thinking of Anita. Twenty-two years old and she still had to tell her father she was staying all night at a girlfriend's. He had tried to persuade her to get her own apartment. With smarts as well as looks, she had a good job—a legal secretary. Shit, she made almost as much as he did. But her family ties were strong too, and never mind persuading her to move in with him. That was out of the question. Her family would disown her. Anyway, he wasn't really ready for that, either. Anita Carrillo was his favorite girl, but not his only one.

When it came down to it, the real problem was that Anita Carrillo didn't like his being a cop. She didn't even like guns, much less the occasional exchange of bullets that was an occupational hazard. Working for a criminal lawyer, she saw enough of the ugly sordidness of criminal activities, and could imagine what it must be like out on the streets.

The only mitigating factor was that he had been in Robbery—not Narcotics or Vice. He didn't think she could take it at all if they put him in Vice. But he was wondering now if she was going to be all that crazy about Homicide.

NINE

AS ARTURO VASQUEZ watched the Immigration officer approach the store, his legs turned to rubber under him and his palms grew moist. He glanced at Miguel Ramirez for some kind of direction or at least reassurance, but the old man also seemed unable to move.

They might never have moved if the calm voice of the girl behind them had not broken the spell. "Step into the back room," she said quietly and without panic. "Quickly—through the curtain."

He found himself standing just inside the curtained doorway in back with Miguel as the bell jangled on the front door and heavy boots thudded across the wooden floor.

"Hello, Rita," a deep masculine voice said.

"Hi, Pete. And what can I serve the Migra tonight?"

"Oh, maybe a pack of Camels, and one of those candy bars over there for my partner—the big ones."

On either side of the doorway, in the back room, Arturo and Miguel remained motionless. Arturo shut even the voices from his mind, concentrating on a far corner of the tiny room where a votive candle flickered beneath an icon of the Virgin of Guadalupe.

He murmured a prayer while his eyes adjusted to the dimness in the room and eventually made out a narrow bed covered with a bright Mexican blanket. A crucifix hung on the wall above it, and in the nearest corner a dark and silent

TV supported a bowl of artificial flowers. In another corner a wrinkled and bony old woman was sitting silently in a straight-back rocker, staring at him with watery eyes. It startled him when she suddenly began to rock slowly back and forth, though she still said nothing.

Through an arched doorway beyond the old woman was a dark hallway that opened into a lighted kitchen, where Arturo could see the grocer bent over a tub, busily cutting up chicken parts. Arturo was aware of the steady beat of an evaporative cooler, laboring somewhere in the back, and the smell of beans simmering on a stove. The ticking of a clock seemed unusually loud, and the old woman's rocking chair began to squeak softly but persistently.

His mind returned to the conversation going on in the front of the store: "—somebody leave without their groceries, Rita?" the deep voice was asking.

"What? Oh, those—a telephone order. They're going to pick them up."

"They'd better hurry, it's about your closing time. And I guess if you haven't got any wets for us, we'll be moving on, too."

"You ought to be ashamed," the girl's voice chided him. "Big men with guns chasing poor Mexicans through the fields. All they want to do is work."

"Then let Mexico give them work," the deep voice said without rancor. "Mexico is their country, and it's a rich one. But I suppose if that happened, your business would drop off a little, wouldn't it?"

"Our business is with anyone who wants it, and if I did know where a *mojado* was, you don't think I'd tell a Migra, do you?"

"No, I don't think you would. But it's always nice talking to you. See you, Rita."

The bell on the front door jangled and the crunch of boots on the gravel echoed through the silent store. But the tension didn't leave the place until the bus with its cargo of illegals pulled away and disappeared down the road. Then Arturo and Miguel returned to the front counter, where the old man whispered, "*Mil gracias, señorita.*"

"*De nada, viejo,*" the girl answered, "but you and the boy should be more careful."

The grocer reappeared then, glaring angrily at his daughter as he wadded up his bloody apron and tossed it into a box in the corner. "That was stupid, Margarita—hiding them. It's against the law!"

"I'm sorry, Papa, but I couldn't just let them be taken."

"We have a business to run, child. We cannot help every *mojado* who walks through the door. We can treat them like anyone else—any other customer—but we cannot hide them from the Migra. I forbid you to do it again."

"Yes, Papa," Rita Sandoval answered.

"We do not wish to make trouble," Miguel told them, and picked up their purchases. "It just happened so suddenly—I forgot how quickly they can appear."

"Do you have a place to work?" the girl asked him.

"Not yet, but we have met some others who know of a citrus ranch that needs pickers. They are waiting for the *patrón* now."

"Just be careful where you go," she told them. "Some places are better than others."

By the time they got back to the silo the moon was high in the sky, its light flooding the clearing, but the interior of the old structure was dark. The fire had been smothered with dirt, and only two men waited in the shadows. A moment of anxiety set their pulses racing before they saw that the men were not Migra but their fellow *paisanos*.

"Where are the others?" Miguel whispered cautiously.

"Gone," the younger of the two explained. "The major-domo came an hour ago with his truck. He took everyone but us." He nodded at his companion, who was older even than Miguel. "He wouldn't take him because he is too old. I refused to go."

"Refused? Why?"

Arturo was barely listening. He was still glancing around them into the shadows, still thinking of their narrow escape back at the store, and of the pretty girl who had saved them.

"I will not work for that *patrón*," the man was saying.

"He doesn't remember me, but I worked on his ranch last year, until I found a way to leave. It was bad—the work, the food, the pay, everything—bad."

"What place was this?" Miguel asked him.

"I don't know the rancher's name, but the foreman who came is called Peralta—Jesse Peralta."

TEN

THEY met for breakfast in the Mexican café across the street from the Sheriff's Department and laid out the day over plates of *chorizo con huevos*, washed down with a pot of strong black coffee.

Gomez especially needed the coffee, and a big bowl of *menudo*, which was good for hangovers. "You've never had *menudo*, Sergeant?" he grinned. "You haven't lived."

"I've never had sex to Ravel's *Bolero*, either," Roberts said, staring with distaste at the bowl of pale white cow intestines.

"*Ay, qué lástima, hombre,*" Gomez went rambling on, "I've really no head for the night life. I went discoing with my Anita. She's a fireball, that one," and he smiled again. "On and off the dance floor."

"Ah, the exuberance of youth," Roberts growled, and refilled his mug from the chrome pot the waitress had left them. "I'm surprised she waited for you."

"For me they'll wait forever, man. What about you? How was this Patricia?"

"She's a nice lady," Roberts answered noncommittally.

"A nice lady? What kind of description is that? Is she old, young, fat, skinny, ugly, gorgeous—and most important, did she put out?"

"Hey, what is this, the Spanish Inquisition? When do you

58

get out the rack and thumbscrews? We just met, for Christ's sake.''

"And you don't kiss on the first date." Gomez's grin splashed all over the table. Then he saw the glare of real anger and backed off, holding up his hands. "*Mira, hombre*— no offense. I'm just sincerely concerned for you. A man needs his little diversions to relax. Especially in this business, no?''

"Okay." Roberts shrugged. "She was pretty—maybe even beautiful if we use the same scorecard. But a nice lady. I asked her for a date and she turned me down.''

"Ah—tough, hombre." Gomez's face clouded with genuine concern. "That must be hard to take.''

Roberts laughed. "That's right, you probably wouldn't know. But believe it or not, I've been spurned before. It's not so bad. The sun still comes up the next morning. Besides, she did leave the door open—a definite maybe, which I think she meant.''

"Ah." Gomez's expression brightened again with hope. "Then I take it you don't have a steady girl, Sergeant— since your divorce?''

"I'm sort of playing the field.''

"Shit, man, I've got three steadies. Well," he hedged, "maybe two of them not so steady, so maybe—''

"Never mind, I'll find my own 'diversions.' And last night wasn't a total loss. I caught the last half of the Giant-Redskins game on TV.'' He signaled the waitress, who cleared their dishes away and brought another pot of coffee. Outside, it was already 79 degrees and heading for a predicted 103, a record-breaker. Roberts wasn't all that eager to leave the air-conditioned comfort of the café.

"So here's where we stand on this letter, Sergeant," Gomez said, finally settling down to business. He spread out a rough translation of what he had been able to make out. "Enrique Vasquez received this from a nephew in Mexico. Something about illness in the family and the nephew is coming north to replace him so he can go home and take care of things. The nephew is only a kid—age fourteen—he brags about it in the letter. He says he's a man now and can take his uncle's place.''

Doug Roberts stared down at the translation and frowned. ''That's it?''

''It's all I could decipher. The ink ran, remember? It wasn't dated, anyway. The kid could either still be on his way or already here. If he came at all.''

''And if he is here—illegally—he's looking for his uncle.'' While they turned that one over, Roberts pulled a paper from his own pocket and unfolded it. ''I stopped and got a preliminary report on the autopsies.'' He smoothed it out on the table. ''Victim number one. Winters, Edwin, age thirty-eight, male Caucasion. About two hours in the water. No evidence of a heart attack or stroke, no drugs, blood-alcohol level 0.08.'' He glanced up at Gomez. ''Under the influence but not really drunk.'' He returned to the report. ''Cause of death, drowning. Right foot bruised and swollen, apparently caught under the brake pedal and he couldn't get out.

''Victim number two. Kathleen Cole, age twenty-three, female Caucasion. Same time of immersion, no evidence of pregnancy or drugs, blood alcohol 0.10. Cause of death, a broken neck, probably sustained in the accident. Died instantly. No rape, not even evidence of recent sexual intercourse. But they did find traces of semen''—he looked up again at Gomez ''—in her mouth.''

''Ah,'' said Gomez understandingly. ''And what about the Mexican?''

''Yeah, the Mexican. Are you ready for this?''

''Is it better than semen in the mouth?''

''All marks on the Mexican's body were antemortem,'' Roberts continued. ''No alcohol or drugs. Extensive blunt trauma to face and neck, numerous hemorrhagic areas; fractures of crania, jaw, and nose. Cerebral edema, a bruised pancreas, lacerated liver, four cracked ribs, a ruptured spleen, pulmonary edema—there was even a quart of blood in the guy's stomach.'' He looked up at Gomez. ''Estimated time in the water five or six hours—but very little water in the lungs and none in the heart.''

Gomez was shaking his head. ''All of which means?''

"He didn't drown. He went into the canal about the same time as the others, but he was already dead. And he didn't die banging around in the trunk. The poor bastard was beaten to death, like we figured. And one more thing—blood lividity indicated the body was moved postmortem, shortly after death."

"Shit," Gomez muttered.

"I couldn't have put it more poignantly." Roberts was pondering the whole confusing situation when his pocket beeper interrupted them. He shrugged. "Our master's voice. I'll go call in."

At the pay phone in the corner, he was put through to Lang's office across the street. "Another homicide, Roberts," the lieutenant said. "A derelict found dead in an alley between Redondo and Thirty-second Street—just outside the city limits, so it's ours. But don't waste any time on it. Pockets turned out, but no visible signs of violence. Autopsy will show dead of chronic alcoholism sure as shit. Just wait for that and file it."

"I gotta at least look, Chief," Roberts said.

"So look, dammit, then wrap it up." The lieutenant then wanted to know if he'd followed up on the lead that the banker and his girl were seen in town Sunday night.

"That's next on our agenda, Chief." Roberts told him about the translated letter and that they'd gotten the autopsy results. "But it's all screwed up. I'll give you a summary. It's just going to take time to straighten out. . . . Yeah, Gomez typed up the initial report last night. It's in your basket."

When he got back to the booth he left a tip on the table and said, "Let's go. We got another homicide. Guy found in an alley with his pockets turned out. Probably committed slow suicide with a bottle—burned his liver out—but you never know. I always like to take a look. Then we'll go check on that lead the chief got on the banker and his girl—remember? It's a strip joint called the Blue Lotus, and it's out that way."

"That's right. That's why I couldn't find anyone who'd seen them in Mimbres Junction Sunday night. They stayed away from the local spots."

"And one other thing," Roberts added, "you did finish that Crime Report last night?"

"Mother's honor, man. I turned it in with all the *t*'s crossed and the *i*'s dotted, and plenty of white-out. One thing about Homicide's the same as Robbery, Sergeant."

"What's that?" They were paying their checks at the cashier's.

"The harrassment by the brass. Too much paperwork and too many cases all coming too fast."

"But without it, your life would be your own," Roberts told him, "and then where in hell would you be? Don't tell me."

As they crossed the street toward headquarters to check out a car, Roberts explained what homicide in Mimbres County was really all about. "So what we've got here with this banker is your garden-variety accident—with a twist. The banker takes the girl out on the town, and coming back after midnight she's feeling so good she goes down on him. His rocket explodes as they hit the bridge, he loses control, and zaps through the rail into the canal—*finito*."

"What a way to go," Gomez said. "But that doesn't explain a beat-up Mexican wetback in the trunk."

Roberts looked at him as they mounted the steps and pushed through the double doors of the Sheriff's Department headquarters. "There was no Mexican," he said.

"What?"

"Not in the trunk."

"But he was killed before he was put in the water. So why wasn't he killed somewhere and stuffed in that trunk, all unknown to the banker?"

"Remember the lab report found that tar on the burlap bags in the trunk? The autopsy didn't mention what was on the Mexican's clothes. I'll ask, but I'm betting there won't be any tar, and not because it washed out. It didn't wash out of the burlap and wouldn't have washed out of the victim's blue denims."

They took the elevator down to the garage in the basement as Roberts continued. "So assuming the Mexican's body was dumped in the canal independently but about the same time as the other two took their drive, it must have floated downstream and caught on the bumper of their car. And that's the only connection, which is really no connection at all. One's a bizarre accident and the other's murder.''

"Then we can close the case on the banker and concentrate on the Mexican, right?''

"Not quite.''

"What do you mean?''

"I mean when we close the banker's case, we're going to have to close it on the wetback, too.''

"I don't get it.''

"Let me tell you about the unofficial kill factor in Mimbres County homicides.'' They had checked out one of the unmarked sedans, and Roberts got behind the wheel. "Take this derelict case we're going to look at. That's rated a zero in the chief's unofficial book. Don't waste a homicide specialist's time on it. I wouldn't even have to go look at it—the autopsy report would do. But a guy like the banker, he's an eight in the chief's book. The girl's more like a five or six—''

"So what's all this got to do—''

"Shut up and get educated. If we write the banker's case off as an accident, which it evidently was, we can write off the murdered wetback, too. It'll go into an open file, and we'll be sent on to bigger things. Because the chief's not going to waste our time on a Factor one kill, which is all the Mexican is, if that much.'' He stared at Gomez. "Sorry, nothing personal. And I didn't make the rules.''

"*Jesucristo*—'' Gomez breathed. "Son of a goddamned bitch!'' He stared at the senior detective. "And that's what we're gonna do? Drop it?''

"I didn't say that, did I?'' Roberts eased into the heavy traffic on Redondo Boulevard and headed for the county line. "All we have to do is *pretend* there's a connection between the two.''

"Pretend?''

"Yeah, you know, make believe. That'll keep 'em both open as one case, and maybe we can find out who killed Enrique Vasquez. Because that kind of beating a man doesn't get in a fair fight. That was cold-blooded and deliberate—a real case of overkill.''

Gomez was thinking about it, visions of suspensions and citations dancing in his brain as he remembered what the chief had said about Roberts' crazy ways. And he had an idea this one wasn't going to end with any citation. But it wasn't fair—it wasn't justice—a kill factor, for Christ's sake. The wetback was a human being—a man, goddammit, the same as them. He glanced again at Roberts. ''You're crazy, hombre, you know that? Faking a connection? That's illegal, immoral, and probably a sin. We could get busted and hung out to dry, at least—maybe put away ourselves.''

''So you want to close it nice and neat as the accident it was? No problem. We'll just let Enrique's killer go. Nobody will care, anyway.''

Gomez exploded. ''Goddammit to hell, man, I'll care! And you should too!''

Roberts smiled grimly, waiting.

''Shit no, man.'' Gomez slammed a fist into his open palm, deciding. ''We can't let 'em get away with that! Let's go for it!''

Douglas Elgin Roberts was still smiling. ''You know, for an ex-Robbery detective, you've got a lot of balls!''

ELEVEN

IT was nearly 9 A.M. when Jesse Peralta came out of his small apartment over the tractor shed with Lupita Morales beside him. They descended the outside stairs together, then he sent her on to his truck while he stopped in the cinder-block building that was attached to the shed and served as a field office for the ranch.

Dutch Masters was inside, pecking away at his adding machine, but he looked up as his foreman opened the door.

"I'm picking up the four new wets I brought in last night," Jesse said. "I'll take 'em past the kennels and see if one of 'em isn't afraid of dogs—then take the others on out to the groves."

Old Dutch nodded absently, relighting his cigar and puffing to get it started. Then he glanced through the open door behind Jesse, shook out the match, and grumbled, "Who's that you got with you?"

"Lupita—my girl."

"I told you I don't like nobody else around here, Jesse, not in the daytime, anyway. Take her home first, then take care of business. And until you do get someone to replace Vasquez, you'll have to feed and water those damn dogs yourself, at least until Jack gets back."

"Jack *is* back," Jesse growled. "He got back late Sunday. He stopped here at the office to pick up some papers, then went to his apartment in town. Said something about he hadn't had any sleep and was gonna crash for a couple of days.''

"Jesus Christ," Dutch Masters said.

Jesse climbed into his pickup, tromped on the clutch, and started the engine, cursing the old man's son under his breath as he drove off. Jack Masters and his goddamned dogs. Sneaking them around all the time for his fucking pit fights, even over the borders into California and Mexico. And all the fucking around with ribbons and papers, pretending he was showing them. Jesse liked a good bloody dogfight as well as the next man, but he didn't like getting stuck with all the work associated with it and none of the gain.

Lupita leaned her head back against the seat and closed her eyes. A barmaid at the Watering Hole in Mimbres Junction, the twenty-nine-year-old Lupita Morales had been Jesse's girl for over a month now, and he was beginning to trust her. There was no reason to haul her ass all the way back to town before making his rounds. And he wasn't about to stop bringing her to his apartment, day or night.

He glanced at her again as the truck jolted over the rough dirt track through the citrus groves. Her blouse was gaping open, and a renewed warmth stirred in his groin as he looked down her cleavage and watched her jiggling breasts, remembering the thick black nipples. She liked his kind of sex— rough, brutal—the more welts and bruises he left on her naked flesh the better she seemed to like it.

His fantasy was interrupted as he pulled up beside an abandoned, weed-grown barracks building and honked. Moments later the four new wetbacks emerged from the dim interior, shading their eyes with their hands.

"*Vámonos, cabrones,*" he called, "*vente pa ca!*"

As the four men climbed into the back of the pickup, one of them paused and asked him in Spanish, "Where can we get some food, *patrón?* We ate the last we brought with us last night.''

"First you work," Jesse told him, "then you eat. Food and shelter and spending money, and safety from the *chinga* Migra, we guarantee it all here. But first you show me you can work like men.''

He drove them out past the groves and up onto the barren mesa where an old guest ranch had been built years ago, in the '40s, long before Virgil "Dutch" Masters had added the acreage to his own. The ranch buildings, built of native stone cemented together, had stood well against the ravages of neglect and time. Several roofs had rotted through and collapsed, but most were still intact and even sound, and still shaded by twin rows of tall salt cedars that could survive about anything.

The buildings were mostly empty now, but crudely built doghouses had been spaced between them; and chained to a stake in front of each one was a scarred pit bulldog. And all of them began whining and snapping and jerking at their chains as the truck pulled past an old swimming pool that had been half filled with dirt and lined with old automobile tires to form a long rectangular pit.

The dog's food and water dishes were all empty. Jesse braked the truck in front of one of the buildings and got out. Standing with his hands on his hips, he surveyed the scene with disgust, then called to the Mexicans in the back of the truck, "All right, *cabrones,* who's going to care for the dogs? They won't hurt you—they just fight each other."

While the dogs continued their raucous uproar the four Mexicans looked apprehensively at each other and shook their heads. "We know nothing about dogs, *patrón,*" one of them said. "We came to pick the fruit."

Grabbing the speaker, who happened to be the nearest, Jesse yanked him bodily out of the truck and forced him over to the nearest building. Pushing him inside, he showed him stacked bags of dried dog food, then turned him around. "You'll sleep there," he pointed to a cot draped with a dirty army blanket that was full of holes. Beyond the cot were stacks of empty wire cages.

"There's beans and flour in that cupboard," Jesse explained, "and the stove's for cooking." Then he pointed to a phone on the wall. "If you have any problems, you call the main house or the shop—the numbers are written right above the phone. And there's a water faucet outside. You'll feed and water the dogs each morning—one dish of food and one of water. Another dish of water in the evening, but no food. The dogs will get used to you, and I'll pick you up later in the morning so you can work in the fields too, but first and last each day you'll care for these *chingado* dogs—and you sleep here. You *sabe?*''

"But I know nothing about dogs, *patrón*. Please—"

Jesse Peralta's lips curled back, his teeth white against the blackness of his beard. "You'll learn, *cabrón*. You'll learn or you'll find yourself in a Migra jail—or worse. Which will it be?" His gunmetal eyes fixed the laborer like a spike.

"I'll learn, *patrón*," the Mexican told him meekly.

When Jesse got back to the truck, Lupita complained about the heat, saying she was sick. "I drank too much wine last night—"

"Shut up," he told her, and glanced at the three Mexicans still crouched in the back of the truck. "*Ya listos, hombres? Vámonos para trabajar!*"

Driving down off the mesa, the foreman entered the groves again, guiding the pickup for a half-mile between the trees before they came to a row of heavy wooden bins resting on pallets. Several tall ladders reached up into the trees around the bins, and on top of each one a laborer was clipping lemons and dropping them in a bag on his shoulder.

The crew pusher, a swarthy Mexican, stepped from the thick foliage and walked over to Jesse's truck, wiping the sweat from his face with a rag. "So you got some more pickers," he said. "*Bueno*. Maybe we'll make the quota today."

Getting out of the truck, Jesse pulled three long canvas bags from a stack and handed one to each of the Mexicans, along with clippers and gloves. Then he pointed to a thin yellow line painted around the inside of a bin, just below the top. "Fill it up to this line, hombres. No more, no less." He motioned to the fat crew leader. "Paco here will bring you a mid-day meal in a few hours—beans and bread and straw-berry Kool-Aid—then you'll work till dark. We've got ten of these bins to fill today. Understand?"

The Mexicans nodded and spread out among the trees, each carrying a long ladder.

"Watch these new ones closely, Paco," Jesse told him, "and don't be afraid to kick ass if they're too slow."

Dutch Masters had waited in the open doorway of the field office, shaking his head as he watched his foreman drive off with the Morales woman and the new laborers. The sonofabitch had been a godsend—he knew how to get the most work out of a greaser. But Dutch knew it was his son, Jack, who ought to be running the crews. Jack Masters was his blood. His daughter had run off to San Francisco with a pinko-liberal hippie after his wife died, and he had disowned her. Now it looked like he might have to disown Jack too if the sonofabitch didn't straighten out.

The whole place would belong to Jack someday, and where in hell was he half the time—off someplace fighting his goddamned dogs. Turning, Dutch went back inside and closed the door, then stood there staring at his cluttered desk where more work was waiting. Jack could be helping out with this too, God damn him, but he was just plain irresponsible, always had been; independent, unpredictable. And then finally, when Dutch figured he'd gotten most of the youthful wild hairs out of his system, off he goes in the army to Vietnam. Back two years later, he was worse than ever. There was no understanding him at all.

Well, he blamed the war itself for that, or rather the bleeding hearts who wouldn't let them go all out and win it—atom-bomb the shit out of the slant-eyes, that's the way it should have been handled. It had sure stopped the dirty, brown-assed little Japs quick enough in his day. He sat down heavily in the chair at the desk and stared unseeing at the glass-eyed javalina mounted on the wall. Now *that* was a war, he thought, *his* war. Not the candy-assed police actions or undeclared pussyfooting in all the years since. World War II had been fought by *men*.

At twenty-eight years of age, U.S. Marine Sergeant Virgil Masters had ended his service in World War II by being carried off Sugar Loaf Hill in the battle for Okinawa. His company had taken eighty percent casualties, and he woke up in a hospital with a Silver Star and a Purple Heart. And nothing that had happened to him since had ever been as great.

But that was when America had been great. And the hatred he had nourished for the little yellow-bellies had grown full blown into feelings that had justified all his prejudice since— feelings that America was for Americans, and real Americans were Anglos, not dark-skinned foreigners with foreign tongues and foreign ways. But these were the ones who were trying to take over, with their civil rights and welfare rights and any other phony right they could come up with. By God, he could understand Jesse's fury with the greasers when they didn't conform to the rules. Except that Jesse overdid it. There might well be a war soon enough over it, right here in America. He even had a hidden cache of food and weapons for just such a holocaust. But Jesse's wasn't the way to do it. That could only bring trouble.

TWELVE

THEY had finished eyeballing the body of the derelict found in the alley. No ID had made him a John Doe for now. No visible marks of violence, no bumps on his head, no visible lacerations or bruises. Apparently a dead alkie, with nothing to indicate he might have been wasted before his pockets were turned out. Roberts made a few notes, but if the autopsy didn't turn up anything unusual, they would be clear on this one.

Driving back into the city to see what Lang's informant might have on the banker's case, they stopped at a taco stand for an early lunch. Roberts was grumbling as they went inside, "I suppose every time we pass a Catholic Church, you're gonna have to go in and kiss the saint's foot, too."

Gomez grinned as they placed their orders. "You've got to humor us greasers, Sergeant, if you want to get the best out of us."

"And what's the best I'm gonna get out of you?"

"I don't know yet. Why don't you tell me about this fink we're going to see?"

The girl brought their orders and Roberts reached for the hot sauce. "He's called Fast Freddie, but his rap sheet says William Frederick Hall—all minor stuff. He's the kind of guy who tippy-toes along the thin edge of legality, and every so often falls off on the wrong side. And he has one little sideline that should interest us. He gets wets 'legalized.' "

"How's that?"

"He arranges for Social Security cards, a driver's license, a *fe de bautismo*—any document to help them appear legal or fake citizenship."

"That *is* interesting."

"And he's a part owner of this strip joint called the Blue Lotus. Funny little guy—an ugly ladies' man, with bug eyes, jug ears, a long hook nose, and crooked teeth, but he's always got the girls around him, like a man with a golden dick."

"Or a silver tongue," Gomez said.

"Whatever. Anyhow, we've got to touch base with him, since he was evidently the last one to see them alive, and he's Lang's pet."

They parked behind the Blue Lotus, which advertised top-less and bottomless dancers, but as they entered the open back door there was only the stale-beer smell of a morning after. The slatted grates behind the bar had been turned up, and an old black man was mopping the floor. Empty beer kegs had been set up on one end of the bartop, and covering the two stools on the far end were the funny little guy and a thin blonde who looked like she might be underage. They were both drinking coffee, and looked up as Roberts walked over and flashed his shield.

Freddie rolled his buggy eyes. "Oh shit, not Vice again."

Doug Roberts smiled and put away his I.D. "Homicide—Sergeant Roberts. This is Detective Gomez."

"Oh." Freddie looked relieved, but all the same he signaled the girl to drop out of sight. She did, taking her coffee with her. "Lang said I should talk to you. I owe him one."

"So talk."

"What about?"

"The banker and his girl—down in Mimbres Junction."

"Yeah, that. You guys want some coffee? It's fresh."

"We just had some."

"Well, I called the lieutenant when I saw the banker's picture in the paper. He was in here Sunday night, him and a young chick, maybe about ten o'clock, watching the strippers.

They were both a little sloshed, but not bad. Nothing happened out of the ordinary.''

"So how come you noticed them at all?"

"It was later—with the Mexican."

"The Mexican?" Roberts glanced at Gomez.

"Yeah, later I saw them out in the parking lot. They had a flat tire, and some Mex was helping 'em change it."

"And?"

"And nothing. That's all. I came inside and never thought any more about it until I saw the paper—dead—and with a Mexican in the trunk. I thought the lieutenant would like an earful, since I owe him."

"We don't know the Mexican was in the trunk," Roberts said. "Do you?"

"I told you what I know, and what the paper said. He wasn't in the trunk when I saw him. The trunk was open, and he was changing a tire."

"Did you know him?" Gomez asked. "The Mexican?"

"Never saw him before. He was just a Mexican—a little guy. There was a light in the parking lot, but they all look alike to me." He lowered his eyes. "No offense."

"Anything else?" Roberts asked him. "Did you happen to see him get in the car—the Mexican?"

"No. I told you, I didn't hang around for the whole performance. I've seen tires changed before. I came back inside."

Roberts excused himself and went to the public phone booth in the corner. When he returned he asked Freddie if he'd ever heard of the third victim, Enrique Vasquez.

"No. Why?"

"Wouldn't know him if you saw him?"

"No. Why should I?"

"I just thought in your varied line of work—" Roberts shrugged.

Back in the car, Gomez asked, "What was the phone call all about?"

"I called the impound yard—asked them to check the spare tire in the trunk. It was flat. So I called the lab—asked them to look again for latents on the tire tools, and anything that might indicate one of them might have been used as a weapon. Maybe we missed something.''

"But that's not likely, is it—finding something after everything was immersed in water?"

"No, but it's possible. And if they *could* find Enrique's prints, we'd have us a new ball game. But I'm still betting it was an accident, just like we figured. And the Mexican in the parking lot and Enrique Vasquez are two different people. But we won't tell the lieutenant that.''

"What *will* we tell the lieutenant?"

"That it probably *was* Enrique, only we can't prove it yet. That they must have given him a ride to Mimbres Junction after he changed their tire. That they were drunk and got mad at him for something, and the banker beat hell out of him, tossed him in the trunk to dispose of out in the desert, but went into the canal instead.''

"Shit, Sergeant, that banker couldn't have beat his way out of a wet paper bag. You saw his hands at the morgue. You read his history. He was a Casper Milquetoast.''

"But a Casper who's mad and a little drunk and has access to a tire iron—no, I don't buy it, either. But I think we can blow enough smoke up the lieutenant's ass so he'll buy it. At least as a possible solution long enough for us to find out who really killed Enrique. I think we're looking for a heavyweight, and dammit, I want the sonofabitch!''

"Shit, man, we don't even know where to start.''

Roberts looked at him. "We'll start with the victim himself. Find me a phone and I'll call the lab again. Then we'll drive back down to that canal in Mimbres Junction. Because it looks like it's going to be up to Enrique to tell us who killed him.''

THIRTEEN

"FORGET the car accident, Gomez. Forget the banker and his girl altogether. Let's just think about Enrique Vasquez and how he might have gotten himself beaten to death and tossed into the water."

"Well, it wasn't robbery," Gomez said. "He had his wallet, and a dollar in his pocket."

"And the lab insists there was no tar on his clothes. There would have been some trace if he'd been in the trunk with those burlap bags, because the tar was still on them. And of course they found no latent prints."

They were back at the bridge over the canal, going over the physical scene once again. They had even reinspected the sides of the road, the tops of the bridge rails, and the banks along both sides, looking for evidence of some other way the victim could have arrived at the bridge canal if not in the trunk of the banker's car. But they had come up with zilch.

"So if he didn't go in with the car, and he wasn't dumped off the bridge or the bank nearby—" Roberts was musing.

"Then we're back to his going in somewhere else—somewhere up the canal and floating downstream."

"Jesus!" Roberts gripped the railing and then pounded it in sudden frustration. All the evidence was negative. There was nothing to place him in the car or anywhere near the bridge. "There's just no positive evidence of Enrique Vasquez at all, except that he was already dead when he went in the water about the same time as the others, and he was caught on the rear bumper of their car when it was hauled out with its trunk hanging open.''

"*Mira, hombre,*" Gomez said, lighting up one of his ugly little cigarillos and consulting his notes. "If he didn't go in the water here, he could have gone in anywhere, because he went in soon after death and didn't get pulled out till five or six hours later.''

"The water," Roberts was still deliberating, staring blankly down into the smooth-flowing canal. Then he looked at his partner. "How fast do you think that water is moving?''

Gomez shrugged, drawing on his cigarillo. "Slowly, man—a mile, maybe two miles an hour. Hey, I get you—how far did he float downstream? Depends on how long he floated. He could have drifted for nearly the full six hours and caught on that bumper just before it was hauled out.''

"He also could have been dumped practically on top of the car right after it went in, and instead of floating downstream, he caught on the bumper—except that there's no evidence he was dumped here. So if not here, where?''

"Yeah, where? That canal is forty miles long. It crosses the whole valley!''

"It sure does. So remind me to call the Irrigation District office when we get to a phone, and find out the exact rate of flow along here.''

"And that will tell us where he was killed?''

"No, but it'll sure narrow it down some. And that's our next step. We know about when he was killed, and we know how. We don't know who did it, or with what, or why or where. So we'll start with where.''

"And most murder victims are killed by someone they know, right? Often a relative. So once we know where—''

"Only here we've got a stranger in a strange land—illegally. Who did he know? His fellow workers? His employer?''

"Or a casual acquaintance in a bar?''

"Maybe. You see, it's starting to narrow down already. Which means we need to know where this guy was in the hours before his death.'' Roberts had pulled out his own notebook now, and he thumbed through it as they walked back to the car. "We need more than the lab gave us in their report. We need a more thorough analysis of everything—his clothes, his boots, his hands." He closed the notebook. "Damn! Everything couldn't have washed out—they just didn't examine him closely enough!"

"Hey," Gomez suddenly smiled brightly around his cigarillo. "What about the other stuff in his pockets?"

Roberts looked at him, remembering. "The book of matches—where were they from?"

"Some bar in Mimbres Junction."

Roberts had already reached the page in his notebook. "The Watering Hole," he said and smiled. "Okay, we'll start there."

There were two bars in Mimbres Junction, one at either end of the main street. The Hanging Tree had a color TV and catered to the ranchers, foremen, and businessmen, while the Watering Hole was mostly a Mexican bar, where the flickering black-and-white TV was tuned to a Mexican station.

Since it was early Tuesday afternoon, there weren't more than a half-dozen patrons. And since the only one on duty turned out to be a Mexican barmaid who was thirtyish with too much makeup and red-dyed black hair, Roberts let Gomez do the honors.

The younger detective, showing her his shield discreetly and mentioning a homicide investigation, flashed her his winning smile. Roberts noticed that his new partner didn't come on strong; it wasn't his style. So he himself just listened in.

Her name was Lupita Morales, and like most people she showed an immediate interest in murder. Yes, she had heard about the car accident and the dead Mexican found with the others; and yes, she knew him—Enrique Vasquez. At least she knew him as a customer. He came into the bar every few weeks. He was quiet. He drank alone. Sometimes he talked with others, but he always left alone. He had to be careful, being a *mojado*—a wetback. She glanced around even now. "We get a lot of wets, and the Migra check this place all the time."

"And when did you see him last?" Gomez asked her.

She had to think about that one, but she finally decided she just couldn't remember—but a couple of weeks, maybe more. She had thought the Border Patrol had nabbed him, until the accident. He had told her they'd gotten him once before.

"What else did he tell?"

"Nothing."

"You don't know where he lived, where he worked? One friend he had?"

"I told you, he didn't talk much. Not to me, not to anyone. He kept to himself."

Gomez handed her his card and flashed his smile. "If you should think of anything else—"

"Sure." She smiled back, but she had a tooth missing and it sort of spoiled the effect.

As they started out, Roberts spotted a pay phone just inside the door. "Wait for me, Gomez. I'm going to call the Irrigation office and try to get the flow rate of that canal."

Outside, it was at least 95 degrees, and even the afternoon breeze was hot. Gomez waited under the shade of the ramada and gazed up and down the nearly empty street. A half-dozen cars were parked at the meters, but there was little movement. Two old ladies, sharing a large white umbrella for shade, came out of the bank just down the street and disappeared again into the corner drugstore. A pickup went by, dragging an empty horse trailer.

Spotting the little Mexican grocery store across the street, Gomez remembered something. When he had checked around town after the accident, he had been inquiring after the banker and his girl. So he hadn't asked in a store with a big sign in Spanish: LA TIENDA SANDOVAL.

"You might ask over there," a voice said behind him as if reading his mind. He turned to find Lupita Morales standing in the open doorway, one hand on a voluptuous hip. She was heavily mascaraed, with tiny black wings at the corners of her eyes, and it crossed his mind that she had looked a little prettier in the bad lighting of the bar. "Pete Sandoval might have known him," she was saying, "or his daughter, Rita. I'll tell your friend where you are if you want to go ask."

*   *   *

The bell jangled over the front door of the store as Gomez entered, and the girl who came through the curtained doorway at the back was a real contrast to Lupita—a fresh and luscious youngster in a bright red dress. "Hi," he said, "I'm Gomez," and he showed her his shield.

She was frowning as she came up to the counter, and even his bright smile failed to move her. "Migra?" she asked.

"No—Sheriff's Department. I'm a detective—homicide."

The frown faded a little, but the suspicion remained.

"And you're Rita, right? See how good a detective I am?" He glanced around, but there was no one else in the store.

At least he'd got a smile out of her. "You probably asked about me across the street," she said. "I saw you go into that bar a few minutes ago. Where's your partner?"

"Hey, you'd make quite a detective, too. I was asking about the accident at the canal bridge Sunday night, the one where they found the third body—the Mexican?"

"I know, I saw it in the paper just this morning." She looked genuinely concerned. "Enrique Vasquez was a customer here, but we didn't really know him—my father and me. He was only in here occasionally."

"And you don't know where he lived—where he worked?"

"He was a wetback—it said so in the paper. They live any place they can—in the fields, the camps. They move around a lot, they have to. He never said where he worked, but there are mostly citrus ranches around here, so he probably worked on one of them."

"When did you see him last?"

"I don't know. Quite a while—two or three weeks I guess."

A man in an apron had come into the store from the back, and the girl introduced him as her father. He claimed he didn't know any more than the girl. He knew Enrique was a wetback, and like a lot of others Enrique kept to himself, or with other wetbacks.

"There was someone else in here looking for him last night," Rita Sandoval said, and Gomez noticed the quick uncertain glance she exchanged with her father. "A boy and his friend. They were illegals, too. The Migra almost caught them right here in the store. The boy asked for him too, said he was his nephew. But we didn't know then who the Mexican was that they found in the car."

"How about them—the boy and this man? Did they give their names?"

"No. The boy was young, maybe twelve or thirteen. The man was about fifty."

"And you don't know where they went? Where they worked?"

Both Sandoval and his daughter shook their heads simultaneously. "They were looking for work," Pete Sandoval said. "I think they just arrived."

Gomez left his card and almost bumped into Roberts coming out of the store. As they walked to the car he told him what he had found out.

"So the nephew *is* here," Roberts said.

"And looking for his uncle."

"Damn—if we could only find them."

"What good would that do?"

"The uncle's letters to the boy's family—maybe they mentioned names, places—trouble."

"Not likely," Gomez said, "if the boy is looking for him, too."

"No, I suppose not. It would be a long shot at best, but that's what you play when there's nothing better—long shots." They had reached the car and Roberts said, "Let me drive," as he slid behind the wheel. "I think better when I drive."

"So what did the Irrigation District office have to say?" Gomez asked as they headed back toward the city.

"Maybe that's a long shot too, but the rate of flow is 1.4 miles per hour. It varies, of course, depending on how much water they're letting out of the dam at any given time, but all this week and part of last it's been 1.4. So with Enrique going into the canal just after midnight, like the others, and pulled out about 6 A.M.—even if he drifted the whole six hours and was caught on the bumper just minutes before the car was pulled out, he had to have gone in within a range of about eight and a half miles of that bridge, certainly no more than nine miles, anyway."

"Nine miles of canal bank is still a lot of ground to cover, man. And looking for what—a footprint, dried blood?"

Doug Roberts grunted, scowling thoughtfully. "There was a map in that real estate office—"

"What?"

"A map. It was color-coded to show types of real estate, and all along both sides of this canal it was colored green—commercial agriculture."

"So? It's still a lot of ground to cover inch by inch."

"Except that since we're probably looking for a specific ranch, I might be able to narrow it down even further back at that real estate office."

"Ah, Patricia Lane."

"Right. And you're gonna be busy, too. Check with the lab again. Ask for Sam this time—he's the Chief Medical Examiner. Tell him what we're looking for—where the body was in the hours before his death. Ask Sam—pretty please for me—to give Enrique and his clothes one more going-over. For instance, if there was no tar, what was there? There had to be something. Then call the office when you find out anything. I'll leave word where I am."

"Shit, man, you really think we're finally onto something?"

Doug Roberts smiled. "I think the music has begun for this one, Gomez. And I'm beginning to get the feeling we've finally been invited to the dance."

FOURTEEN

PATRICIA Lane wasn't in her office, but she was expected within the hour, so Roberts waited. And while he waited he studied the large color wall map of Mimbres County.

Gomez had probably been right. It wouldn't narrow it down that much. There seemed to be several large ranches bordering both sides of the canal, all within the nine miles upstream from the bridge.

"You seem to find our map irresistible, Sergeant Roberts," a familiar female voice said behind him. He turned.

"Hello, Mrs. Lane." He actually felt embarrassed, sensing she would guess that the map business was only part of the reason he was here. But he was surprised himself at the pleasure it gave him to see her again. She was even prettier than he remembered, her eyes sparkling and her dark hair swept to one side of her face. "I did want to check your map again," he said, "and to ask you some questions about it."

"Fine. Just give me a minute to make two quick calls and I'll be with you."

He watched her retreating figure—tan blouse, tight brown skirt, and knee-high boots—and knew he was going to have to devote more time to relaxation. All work and no play—

She was back as quickly as promised, and the scent of her perfume, arriving a minisecond ahead of her, was a little devastating as she stopped beside him in front of the map.

"Now, what do you need to know? It's still about the bank-er's case, I presume."

"Uh, yes." He pointed to the area along the canal. "These are color-coded green—agricultural land, ranches—but do you know what they are specifically? What kind of ranches and who owns them. Here," he pointed, "within this nine miles or so above the bridge."

"Some cotton and lettuce," she said, "but citrus mostly. Huge groves. I'd have to look up most of the owners—it'll only take a minute. Come on." She led him back through the swing gate in the wooden railing to her desk, where she thumbed a small circular file. "Here's two—both absentee owners."

"I need to know who's actually farming them—who would be hiring workers."

"They're leased to the same party—a man named Hughes. Dwight Hughes. He grows the cotton and lettuce. And there's this two-hundred-acre parcel for sale by the owner—Jim Anderson. But it's way overpriced. It's lying fallow. And here's one citrus grower, a small one named Kyle Ross—two hundred fifty acres. But the largest acreage along that part of the canal is here. It runs six to eight miles above the bridge and belongs to a man named Masters, Virgil 'Dutch' Masters. He has six hundred acres of citrus—oranges, lemons, grapefruit, tangerines. He uses a lot of hand pickers during the harvest, which is starting now." She watched the detective as he added the names and information to his notebook. "Does that help you?"

"I hope so, Mrs. Lane, I certainly hope so."

"It's Pat, Sergeant. Anything else I can do? I saw in the paper they identified the dead Mexican who was found with them. Is that what this is about?"

Roberts was looking again at her desk. "Is that a piece of tracing paper? I'd like to overlay it on the map and trace these locations along the canal."

Walking back to the map with him, and watching while he made the overlay, she tried again. "You think the Mexican's death was somehow separate from the banker and his girl, don't you, Sergeant?"

Finished, he looked around and smiled as he pocketed the paper. "You're very perceptive, Mrs.—Pat. We ought to get together and talk about it over dinner sometime."

"How about now?" She glanced at her watch. "It's only five—a little early, but if you're as hungry as I am . . . ?"

"Now?" She had caught him completely off guard.

Her smile was captivating. "C'mon—my treat." God, he thought, she's prettier than Gomez. "Detectives do take time out to eat, don't they? And so do real estate agents—unless you've made other plans?"

"Uh, no—it's just that you turned me down *last* night."

"Well, tonight you're in luck. As to why, it's multiple choice. (A) I know you better now. (B) I want to pump you about your case. Or (C), both of the above. But seriously, I'm celebrating. I just closed a very lucrative deal with wrap-around financing—my first this month. Don't make me celebrate alone."

"I'm sure you've got a boyfriend—"

"Oh, I have—but he's out of town."

"In that case, I accept. But I warn you, I'll be a poor substitute."

"Why not let me be the judge of that?" And she took his arm as they stepped out the door. "You like Mexican food? I know an excellent place close by. El Pajarito—the Little Bird."

Roberts gritted his teeth and smiled, trying to forget about the enchiladas and burritos he and Gomez had washed down with beer at lunch. "Just let me call in," he said, "and leave word for my partner where I'll be."

El Pajarito had an enclosed courtyard filled with lush tropical plants with caged and colorful parrots hanging everywhere among them. There was even candlelight and wine, and the food was really excellent, from his sautéed shrimp on Mexican rice to her Flautas Magnífico. And over dishes of Almendrada served for dessert, they talked.

A divorcee for fourteen months after a three-year marriage to a fireman, she'd been badly bruised emotionally, and a little of the bitterness still showed through.

"No kids?" he asked.

She shook her head.

He told her about his own boy, Chris. Age thirteen, eighth-grader, one-hundred-twenty pounder on the school wrestling team. "He set a national record with a seven-second pin. He's got a match tomorrow night, first of the season. I've got to try and make it."

"Sounds like fun."

"You're welcome to come along, if you like the noise and smell of gymnasiums. I'll even pick you up—business permitting, of course."

"My business too—I never know. Let's make it tentative."

Roberts smiled. "Sure—in case the boyfriend gets back?"

She met his eyes. "There is no boyfriend. At least no one steady, no one serious."

"Then my luck still holds."

She turned suddenly serious. "There's something about my ex I feel I ought to tell you. I haven't told anyone else I've dated but—maybe it's because you're a cop."

"You're not going to tell me you were a bank robber's moll. I don't hear confessions over dinner."

She smiled, just a little. And her eyes, which he had decided were hazel, looked greenish-gold in the candlelight.

"Danny—my ex—was gay. When they all started coming out of the closet, he did, too."

"Jesus—three years, and you didn't suspect?"

"He was good at pretending. He even said he enjoyed both." She took a long sip of wine as Roberts watched the color rise in her cheeks. "But he liked men better. I just needed to get that out in the open. I haven't really dated all that much because of it. But I feel strangley comfortable with you." She had taken a pack of cigarettes from her purse, and he picked up a book match from the table and lit one for her.

"Didn't anyone ever tell you that those coffin nails'll kill you? It says so on the package."

"It only says they're dangerous, but I am cutting down," she added apologetically. "I notice you don't smoke. How'd you quit?"

"It was simple." He smiled, pouring them more wine. "I never started." Though I'll tackle a pipe occasionally."

They sat in silence a moment. Somehow the empty time was neither uncomfortable nor embarrassing; it was just there, a silent gathering between them. "You know," he said finally, "you're right to get something like that out. Get it behind you. It wasn't your fault. Now I was the heavy in my own marriage."

"You?"

He nodded. "I've got an incurable disease—chronic lack of ambition. No desire at all to make lieutenant or captain, or run for county sheriff. The only reason I'm a sergeant is that it got to be embarrassing for the Department—fifteen years a homicide detective. I'm forty-seven next month, but all I want to do is work homicides. There's something extremely satisfying in hunting down killers. I'm almost in love with it or possessed by it, if that's a perversion. Anyway, my wife couldn't take my refusal to play the political game and climb the inevitable ladder to success. I was just an unwashed street cop at heart. Even with the horrendous paperwork, and usually being up to my ass in alligators of one kind or another, or on somebody's shit list, it's all worth it—to me. I'd rather run with the hounds than be one of the hunt masters."

"Well, you *are* a sergeant," she said, "and you enjoy your work. So why put yourself down?"

"I don't. Not really. I close a lot of cases with positive terminations—more than most." He smiled. "That's the only reason they put up with me at all."

"And are you going to solve this case you're on now?"

They were interrupted by the waitress calling, "Is there a Sergeant Roberts here? Telephone. You can take it in the booth by the cashier's."

"You see?" Roberts said, rising and excusing himself. "Duty calls. I'll be right back."

At the phone booth he put the receiver to his ear. "Gomez? What did you get?"

"Bingo, man. Sam was very cooperative when I mentioned your name. He called you a sonofabitch, but he sounded like he was smiling. What have you got on him?"

"Never mind that. What did you get?"

"The clothes first. Trace evidence of a common commercial fertilizer used on farms around here, along with common grasses and weeds. Also grease stains, like in a garage. But best of all, his hands, man—he'd handled a lot of citrus fruit recently. Trace evidence of citrus residue still under his nails. And get this—also under his nails and ground into the soles of his boots, tiny, undissolved grains of commercial dog food."

"Dog food?"

"And a few dog hairs still on his pant legs, for whatever that's worth. Now what happened on your end?"

"How's this—the biggest grower along that nine-mile stretch of canal is a citrus farmer."

"Beautiful, man—so what do we do now?"

"Nothing. Take the rest of the night off, pal. I'll do the second homicide report myself and give it to Lang in the morning. Tomorrow's our regular day off, so we'll be on overtime—something more for him to bitch about when I present him with the big smoke job."

"What if he doesn't swallow it? What if he really reads the lab reports on the banker and the girl—in detail?"

"He won't. I've seen him leaf through too many summaries. The man hates to read anything but the crossword puzzle and the sports section of the paper. Besides, you don't know what a smoke-blower I can be."

"I'm beginning to get an idea, man. But don't you want some backup?"

"No. I'd better face our fearless leader alone. See you."

"Hey, I almost forgot. Sam gave me something on the weapon. More than fists did the job—a blunt instrument. Something metal, like a piece of pipe "

"A pipe?"

"Not a pipe, man, something *like* a pipe.

"Jesus!" Doug Roberts said.

Inocencio Gomez hung up the phone and groped his way back to his table by the flickering strobe lights. Anita Carrillo was still waiting, but she wasn't smiling.

"Hey, cheer up, *querida*. I got the rest of the night off."
The heavy disco beat pulsed in rhythm to the flashing multi-colored lights, and the dance floor was packed with gyrating happy couples, but he knew his own evening was a washout. "I had to get some information to my partner, Anita, I told you that."

"It's always something," she pouted, poising moist red lips around a cigarette while he lit it for her.

"Anita baby, it's my job."

She tossed her head, jetting a stream of smoke at the ceiling. "*Chingado cabrón, hombre*, it's always your damn job—first burglary and now murder."

"Robbery," he corrected her. "It was Robbery detail."

"Stealing then—okay? But murder is worse. Ugh. And why is your gringo partner the sergeant? When do you make sergeant. eh?"

"Hey, Anita, lighten up. The guy's almost fifty—he's got fifteen years on the force. He's been a cop for over twenty. This is only my fourth year, for Christ's sake." He lit a cigarillo for himself, wishing they could get on another subject. "The guy is good, Anita. I can learn a lot from him. He oughta be a captain, or at least a lieutenant, but he likes working cases."

"Huh," she muttered, still unimpressed.

"Aren't you even interested in the case, Anita? A Mexican national was killed—a wetback. Maybe he just happened to be at the wrong place at the wrong time, but he's dead. And nobody seems to care but Roberts and me."

"What was he doing with a banker and that girl, tell me that. Beaten up, like it said in the paper, and in their trunk?"

"We don't even think he was in the trunk. Don't say anything, but we don't even think the one had anything to do with the other. We think the Mexican was killed somewhere else and dumped in the canal, and just happened to get caught on the bumper of the car before it was pulled out. We think the car wreck itself was an accident."

"So why don't you just say so?"

"Two reasons. One is we'd have to close the case. The death of a prominent banker is a must-solve on the brass's list, but the death of a wetback is only zilch. And two—why let the killer know we're onto him?''

"You mean you know who killed him?''

"Not yet, but we're beginning to put together *where* he was killed, and that's going to give us some suspects.''

"But it's dangerous, *querido.*''

"That's why a detective carries a gun, Anita.''

FIFTEEN

NEAR Mimbres Junction, Arturo Vasquez and Miguel Ramirez rested beneath a palo verde tree beside the road, ready to leap into the sanctuary of a nearby weed-choked ditch if the need arose. The thin green limbs and fragile fronds of the tree offered only a splotchy, broken shade; but that, along with their wide-brimmed straw hats, was shelter from the relentless September sun as Miguel tugged at the water jug and passed it to the boy. "Do not despair, *chamaco*," he said. "We will find work."

Arturo was not so sure. He drank deeply and restoppered the jug. Since they had left the store Monday night and returned to the silo to find all but two of the other illegals gone, things had not gone well. "We were almost caught again," he said dejectedly, remembering how another contact had been made and the pickup set for dawn this morning. But instead, just before daylight, a pale green Border Patrol van had come slowly down the narrow, weed-grown trace toward the silo with its lights out, and they had barely awakened in time to flee. Arturo remembered his panic. For an instant he couldn't understand what he was doing so far from home in an alien land.

But Miguel was smiling reassuringily now. "You did well, Arturo," he placed a callused hand on the boy's shoulder. "You are learning the life of a *mojado*." Scattering into the nearby groves, he and the boy had quickly rejoined each other, but they had lost the other two. It was eight o'clock in the morning before they had dared come out of the groves and up onto this barren mesa, following an old back road.

"But what will we do now, *viejo?*" Arturo asked him. They had walked for nearly two hours before stopping beneath the palo verde tree to rest, and he wondered if the old man had any plan or purpose. As he followed Miguel's gaze across the road where the property was enclosed by a chain-link fence and padlocked gate, he began to suspect that the old man was only groping blindly. Behind the enclosure was a scattering of apparently abandoned old stone buildings shaded by rows of salt cedars.

"Let's try over there," Miguel said, but when they started across the road to investigate, several dogs began barking and they retreated quickly back to the tree.

"I don't think we'll be welcome there," Arturo said. The dogs were evidently tied, because none of them came up to the fence, But Miguel agreed it would be best to stay clear of any place with that many dogs.

"Maybe we should—" Arturo started, then saw in the distance a pickup truck coming down the road so fast it carried a cloud of dust behind it. The panicky taste of fear rose again, his every instinct screaming at him to run. But before he could act Miguel grabbed his arm and dragged him back into the tall weeds of the ditch.

Unconsciously, he drew closer to the old man, though Miguel too seemed uncertain, helpless and alone as they watched and waited while the truck braked in front of the gate and the driver got out to unlock the padlock and push the gate open.

The truck was loaded with empty wire-mesh cages, and they watched the man drive it on through and then get out and close the gate behind him. He left the chain and padlock hanging free, and as he drove the truck on in among the trees they could hear the dogs barking furiously. Then the truck disappeared behind one of the old stone buildings.

"Let's go, *viejo*," Arturo whispered.

"No," Miguel said softly, decisively. "We'll wait. I have an idea."

It was almost twenty minutes later when the truck came out again. This time, the cages had been left behind, and as the man got out and was locking the gate behind him, Miguel Ramirez stood up and motioned to the boy. "C'mon, *chamaco*, let's see if he knows of any work around here."

Jesse Peralta, sitting on the edge of his bed in his apartment over the tractor shed, was carefully cleaning a .357 Magnum revolver when he heard the commotion outside.

Setting the gun aside, he walked to the window and looked down into the yard where Jack Masters' pickup had just pulled in. The dust was still settling around it as he parked, and old Dutch was yelling something at his son as he hurried over from the office below. Jack must have finally rested up from his trip and was ready to do some work, Jesse thought bitterly. He even had two Mexicans with him, an older one beside him in the cab and a kid in the back. He wondered where in hell Jack had picked them up.

Descending the outside stairs to the yard, he walked slowly over to the pickup where Jack and Dutch were still arguing. Jack hadn't even had a chance to get out of his truck before the old man jumped him, and Jesse felt a little sorry for him. He'd always had mixed feelings about Dutch's son—jealousy, mostly, of Jack's independence, his educated arrogance. But he admired him too, even feeling that under different circumstances he'd be a lot like him. Jack didn't take any shit off of anybody, especially old Dutch.

The argument now seemed to be about the usual things: the fact that Jack hadn't reported in on Sunday as soon as he got back, and that for months now he had been putting more and more time into fighting his pit bulldogs in three states and old Mexico. With all their scars, Dutch couldn't understand how he could keep passing them off as show dogs if anybody got curious, even if he did keep a fistful of ribbons in his glove compartment. And it galled him, the time Jack spent away from the groves, especially at harvest time.

"Back off, Pop," Jack was placating him, "I was thinking about you—see, I brought a couple of wets to help out."

"Sure you did," old Dutch's voice would have scalded a

cat as he ground out his cold cigar under his boot. "A wore-out old man and a skinny kid—what good are they gonna be?"

"I can use the kid out there at the kennels," Jack told him. "I had to feed and water the dogs myself just now. Where's the Mex that was out there?"

"He left a week ago, Jack," Jesse cut in. "I've been taking care of 'em till we got a new one in just yesterday. I took him out there myself. Where was he?"

"Gone. There's nobody there now. Then I get here and the old man starts in on me."

"Goddammit," Dutch grumbled. "Nobody'll stay with those fucking dogs—they're more trouble than a bunch of kids."

"They're worth big bucks, Pop, and you know it. You ought to get to a fight once in a while, put some money down."

"And just let the place go to hell in a bucket, I suppose."

"Hell, Jesse can take care of it. He doesn't need—"

"The shit he can! It's more than the *two* of us can handle. If you can't see that—"

Jesse had walked around to the other side of the truck while they continued the same old argument, sure that nothing would be settled this time, either. It never was. He inspected the two new arrivals more closely. The one wasn't as old as he had looked from upstairs. He might still be good for a long day's work. But the kid was really young—and skinny. Maybe he'd do for the dogs like Jack said.

Dutch had stopped arguing long enough now to walk around and take a better look himself as Jesse opened the pickup door and motioned both Mexicans out. "What's your name?" the foreman asked the older man.

"Ramirez, *patrón*,—Miguel Ramirez." He had swept off his hat with the servile respect of the old ones. "And this is Arturo Vasquez. He is looking for work too—and for his uncle, Enrique Vasquez, who is supposed to be working somewhere around Mimbres Junction."

Jesse frowned, and exchanged a sudden glance with Dutch, but neither of them said anything.

"There's no one here named Enrique Vasquez," Dutch offered finally, "but there's plenty of work if you want it." He looked at his son. "Jack, why don't you take the kid out to the pit and introduce him to your dogs? Jesse can take Ramirez to the groves and get him started."

Jesse took the Vasquez boy out to the kennels, showed him what to do, and left him. At least he didn't seem afraid of them. When he got back he sought out Dutch. The old man didn't think it meant anything, the kid turning up and asking about his uncle. It was just a coincidence. The news story was already only a couple of inches buried on the back page.

"Jack might hear about it, all right," Dutch said, "but he won't connect it with this place."

"Unless the kid keeps after him about his missing uncle, and Jack starts asking around here," Jesse reminded him.

"So who remembers names?" Dutch insisted. "The wetbacks come and go all the time."

"Someone might," the big foreman answered, still worried. Because Jack had told the boy if he stuck around Mimbres Junction, maybe they could find out something about his uncle. Jesse thought maybe he should make up a story that the uncle had gone north, or over to L.A., but Dutch had said to let it alone. "If Jack does hear anything, we'll say we don't know what happened to him—he just disappeared."

Maybe so, Jesse thought as he climbed the stairs to his apartment over the tractor shed. But if Jack *should* start asking around, then something would have to be done. And sitting down on his bed again, he finished cleaning his revolver and put away the kit. The Magnum was his prize possession. Picking it up again, he wiped the blue steel lovingly with a rag before raising the barrel and sighting it between the tits of the *Playboy* calendar hanging on the far wall. Cocking it and dry-firing, he clicked off the empty chambers; then he loaded it and slid it into the oiled leather holster before placing it beneath the bed.

Oddly enough, he had never killed with it. He seldom even fired at targets. He just liked the feel of it, and the idea of owning such a powerful weapon; such a cold, steel, killing thing. His killings had all been beatings, so far, and he took great satisfaction in them. It was a kind of fulfillment—almost a religious experience.

But he had always liked the feel of a gun too, and the sense of supreme power it bestowed upon the holder. Not even a woman felt so good in his hands.

SIXTEEN

"WHAT the shit is *this*, Roberts? Was it an accident, suicide, murder and suicide, or what? What the fuck am I supposed to make out of this?" Lang tossed the report angrily across his desk. "It doesn't say a goddam thing!"

Roberts watched him reach for a cigar and fumble with the bronze horse lighter on his desk. "That's because we don't know a damn thing yet, Chief," he said calmly. "We've got a lot of negative evidence—things that didn't happen—but nothing positive. We've got two people going off a bridge into a canal: one drowned, one broke her neck—apparently in the fall. We've got a third body brought up with the car that hit the water about the same time as the other two, but he was beaten to death someplace else."

Lt. Walter Lang shook his head. "A fucking wetback in the trunk. What the shit's the connection?"

"That's the puzzle, Chief. You read the autopsies and lab reports closely?"

"Of course I read them." But his face flushed just a little as he puffed to keep his cigar going, so of course Roberts knew he hadn't, and he felt the earth steady under him. It was going to go.

"Then you can see we've got zip. We can't tie the Mexican to the accident with hard evidence, yet he *was* there, so we can't separate him, either. And there's that butcher knife found on the floor of the back seat—"

"But nobody was killed with a knife, Roberts," Lang pointed out unkindly.

"Right, but what was the knife doing there? What was the wetback doing there? You know Mexicans and knives, Chief," Roberts suggested evilly. Sure enough, that one brightened the lieutenant's day. He could hang his fucking hat on that one.

"Yeah, yeah," Lang mused, cigar going like a steam locomotive. "That makes sense."

"Your own informant—Freddie—saw a Mexican changing their tire that night in the parking lot. And the spare *was* flat. We tried to get a latent off the tire iron or jack, but nothing there, either. The canal did a pretty thorough wash job on the whole car. We might be able to trace him to where he worked and start from there, but it's going to take time."

"Shit," Lang growled. "This one should have been open and shut—accident, suicide, or murder. Instead, we've got that damned spic involved."

Roberts gave him a questioning look. "The one in the trunk or the one in the parking lot?"

"My God, aren't they the same spic?"

"We can't prove it, Chief—yet. But sure, they're the same. We figure the banker gave the Mex a ride. The banker was a little drunk—that showed in the lab report—and for some reason they got in an argument—maybe the Mex tried to hold him up with the knife, eh? Anyway, the banker beat him to death with the tire iron, tossed him in the trunk, and went looking for a place to dump the body, but lost control on the bridge and took a dive into the canal instead."

Lt. Lang shook his head skeptically. "So why don't you write it up that way and close it the fuck out with some evidence?"

"Because we've got no evidence, Chief, no positive evidence it did happen that way. It just could have."

"So because you can't put it together, you give me this garbage"—he pointed to the new report—"and this one, Gomez's initial report." He tossed it on top of the new one. "Both a lot of hogwash that doesn't say anything positive."

He leaned forward suddenly, jaw clamped fiercely around his cigar. "I could take you off this case, Roberts," he warned.

Roberts met his gaze, determined not to be the one to look away first. But you won't, he thought; you goddamned skin-headed ape, you won't.

"But I won't," Lang said and looked away, staring now at his bronze horse lighter. "Dammit, I won't and you know I won't." He looked again at the detective, resignedly now. "You're good at these puzzlers, Roberts," he added grudgingly. "You put your teeth in 'em and you don't let go. So okay, stay with it awhile longer— but goddammit, I want some results, positive results, not this negative shit!" He pushed the reports aside. "And I want 'em soon."

Doug Roberts heaved a barely perceptible sigh. Someday he was going to push Lang too far and the sonofabitch would call his bluff. But the lieutenant was leaning back in his chair now, his feet on his desk, the decision made and off his shoulders, at least for now. At least until another eight or better turned up to put Roberts on. "So how is Gomez doing?" he asked. "Maybe *he's* the problem—slowing you down."

"Hell no, Chief—he's catching on good. Besides," he glanced over his shoulder as if afraid someone might be listening, and then he winked lasciviously, "can I confess something, Chief? Just between us?"

Lang took his feet off his desk and leaned forward again. "What?" he asked expectantly.

"I like him, Chief. The kid is really beautiful. In fact, I think I'm in love. Christ, if he'd grow a decent set of tits on his back, I'd marry him."

"Jesus, Roberts," Lang drew back angrily. "You're disgusting."

"That's what makes me so likable, Chief."

"Get out of here, Roberts. I want this case wrapped up in another seventy-two hours, one way or the other. You'll be on fucking overtime today, and you know the budget can't stand much of that."

At the door Roberts paused, his hand on the knob, and looked back. "One more thing, Chief—the letter."

"What letter?"

"In the report—the one that was found on the Mexican's body and Gomez translated, from the nephew in Mexico."

"Yeah, what about it?"

"Release the info in it to the press."

"What for?"

"The nephew's here—somewhere. We're looking for him now. He's a lead. Maybe if you put that in the papers, someone will call."

"You mean he bought that bullshit, man?" Gomez was incredulous.

"More or less," Roberts said. "He really didn't have much choice, since he hadn't read the reports that closely. But I had to promise him we'd wrap it up in seventy-two hours—one way or another."

"And will we?"

"Not likely. But you have to give the chief a pacifier. He doesn't handle stress very well."

They were having brunch—in the basement cafeteria of the Sheriff's Department instead of a taco joint for a change—and Roberts was on his third glass of iced tea. "So where to now, Sherlock?" Gomez asked him.

"Well, assuming we know what happened to the banker and his girl," Roberts explained, thinking out loud, "the victim we're concerned about is a wetback who just happened to be found with them. And who knows the most about wetbacks?"

"Another wetback?"

"Sure—specifically the nephew, but we haven't found him."

"So?"

"So there's a Border Patrol agent I did a favor for once. Let's go find him."

"A homicide detective? Baby, that's worse than a fireman."

"I know," Patricia Lane admitted, shrugging and dipping her straw deeper into her frozen daiquiri. "But I can't help it—it's the way I feel." She was having brunch with a friend. But in more elegant surroundings than a basement cafeteria. She had agreed to meet Jack Masters one last time, here where they had met the first time—in the Brave Bull Lounge, a piano bar a few blocks from her office.

"I can't figure you, Pat. I thought we had something going, but I go off on a business trip for a couple of weeks, and when I get back you're going out with a goddamned cop. Where'd you meet him?"

"At the office. I had to settle some details on the sale of his ex-wife's house. But it doesn't matter where, Jack, or what he does. I met him and that's that. Besides, I've found it does matter to me what business you're in. It's cruel and inhuman—and illegal. You said it was only a hobby, but it looks to me like a full-time job. Your father has to run that citrus farm without you most of the time."

"And you think a cop—a homicide dick—is better? That's a laugh." He tossed his long dark hair and his teeth showed in the dim light of the bar. "Half of them are on the take, and the other half are practicing to be. I suppose you're gonna turn me in?"

"No. I just don't want to see you anymore, Jack, and I don't want to argue about it."

"Look, baby," he started pleading now, "I'm sorry I ever took you to that dogfight. It was a mistake. But there's nothing wrong with it. It's nature. Dogs fight each other all the time."

"Except for one distinct difference," she pointed out bitterly. "When they fight on the street and one is winning, the other can quit and run away. It has a choice. You throw dogs in a pit and make them fight to the death while a mob around them roars for blood. Neither of them can quit or run away. Half the time even the winner dies of his wounds. It's sickening, and betting money on the outcome only makes it worse."

"It's a better living than I'll ever make scratching around my old man's groves, Pat," he insisted. "There's big bucks in the gambling that goes with fighting dogs—" But he saw that he was beating a dead horse and he left it hanging there.

She had wanted to tell him then about Roberts' interest in his father's farm and ask if he knew about the dead wetback, since he probably hadn't seen a local paper yet. But somehow she thought it best not to mention it. She was beginning to wonder herself if there was some connection with Masters' place.

She knew, of course, that old Dutch worked wetbacks, but everyone did. Only everyone didn't beat them to death. She caught herself staring at Jack Masters' hands—the callused palms, the strong thick fingers—and remembering the cruel "sport" he indulged in, she shuddered involuntarily and looked away.

SEVENTEEN

ROBERTS had shouted himself hoarse in the noisy, stale-sweat rankness of the gym. But in spite of his vociferous support, his son's team had lost by four points. Still, Chris had pinned *his* opponent, and so at least had the satisfaction of a personal triumph.

Climbing down from the wooden stands, Roberts shook hands and congratulated him. At thirteen, Chris was already up to his father's eyebrows, and building muscle day by day. He'd made the varsity his first year, and his national record for fastest pin had surprised everyone.

But as far as Roberts was concerned, the boy could have been a champ at tiddly winks or at nothing at all and he would have been just as proud. Or almost as proud. Because Chris was a good kid.

He introduced Chris to Patricia and she too congratulated him on winning his match and wished the team better luck next time. Roberts saw the usual reaction in the boy's eyes—the quick appraisal, the wondering if this would be the one, along with a touch of adolescent jealousy; but admiration too as he smiled in his quick, easy way and thanked her. Then Chris asked his father if he could see him a minute alone, and they walked together over by the wall under a folded basketball hoop.

"Dad—Mom's getting married again."

"I know," Roberts answered, "she told me."

"And you're going to let her?"

"I can't stop her, Chris. It's over. It's been over a long time. But not with us—never with you and me."

"I guess a lot of families are breaking up."

"The whole world's a little crazy, Chris. It always has been."

"I know—and something else." He met his father's eyes. "I've decided I don't want to be a cop anymore. Nothing against it. I just want to be an archæologist."

Roberts smiled and gripped the boy's arm. "An archæologist is fine, Chris. Whatever you want. I've always told you that, haven't I? Every kid starts out wanting to be a cop—or a fireman."

"But you *are* one—a good one."

"It just happened, Chris. It's no big deal, mostly a lot of paperwork and aggravation." But he knew it wasn't, not for him. It was a way of life.

"Thanks, Dad." The boy excused himself to help roll up the mats, while Roberts walked over to where Pat was waiting by the drinking fountain.

"He's a handsome young man, Sergeant," she said. "Must take after his mother." But her warm smile took away the sting. "And do I really have to go on calling you Sergeant? What do your friends call you?"

"My name is Douglas E. Roberts. They called me Dougie when I was a kid. Now they just call me Roberts."

"And what does the *E* stand for?"

He smiled. "You don't really want to know."

"Try me."

"Okay—Elgin."

"Ugh. I think I'll call you Doug."

"C'mon," he took her arm and guided her through the crowd toward the doors. "I don't care what they call me, as long as they call me in time to eat. It's my treat for dinner, and you said you liked spaghetti."

Vini's Spaghetti Palace was tucked away in a fold of the foothills that climbed to become a mountain north of the city. The Palace was rated three stars in the tourist guides and deserved it. The food was excellent, the red wine exceptional, and the candlelight made all women look, or at least feel, beautiful.

Patricia Lane's eyes shone in a special kind of way. "You miss your boy a lot, don't you? Being with him, I mean."

"Yes—though I think I see more of him now than when Liz and I were married. I don't know how it'll be when she's married again, but at least the times I see him seem more meaningful. Or maybe it's just because he's growing up."

"Or you are."

"That, too. I took him with me on my vacation this summer—two weeks camping and fishing in western Colorado. It was the best time of my life."

They were silent awhile, sipping the wine, and again neither of them found the silence awkward or embarrassing. They didn't seem to need small talk.

"I've thought a lot about this Mexican kid we're looking for," he said finally. "The nephew of the one who was killed. You know he's only a year older than Chris? He mentioned it in the letter my partner translated—having completed fourteen years and being a man and used to work. That's probably all a kid like that *is* used to—hard work. The kids of the *ricos* down there have it made, but the kids of the working class and poor learn to hustle right out of diapers. No unemployment insurance, no welfare, no food stamps. It's work or starve, so they become very good workers."

"And you really think you can find him?"

Roberts shrugged. "The proverbial needle. Gomez and I talked to a Border Patrol agent this afternoon. He's passed the word at his sector headquarters in case they pick up a fourteen-year-old named Vasquez. But he could be anywhere, or nowhere. He could have given up looking for his uncle and caught a freight train to Phoenix, or L.A. for that matter, or just turned back to Mexico. In a way I hope he has."

"Why do you say that?"

"Because I don't imagine whoever killed his uncle will want a nephew nosing around asking questions. It could be dangerous. That's another reason I'd like to pick the kid up first."

"But you're fairly sure it's a citrus ranch he's headed for, so that should narrow the search a lot, shouldn't it?"

"There are over twenty citrus ranches in this valley around Mimbres Junction, and according to the Border Patrol they all work wets at one time or another, especially during harvest. And there are probably fifty small, clandestine camps hidden away where wetbacks stay. Sometimes they're full, sometimes deserted. Most illegals are extremely mobile."

He shook his head and sucked at his cold pipe. "I released the information that Gomez translated from the letter to the newspaper in hopes that somebody else knows one of them—the boy or the uncle—but it's a long shot. Everything about this case so far is a long shot, Pat. There's just no firm lead to follow." He poured them both some more wine as he continued. "But I think we have narrowed the murder site down to those nine miles of canal bank above the bridge where the victim was found. And there are only two citrus ranches along there—the two on your map."

"So what's the problem? If they're working illegal aliens, why can't you go in and look?"

"It's not that simple. Within twenty-five miles of the border, the Border Patrol has a fairly free hand. But beyond that—and we're well beyond that—they're subject to search-and-seizure laws, like anyone else. And there's no law against working illegals, that's the Patrol's biggest problem. It's only against the law to transport them or hide them, and it's hard to catch them doing that. The ranchers don't even have to pay them, and some of them don't. On payday they just call the Immigration to pick them up, then they hire a new crew."

"And you can't go in yourself?"

"Not without a warrant. And without some hard evidence of probable cause, no warrant."

"But how can you get evidence if you can't—it's a Catch-22!"

He smiled. "I wouldn't want to spook 'em anyway, till I do have some evidence."

When they left the restaurant, it was nearly ten o'clock. They drove along the foothills road in Roberts' '49 Plymouth, stopping at a parking bay that overlooked the lights of the city. Behind them a moon was rising above the mountain and the night was warm. With the car windows rolled down they could hear the breeze sighing through the cacti and mesquite, and the chirp of crickets in the brush along the roadway, but eventually only their own heavy breathing as they kissed.

It was obviously a time for love. But not here. There were too many muggers. They discussed it sensibly, like grownups, and discovered her place was bigger and nicer, while his was smaller and messier—but closer. And time seemed suddenly of the essence.

Minutes later he pulled into one of a row of carports behind a large apartment complex. They went in through a back gate and followed a little winding walk beside a lighted swimming pool. He unlocked the door of number 112 and reached in ahead of her to turn on the light.

At first she thought he had been burglarized. But he apologized for the mess, including the dirty dishes still in the sink, explaining that the maid must be sick. She suspected, correctly, that he didn't have one, and began immediately picking up things. "This is where you bring your ladies?" she asked.

"I don't usually go out with ladies. You're the exception." He was tugging the holstered snub-nosed .38 from his belt, along with his handcuffs and beeper, and laying them all on the breakfast bar that separated the living room from the kitchen.

She had moved to the open bedroom door and was looking in as he dialed the office and let the switchboard know he was home. "I know," he said, hanging up and sensing her despair, "the bed's not made, either. It's just a waste of time when I'll only mess it up again. I do change the sheets once a week—whether they need it or not."

Then she was glancing into the bathroom, switching on the light there, too. "Well," she called back, "now I do believe in miracles—your bathroom looks like Mr. Clean!"

He was busy in the kitchen pouring two glasses of wine. "I've got a thing about bathrooms," he answered. "I think I must have been toilet-trained too early!"

When she came out he handed her a glass of Burgundy.

"I'm afraid this is just a place to sleep, Pat," he said. "To flop between cases, to shower and shave and change clothes. I don't call it home yet. I guess I still miss the old place."

Their eyes locked over the tops of their glasses, and this time he was first to look away. "Why don't you see if the stereo still works," he said. "The switch is over there."

The apartment quickly filled with the lilting strains of Dionne Warwick's "After You." By the time the needle reached the end of the record and Dionne was singing "Déjà Vu," the homicide detective and the real estate lady had reached an exquisitely embarrassing degree of undress. Leaving the two empty wineglasses behind on the coffee table, they found the bedroom and the unmade bed together.

In the darkness her aggressive, nearly desperate hunger surprised him. And later, when she asked, exhausted but smiling, "Will you respect me in the morning?" he held her close and whispered, "Do bears sleep in the woods?"

And later still, as she lay propped up on a pillow, smoking, he watched the red arc of her cigarette in the darkness as she said quietly, "There's something else you should know, Doug."

"Sounds serious."

"It is." The cigarette arced again. "My boyfriend is back in town—my ex-boyfriend. We broke up this morning."

"I see," he said slowly, surprised by the painful jab of jealous anger. "Over me, I hope."

"You—and other things. Anyway, it's his name that should interest you. It's Jack Masters. His father is Dutch Masters, owner of the largest of those two citrus ranches along that nine miles of canal above the bridge. I thought I should tell you, for what it's worth."

"You *are* full of surprises," Douglas Elgin Roberts said.

The jangling of the bedside phone interrupted them. He found the receiver in the dark and held it to his ear. "Roberts here. . . . Yeah, Gomez, what is it? I'm listening. . . . Jack? Jack who? . . . Yeah—dogs? *Fighting* dogs? . . . Yeah, sure it's interesting. Things are beginning to fall into place bit by bit. I'll see you in the morning. Hey, what's that splashing sound—you at the beach someplace? . . . No shit,

I'll have to try that sometime. So long." He felt for the phone cradle and hung up.

Patricia had put out her cigarette. "What was that all about—'Jack' and 'fighting dogs'?

"Gomez is at a spa—hot tubs. Says he got an anonymous tip from the news story about the letter. Somebody saw two Mexicans—a young boy and an older man—getting into a pickup this afternoon near Mimbres Junction. Said the truck belongs to a guy named Jack who raises pit bulldogs for fighting."

"Jack what?" she asked cautiously.

"The caller claimed he didn't know the last name, but it's an interesting coincidence, don't you think?"

"It's more than that, Doug." She sighed heavily. "Jack Masters keeps fighting dogs—it's his hobby. It's the business he was out of town on, the main reason we broke up."

EIGHTEEN

RABBIT GOMEZ hung up the phone. Naked, he slipped on the wet wooden grating getting back to the hot tub, but caught himself on its edge and climbed back in. Sinking into the swirling, steamy water beside the equally steamy redhead, he sighed heavily and flashed his smile. "That's called business before pleasure, Vicki."

"I didn't think the tip was that hot," Vicki Taylor said. She was the TV news reporter who had interviewed him at the scene of the accident. "Now I gave you something," she added, "how about giving me something?"

Gomez flashed his smile again. "I thought that's what we're doing here among the bubbles. Or was this date just arranged to pump me?"

"A little bit of both," she answered frankly. "That Lieutenant Lang is a creep. I can't get a thing out of *him*."

"Not even this way?"

"I couldn't stand *him* this way—not even for my job. You I can enjoy pumping."

"And I thought it was just my dazzling smile that attracted you."

"It sure as hell wasn't your modesty, Rabbit—stop that!" She moved suddenly away from his groping hands, her twin white mounds bobbing enticingly. "What I don't understand," she continued from the opposite side of the tub, "is why you're still trying to tie the three deaths together. Isn't it more likely the wetback was killed separately and disposed of in the trunk of the banker's car—all unknown to him?''

"Say, did you ever think of changing jobs—becoming a detective?" He splashed her with a jet off the heel of his hand.

"I'm serious—maybe it's the clue you withheld that explains it. Don't detectives always withhold something only the murderer would know?''

Gomez just smiled furtively and splashed her again.

"Or was the letter you just released the secret clue? You finally got that desperate?''

"If I told you, it wouldn't be a secret anymore. But publishing that letter did pay off, didn't it? Someone called you.''

"I don't think I got much. A guy named Jack who keeps fighting dogs? That's illegal, isn't it?''

"A felony. But it's seldom enforced. Why don't you do a story about that?''

"I'd like to do both stories, but murder always has priority. So what about the weapon used?''

"Weapon? What weapon? You mean the knife?''

"Don't be devious, Rabbit. The knife was there, but it wasn't used. The victim was beaten to death. But how? With just fists, or a weapon?''

Gomez smiled. "Why don't you use that for the secret clue—the weapon? We're still looking for it.''

"And meanwhile those fists, whoever they belong to, are healing.''

"That's a thought—unless he wore gloves. I still think you should have been a detective.''

She shook her head. "I wouldn't have the patience—or the guts. Things do get a bit hairy sometimes, don't they?''

"Only when I forget to smile. But haven't we talked enough business for now?" He moved across the tub toward her. "Isn't it time for a little pleasure?''

And this time Vicki Taylor rose, dripping, and met him halfway.

NINETEEN

"SO we've got a guy named Jack who fights dogs," Gomez said.

"Which is illegal, for what that's worth."

"And a description of the guy—six feet, one-eighty, mid-thirties, long dark hair, clean-shaven, and sharp-looking with no scars—Mr. Average with no last name."

"We've also got a last name," Roberts said.

"We have?" Gomez was beaming. "Where did we get a last name and what is it?" They had mounted the stone steps of the old Mimbres Junction Court House and Jail, and Gomez held open the door as they got in out of the morning heat.

"Masters," Roberts said. "Jack Masters—son of Virgil 'Dutch' Masters, who has the biggest citrus grove along that nine miles of canal above the bridge. Jack is also an ex-boyfriend of Patricia Lane."

"*Our* Patricia Lane?" Gomez grinned. "*Chingado, hombre,* what do they say about a small world?"

"Especially where murder's concerned."

Walking down the long hallway, the ancient hardwood squeaking softly underfoot, they went into the chief deputy's office where they found the black deputy, Link Johnston, on the switchboard. "Chief still in the hospital?" Roberts asked.

"Naw, he's home now—'convalescing.'" He made it sound like a disease itself.

"And Louise—my favorite switchboard artist?"

"She's sick too—a bad cold, she says. Afraid I'm it, gents. What can I do you in for?"

"We just want to use the old courtroom," Roberts said, "sort of lay out what we've got and where we're going on this Winters case—okay?"

"Sure, help yourself. Coffee too, if you like—just leave a dime in the jar."

"Thanks." Roberts poured two white "guest" mugs, dropped two lumps of sugar in his own, and two dimes in the jar.

"You guys figure it was murder, suicide, or what?" Link asked. He had walked over to the soda machine for a can of Coke. "The banker and his girl, I mean. Obviously the wetback got his ticket punched, but what about them? The paper says you're looking for a Spanish kid who wrote that letter. You don't think he did it, do you?"

"We don't know what to think yet, Link, about any of it. That's why we came down here to lay it out where we won't be disturbed. If Lieutenant Lang calls, you haven't seen us, okay? Take a message."

Across the hall, in the old courtroom, most of the scarred benches had been removed, but the tables and chairs were still set up between the railing and the judge's high bench. And there was still the blackboard that had been used to diagram traffic accidents, and even a piece of chalk and a rag.

An hour later they realized how little they really had to go on. From their notes laid out on the table, along with the sketch and photographs of the scene, and the autopsy reports, Roberts had condensed everything on the blackboard. He even listed the contents of the Mexican's pockets, including the cashier's slip with numbers adding up to 42 that was probably a grocery order at that store where he traded.

"So what does it all add up to, man?" Gomez asked.

Roberts shook his head and tossed the chalk in the trough. "We haven't got shit, Gomez," he answered grimly, dusting his hands.

Gomez was still staring at the board. "What we need right now is a physical search," he said.

"Right—and search for what?"

"The exact scene of the killing, man, which should be one of those citrus farms—and only Masters' place has both citrus *and* dogs, besides using a lot of wetback labor."

"Okay, and the stuff in his pockets should help. Like that key. Certainly not a safe-deposit box—more likely a footlocker?"

"Sure—where he kept his clothes, in a camp or barracks or whatever. He'd been here long enough to buy one."

"And what about that lubricating grease on his clothes?" He looked at Gomez. "A garage? A mechanic's shop?"

"A maintenance shop, man. A farm that big would have someplace they do minor maintenance and repairs on their tractors and equipment, right?"

Douglas Elgin Roberts smiled. "Okay, Gomez, now you can go to the head of the class if you can answer this next one—what else are we looking for on that farm?"

"The weapon, right?" Gomez had turned back to the board. "Something heavier than fists—something metal like a pipe, but not a pipe. Something like a tire iron or a poker—or some farm implement?"

"Fine, you get the gold star. Except we've still got the one big problem—the search warrant."

"*Hijola*—shit, man, you're right. With what we've got, there's no way we'll get one."

"We can try," Roberts said, and he began erasing the blackboard with the rag. "We can sure as hell try. But first I want to call Sam once more at the lab. And I've already arranged with the Border Patrol for a flyover along that canal to at least have a closer look at Masters' ranch."

Deputy Link Johnston put the call through.

"Sam? Roberts. Don't get your balls in an uproar, but I need more on the Vasquez victim. Yeah, you're a bastard too, Sam, but he hasn't told us quite enough yet. The grease and fertilizer were good, and the citrus residue, and the dog food and hairs were sheer genius. We're getting there. With just a little more—anything—we're going to try for a warrant, but—what? Okay, fine, Sam. Thanks. I owe *you* now." He hung up and looked at Gomez. "He's going to take one more close look, but anything new will have to go to the FBI lab in Phoenix for analysis."

He had Link Johnston put a call through to Lang then, and told the lieutenant that considering what they had now, he wanted a warrant to search Dutch Masters' farm. Lang's raucous laugh was irritatingly to the point, but Roberts finally convinced him he was serious. "The Border Patrol is going to fly us over the place for a look, but we need that warrant."

"I'll try, Roberts," Lang gave in grudgingly, "but what will you do for me?"

"I'll close this triple homicide with positive results, Chief, okay?"

"You better, Roberts. Captain Trudeau is getting antsy about this one. I think he's gonna want to look into it personally."

"Shit," Roberts said as he hung up the phone.

"Trouble?" Gomez asked.

"Lang says the chief of detectives is getting antsy and may look into this case himself. Snowing the Homicide chief is one thing, but Trudeau is a horse of a different hue. He's a hard-nosed, egotistical, arrogant ass, but he's got more than shit for brains." Roberts stared hard at Gomez. "We better hope Sam comes up with something solid, or that Lang gets that fucking warrant."

"And if they don't get either?"

"If they don't, we'll be up that old familiar creek without even a boat, much less a paddle. And that'll leave us with one choice. One of us will have to go under cover. And it's sure nobody in his right mind would ever take *me* for a Mexican."

TWENTY

"WON'T we spook 'em if we get down too low?" Roberts asked.

Larry Preston, the Border Patrol agent seated beside the pilot, laughed. "They're used to 'harassment' by the Migra. It's about all we have manpower for. It's an attempt to keep 'em honest, but it doesn't work."

The Cessna 210 banked sharply to the left, and both Roberts and Gomez leaned instinctively the other way as Preston nodded to the pilot and pointed out the various features on the Masters ranch. "That big Quonset hut is for storage, machinery, wets, whatever." The curved corrugated metal sides glinted silver in the sunlight against the dark green foliage of the surrounding groves.

In another clearing, a long, wooden, apparently abandoned barracks building was surrounded by weeds. "What's that?" Roberts asked.

"Just what it looks like—a barracks and mess hall. It was used back in the '60s when they had legal Mexicans working—the *braceros*. The wets have to fend for themselves."

The plane banked sharply again, and Roberts felt a slight queasiness in his stomach as they straightened out and headed in low along the winding canal that bisected the northern section of the ranch. Narrow dirt roads branched out in several directions through the groves, but two converged on a large clearing with a two-story building and attached shed

115

surrounded by rusting equipment. Roberts tapped Preston on the shoulder and pointed, "What's that—near the canal?"

"Maintenance shop and office."

Roberts glanced significantly at Gomez, and then asked Preston, "How come we don't see any people?"

"They're there. Among the trees—in camps along the ditches. There's the main house and outbuildings coming up now."

Below them a modern sprawling brick ranch house loomed out of a clearing in the dense groves. A wide, dusty yard with garages and storehouses and a broken-down corral, and Roberts spotted a girl hanging wash on a line. She waved as they passed overhead. "Who lives there?" Gomez asked. "Besides Dutch and his son?"

"Not Jack," Preston answered. "He's got an apartment in town. And the old man's a widower. No other family. That girl's probably the maid—and probably wet. He's got a foreman named Jesse Peralta, and a crew pusher—Paco Cruz. But Cruz lives in town, too."

Roberts looked at Gomez. "When we get back I want a make on all four of them, got that?"

"Jack, too? He wasn't even in town—"

"Especially Jack. We don't know where he was."

The Cessna was flying level now over a barren mesa that had suddenly jutted up above the groves. "This still Masters' place?" Roberts asked.

Preston nodded. "I want to show you the dogs." Moments later he pointed to the large fenced enclosure of several acres, and the salt cedars with the ramshackle stone buildings scattered among them. As the plane banked and began to circle, Preston added, "See them—chained to individual doghouses."

There seemed to be no one around down here either, not even a parked truck, though an aluminum travel trailer was parked under one of the trees. "Used to be an old guest ranch," Preston was saying, "but it went broke. Dutch bought it up and planned to expand his citrus acreage up onto the mesa. There's a good well, and you can see the old water tower."

"Why didn't he expand?" Roberts asked.

"Jack, his son, has no interest in the citrus business. He's the one runs the 'show' dogs and uses the old guest ranch for his kennels. See the old swimming pool with no water? It's half full of sand and used as a fighting pit."

"All illegal now, of course," Gomez commented. "California and Arizona both have made it a felony."

Larry Preston shrugged. "One more law made to be broken."

They flew back over the main ranch once more, but nothing was stirring. Even the girl hanging clothes had gone back inside. "Seen enough?" Preston asked, and Roberts nodded. The Border Patrol agent signaled the pilot, and the plane banked again and streaked away over the maintenance yard and along the canal toward the highway.

"Shit, man," Gomez said to no one in particular, "I'd give my left nut to know what's going on down there right now."

Down below, Lupita Morales was writhing in ecstasy under Jesse's stinging lash. He had her hands bound to the metal bedstead in his apartment over the maintenance shed, and she was lying naked, face down, twisting and turning and moaning as he used his leather belt expertly across her back and buttocks; not quite hard enough to rip open flesh, but enough to raise beautiful red welts that, combined with the inability to move her wrists, drove her into a sexual frenzy.

She panted and sweated; her eyes blurred and her heart pounded; and when he finally pulled her to her knees, still bound, and mounted her like a dog, she shrieked with pain and delight, reveling in the sheer brute strength of his thrust.

Jesse Peralta was sweating, too. Finished, he was breathing hard and barely aware of the sound of the plane passing overhead as he released her hands and sat down beside her on the bed. He watched Lupita roll over, rubbing her wrists, her face still flushed, her dark eyes bright and almost unseeing. The fucking spic bitch, he thought, and watched her get up and disappear into the bathroom.

Down in the yard outside, the sun shone hot and bright and the surrounding orchard was still. The digital clock beside his bed read 12:38, and the thought flashed through his mind: Lupita Morales was always good for a nooner.

When she came out, and began to dress, she felt his eyes on her and knew the familiar feeling of genuine fear. It was almost a tangible presence whenever he was near her; a fear that remained with her, deliciously sweet, like the pain he inflicted, long after he was gone. But she knew the fear, like the pain, was an innate part of their relationship—maybe the best part. Because it was the instinctive fear of him that had attracted her most. And she was deathly afraid of Jesse Peralta most of the time. So she almost didn't mention what was troubling her, except that she was also curious about his reaction. And as her curiosity gradually overcame her fear and common sense, she told him about the two detectives who had come into the bar Tuesday afternoon.

Jesse's face grew dark and furtive, his gray eyes hooded and dangerously angry. "Detectives? Cops? What did they want?"

"They're poking around those canal deaths," Lupita told him, already regretting her decision to speak of it. "You know—the banker and his girl and that wetback, Enrique Vasquez. It was in the paper. He came into the bar a few times, but I never knew where he worked. They're looking for his nephew now, a kid. Paper said he's supposed to be around here, too. Did Vasquez ever work for you?"

Jesse crossed the space between them so suddenly, so savagely, that she flinched reflexively and caught her breath as he gripped her arm in his strong hairy hand. She was in her bra and panties now, her blouse half on, but the pain was shooting clear up into her shoulder, and she was afraid to cry out or try to pull away. "What did you tell them?" he snapped.

"Nothing. Honest, Jesse, *por seguro. Híjola, hombre,* what could I tell them?"

He relaxed his grip then and she pulled away, rubbing her arm where he had held it. "What in hell's the matter with you?" she said.

But Jesse Peralta had stepped to the window where he stood staring down at the yard while she finished dressing.

"He never worked here," he said at last, his back still turned to her, "and I don't want you talking to any cops again, Lupita. Not about anything. I don't like cops." He looked around then and waved, "Go on—get out of here. I'll call you later."

He watched from the window as she descended the stairs and crossed the yard to her battered Chevy pickup. When only the dust of her departure remained in the yard, he turned back to the rumpled bed and sat down. He stared around him at the shambles of a room. The dirty dishes from breakfast still on the table, the box of dirty laundry almost a week old beside the closet door. The morning newspaper was still open on the chair beside the bed, folded to the story of the letter in Spanish that had been on the wetback's body—a letter from the fourteen-year-old nephew who was sought now by the police for questioning.

Jesse thought hard about the boy—Arturo Vasquez—out there with Jack's dogs. And he thought too about the two detectives who had questioned Lupita.

Moments later he had the box containing his Magnum from under the bed. Slowly, methodically, he began to clean and oil the weapon all over again.

He would have to do something about that kid.

A mile away, in the main house, Virgil "Dutch" Masters was getting a "nooner" too. Sprawled naked in his lazy-boy recliner by the cold rock fireplace in his den, he ran his hand through the mat of gray hair that blanketed his chest and belly while his "wet" Mexican maid, Juana, knelt between his thighs and serviced him with her mouth and tongue. At sixty, Dutch needed a little help keeping it up.

A widower for three years, he took great pleasure in his new freedom. Not that Hannah hadn't been a good enough wife as wives go. She'd bitched and nagged and whined no more than most he knew of, but after thirty-two years of it—the money for all this being on her side of the family—it was actually pleasing to be alone. Or not alone when he chose, like now. He patted Juana's head while she worked.

He needed something now and then to relieve the tensions; and fortunately, little Juana never refused. How could she? Two years ago, at eighteen, she had come to him from a friend in Hermosillo—a Mexican friend he had dealt with before in matters of illegals. It was a solution to both their needs, his and his friend's, since the friend had gotten the girl in trouble and she was pressing for marriage after her family turned her out.

Dutch had seen the advantages instantly. Tired of an occasional whore and badly in need of a housekeeper, he had smuggled her with her swollen belly north into the U.S. in his camper. And she had been with him ever since—her and her brat, which was part of the hold he had on her.

Cook and scrub, fuck and suck, she did it all for forty dollars a week and board. And even from that he deducted Social Security and taxes, which never went to either office; fuck the bleeding-heart government, too.

Best of all, she never had a "headache." Anytime he didn't get instant obedience—if she didn't scrub hard enough or suck deep enough—he threatened to turn her and her brat over to the Border Patrol, and she was more afraid of this than of him. And since she didn't seem to know, he didn't bother to inform her that her baby's birth in the U.S. made it a citizen, and she could probably become legal, too.

He suspected that another reason she put up with him was an uncle she had told him about, the only one who might take her back if she went home, and for the same services that she rendered to Dutch. So he could relax. Juana's services were one thing he didn't have to worry about.

If only he could say the same for everything else. Because for Dutch the world was changing too damn fast. And for the worse. Even his small sphere was intruded on; browbeaten by federal regulations, by inflated costs, impossible interest rates; the land continually encroached on by big developers. It was worth far more now if he sold it for a future subdivision like Jack wanted to do.

And now there was this police thing. Another dead wetback. He had to admit that he'd made a mistake having Jesse put him in the canal. Burying had been best. The big foreman had put away maybe seven or eight of them since he'd been on the place, and those were the ones that Dutch knew of. God only knew how many the bastard might have done in secretly.

But why were the cops so persistent about finding the killer of a dead wet? And what did the deaths of the banker and his girl have to do with any of it anyway, besides being a coincidence? Dutch had asked around discreetly, like everyone who was curious did, but no one had any answers. And now with the story in the paper about some goddamned letter they'd found—Jesse hadn't even known enough to empty the greaser's pockets—and the nephew turning up at Jack's kennels looking for his uncle, Dutch didn't know what the hell was going on.

Should they run the kid off? Or risk telling Jack what had happened, before he started asking questions?

"God," he murmured, and issued a long, drawn-out groan of ecstasy, grabbing Juana's head, his thick fingers knotting in her shimmering black hair.

TWENTY-ONE

"JESUS H. Christ, not so damned much, kid!" Jack Masters yelled, yanking the feed bucket out of the boy's hand. "Don't you *sabe Inglés?*"

"*Sí, señor.* I learn with the *turistas* in Guadalajara."

"Then pay attention! I told you the size ration for each dog, once a day. You're giving 'em too fucking much!"

"But they are thin, señor. And there is so much food stored in the—"

Jack struck him a stinging backhand across the face. "You're not listening, kid, goddammit. Just do it like I tell you, if you want to work here. The dogs are meaner if they're lean and hungry. They fight better. *Sabe?*"

Arturo Vasquez nodded, rubbing his stinging cheek.

"Sorry if I got sore, kid, but you gotta learn. You gotta do things like I tell you, and only like I tell you if you're gonna work here. I can't be around to watch you all the time. Now finish filling their bowls and put the bucket away. You can clean up the shit later. I want to show you the fighting pit and tell you what to do there. Then I've got to go into town."

"*Sí, señor,*" the boy nodded obediently. Jack watched him refill the bucket from a big bag of dry dog food and then cup out a portion for each individual bowl. At least the boy wasn't afraid of the dogs. Harmless to humans, the pit bulls hated each other fiercely, so each was chained to a stake in front of its own shelter and well away from the other dogs.

And each had its own food and water dishes, buried in the ground to keep them from being turned over.

The tall salt cedars gave them shade from the heat, and they got all the exercise they needed from fighting. The only attention they needed was for feeding and watering and untangling their chains when they wound them around their doghouses. Jack decided the boy was better than any adult he had had for a long time. A little young, but that was even better. He trained easier and he scared easier. Jack wondered why he hadn't thought of it before—getting a kid.

The only thing that worried him now was this particular kid. From what Jack had heard around town, the uncle Arturo was looking for was the same Mexican who had been found dead in the canal along with the banker, Winters, and his girl. And now the fuzz wanted the kid for questioning.

There wasn't much chance they'd find him here of course, unless—and he realized his momentary anger with the boy had really been a spillover of his fury at his sudden breakup with Patricia Lane. He was still sore at being dumped—and jealous. And angry for being jealous. But after all, he didn't own her. She wasn't one of his dogs, even if she was a bitch sometimes.

Yet what if she mentioned the dogfighting to her new boyfriend? It *was* a felony now, even though seldom enforced. Shit, he thought, that's all he needed. To get caught with illegal pit bulls and an illegal alien kid who was also hunted by the police. And Dutch with illegals all over the place working the citrus. At least he knew Jesse Peralta could handle them and keep most of them out of sight—the guy had a real mean streak in him. But maybe it would be better to get rid of the boy after all, send him on down the road and not take a chance. He'd have to think about it.

When Arturo returned from putting away the feed and buckets, Jack took him around to what had once been the guest-ranch swimming pool and was now the practice fighting pit.

He showed the boy where he stored the iron rake in the old bathhouse. He also kept the portable bleachers there, for use when he had a fight here. "You keep the sand raked smooth and even," he explained. "After a fight there'll be a lot of blood, and you'll have to throw fresh sand over it and rake it in, *sabe*? I'll show you how we set up the bleachers later."

"*Sí, señor*. And the next fight—when will it be?"

"Soon. But not for a couple of weeks. You'll know how to do everything by then, okay?"

Arturo Vasquez smiled. "Okay."

Later in the afternoon, Jack took Arturo with him as he made the rounds of the ranch. Since Dutch and Jesse and Paco looked after the citrus business, the dogs were his only real concern. Still, he always liked to look the place over when he got back from a trip, just to make sure. After all, he reflected, he had a financial interest in it. When the old man was finally gone, it would be his to sell or develop or whatever the hell he decided to do with it.

He drove over to the canal to check on Paco and a crew that were picking there, and then back past the maintenance yard to stop by the office. Neither Dutch nor Jesse was anywhere around, so he drove on over to the main house and parked in back.

Arturo, watching Jack disappear into the big, two-story brick structure, wondered how long he would be. He had decided he was going to like working with the dogs, but it didn't solve the problem of finding his uncle. So he would be able to stay here only a little while and then, if he learned nothing of Enrique, he would simply have to move on and ask somewhere else.

When a side door of the house slammed suddenly, he thought it was Jack Masters returning, but it was a girl—a Mexican girl—running across the yard right in front of the truck. She looked about the same age as the girl back at the store in town, but not as pretty. He called to her.

She stopped, hesitant, then glanced back toward the house before coming over to the truck. When she got closer, he saw she'd been crying. "What's the matter?" he asked her. "Are you hurt?"

"No." She wiped her eyes with the back of her hand. "Who are you?"

"Arturo Vasquez. I'm working for the Señor Masters—with the dogs."

"Oh, him—the young one. You're lucky you don't work for the old man—that *pendejo*!" She spat into the dirt beside the front wheel. "May his eyes rot out and his heart be eaten by ants!"

"You don't like working here?" Arturo asked her.

"I hate it."

"Then why don't you leave?"

"I have a baby, only a year old. Where can I go?" She brushed her hair back out of her face then, and peered at him more closely. "You say your name is Vasquez? There's another Vasquez working here. Enrique Vasquez."

Arturo's face brightened. "Enrique? He's my uncle—I came north to find him!"

"Well, he's here. Only, I haven't seen him for several days. He works for Jesse, the foreman."

"I think I met Jesse, but he didn't say he knew my uncle. Where can I find him?"

She shrugged. "He's around someplace. But I haven't seen your uncle since last week—no," she frowned, "Sunday—it was Sunday afternoon. Maybe he's gone."

"Did he say anything about leaving?"

"No. He was here fixing a plugged toilet for the old man. He said he'd been repairing a tractor at the shop, and that Jesse was after him to finish that job by Monday. But he didn't say anything about leaving." She looked around as Jack Masters came out the back door. "You might ask him," she said. "He came by Sunday afternoon too, and he gave your uncle a ride back down to the maintenance shop. Now I've got to go."

"What's your name?" Arturo called after her.

She turned, breaking into a run. "Juana," she called back over her shoulder. "Juana Lopez!"

Jack Masters drove out of the yard with the boy beside him. He suspected he'd interrupted something between the old man and that maid, Juana, and he smiled to himself. The old fart still had some fire in his furnace.

He'd mentioned what he'd heard around town about the banker and the dead wetback, and that the wetback was evidently the boy's uncle, but Dutch had said he didn't know of any Enrique Vasquez ever working for them. "Of course he could have been here," Dutch had said. "Wetbacks come and go all the time." But he didn't see it as any reason not to keep the boy around if he could handle the dogs.

Then the voice of the boy beside him interrupted his thoughts.
"—my Uncle Enrique."

"What?"

"That girl back there—she knows my uncle. He works here. She said you gave him a ride back to the maintenance shop last Sunday."

Jack Masters stared at him. "Last Sunday? Yeah—that's right—I'd just got back and stopped at the house. I did give a Mexican a ride down to the shop. I had to pick up some papers at the office. But I didn't know his name. That was your uncle?"

Arturo nodded. "Can we go find him?"

Jack swung the truck onto the road that led back up to the mesa. He didn't answer the boy. He was trying to think. What the hell had gone on while he was gone? If that was Enrique Vasquez he had picked up Sunday afternoon, and Monday morning he was pulled out of the canal a few miles away, all beaten up— He glanced at the boy beside him. "He's gone, kid," he said. "Your uncle quit and left the ranch—last Sunday afternoon. He didn't say where he was going. So you might as well forget him. You've got your own work to take care of here now."

But later, driving into town alone in his pickup, Jack still hadn't decided what to do. Even if the dead Mexican had been working here for Dutch, it didn't mean anything had happened to him here. And since he was dead, there was no point in upsetting the kid. Maybe if he kept the boy out on the mesa with the dogs . . . but there was still the question of Patricia and her goddamned detective friend.

In Mimbres Junction he went first to the Hanging Tree.

When he learned that the barmaid, Lupita Morales, had moved over to the Watering Hole, he drove over there, pulling up in front of the huge plaster-of-paris cow skull that was surrounded by a ring of whitewashed rocks and bleached cow bones and cacti.

It was still early, not yet six o'clock, and there were only a few customers inside as he slid over a stool at one end of the bar. Lupita brought him his favorite drink without being asked and he smiled. "You remembered."

"Sure I remember. Did you ask for me over at the Tree?"

"They said you'd moved over here. How come?"

"Better pay—what else? So what you been up to, Jack? Off on another one of your trips?"

Jack Masters nodded. "New Mexico—made a few bucks. How's your love life, Lupita?"

She smiled, exposing her missing tooth. "I'm not hurting. I've got a new guy."

"Yeah, who's that?"

"Huh-uh," she shook her head. "I'm not telling. He's very jealous."

Jack shrugged, and while he drank their conversation turned to the three recent deaths at the canal bridge. It had been four days now and the whole thing seemed to be cooling down. The cops had no new leads, and Lupita didn't think they would keep looking for the killer of a wetback. It was the banker and his girl they were really concerned about, and that had probably been an accident.

While Lupita went down to the other end of the bar to take care of a customer, Jack stared at the small black-and-white TV screen with its fuzzy picture. The sound was turned down so low he could barely hear the music of the costumed *mariachis* who were playing. He decided he would chance keeping Arturo on, at least for a while.

He even wondered for a moment who might have beat the Mexican to death, and then decided it must be tied in some way with the banker and his girl, since he was found with them. As he ordered another drink, Jack wondered if he ought to hit on Lupita just for the hell of it. It had been a long time since she had been his girl.

But as she came down the bar, bringing him another drink and a dish of peanuts, he found his eyes had grown accustomed to the dim interior lighting, and he noticed the fresh bruises on her bare shoulders and arms and wondered briefly just who her new boyfriend might be.

TWENTY-TWO

IN the big L-shaped Sheriff's Department building in the city, Roberts went up to the second-floor detective squad room and checked in. It was 7:10 Friday morning and other than the duty officer and a couple of detectives just in from a stakeout, he had the place to himself.

Sitting down at the desk he shared with Gomez, he went through the messages on the spike. Nothing urgent. Another body found, this time in a desert wash, evidently an OD; Lang was turning it over to the narcs. The judge had denied the warrant—not enough probable cause. And Sam had just called at seven. Good old Sam. Roberts picked up the phone and dialed the Medical Examiner's number. "Sam? Roberts."

"About time you got on the job," Sam said. "I got the lab report back from Phoenix."

"That fast? You must have a magic wand."

"They owe me too—you taking notes?"

"Shoot." Roberts had his pad open, his pen poised.

"One—microscopic flecks of metal rust in flesh of victim's face and head, but still no better clue to the weapon except that it was old and rusty. Two—lint and fibers under his fingernails were from khaki cloth—not his own blue denim. Three—two strands of dark brown, human scalp hair, with human blood on them. Blood same type as victim's, but hairs not victim's. And hair cream on the two hairs, but none on the victim's hair."

"Hair cream?"

"Right. Cream, not oil. Not Vitalis or Brilliantine—maybe Wildroot or Brylcreem. It's hard to match up hairs. But I'm afraid that's all our friend Enrique is going to tell us. It's not much."

Sam was right, Roberts thought, scribbling rapidly. It wasn't much. "Thanks, Sam. You know what they say, every little bit—" He closed his notebook and hung up the phone. A blunt, rusty metal object, he mused; khaki cloth worn by the assailant, and dark brown hair with hair cream. "Shit," he mumbled. He *had* been hoping for more. Something—but he should have known. He seldom got the "something" handed to him. He usually had to get it the hard way.

He glanced up at the board, but Gomez hadn't checked in. After the flyover yesterday afternoon, he'd sent his partner to run the make on their suspects and then told him to take off and go see a movie, get his mind off the whole case for a while. Roberts had stayed at his apartment, relaxing with a TV rerun of *The Rockford Files* followed by a long hot shower and a few chapters of an historical novel. But that was yesterday, and Gomez was due on at seven, too. So where in hell was he?

Rabbit Gomez had started in on time, but a friend had flagged him down and told him his cousin, Raul, was looking for him. He had a tip on the canal deaths down in Mimbres Junction. Raul would be at home till nine or so this morning if Gomez wanted to talk about it.

So Gomez stopped at a phone booth and called in. "Sergeant?"

"Where the fuck are you?"

"I got a lead needs checkin', but it's down in the barrio and he'll only be there till nine. You want me to pick you up or go on down alone?"

"Where are you?"

"Corner of Ninth and Saguaro Drive—in a phone booth."

"Sit tight. I'll be there in fifteen minutes. We'll park my heap and go in yours. I've got news too—no warrant. And the Phoenix lab report is back."

* * *

In Gomez's shining metallic-silver Trans-Am, with its tape deck and dual rear speakers belting out the fiery "La Bamba," they headed south across the tracks and into the historic Mexican Barrio with its twin-towered, Spanish-style churches and ramshackle adobe houses that featured tiny fenced yards with bright flowers. Here the graffiti on the walls of abandoned buildings was mostly Chicano. Spray-can specialties included VIVA LA RAZA, BARRIO LIBRE and GRINGO GO HOME.

"I used to go to school down here," Gomez was saying, trying to talk above the blaring music until Roberts signaled him to turn it down.

"That's better," Roberts said. "Now what about school? I thought you were from some town on the California border."

"I am, but there was family trouble for a couple of years and I had to live over here with an aunt. My cousin lived with me, and we went to grade school a couple of blocks from here. Got chased home nearly every day by bigger kids." The radio was playing a more soothing "Malagueña Salerosa" as he continued, "My aunt still lives in the old neighborhood. She'd never move. All this—the crumbling decay, the garbage, the potholed streets—it's home." He shook his head. "But I'll never understand the old ones."

Roberts thought he could understand. Maybe because he sometimes felt he was becoming an "old one." It was a part of the culture, the heritage, the sense of belonging. He was surprised at how many modern Hispanic kids couldn't even speak the language, much less read and write it. While on the edges of the barrio, the old places were being bought up and restored and turned into quaint restaurants and offices for lawyers and accountants. But all he said was, "You sure I'm gonna be safe on this trip?"

"As a baby in its crib, Sergeant." And he laughed. "You got me to guide you."

Minutes later they pulled up to the curb across the street from a low-income housing project where several old-model cars, mostly Chevys and Fords, were parked helter-skelter in the parking bay. One vehicle was jumping up and down in one spot while a dozen Hispanic males gathered around to watch.

"There he is," Gomez said, "my cousin Raul. Belongs to a low-rider club—he's the one in the car. I'll go talk to him. You better wait here. These low-riders got no love for cops. They get hassled too much—and usually deserve it."

"Okay," Roberts said, "if he'll stop playing jumping jacks long enough to talk to you. Sure you don't want a backup?"

"Hey, it's family, man." Gomez was already out of the car and waving to his cousin.

Roberts watched him cross the street, and only then noticed on the broad brick side of an old building a block farther down a giant red and black mural depicting violent revolution. He wondered what it was all really coming to in America.

He watched the club members give way as Gomez walked over, and his cousin Raul's car stopped hopping. Gomez got in, and after a collective glance in Roberts' direction, the others drifted back to their own cars.

It didn't take long. But when Gomez returned, his usually bright face was clouded. He leaned down on the edge of the open window to talk. "We might be in trouble, man. The Mexican who changed the tire that night for the banker is alive and well. My cousin knows him. He's a wetback too, and he works as a dishwasher someplace. He won't talk to anyone but my cousin, but he confirms Freddie's story. He was cutting through the parking lot to his job when he saw them, and the banker gave him five to change the tire. He threw the spare and jack back in the trunk and that was that. He said they both seemed a little *borracho,* but not bad. No arguments, no trouble."

"So that shoots down our smoke job that he might have been our victim and the banker his killer."

"Does it have to go in the report right away?"

"No, not right away. It's only hearsay if the guy won't talk to us directly. But the lid is closing down fast, I can feel it. Get in. Let's make a quick call to the Border Patrol, and then we'll go get some breakfast and I'll tell you about the Phoenix lab report before we figure out what to do next."

* * *

In the Mexican café across the street from the Sheriff's Department, over tall, cold glasses of orange juice, plates of *huevos rancheros,* and coffee, they plotted their next move. Roberts knew they had to keep the momentum going. If they let down now the whole thing would slip away, out of control. But tying the wetback's death to the banker and his girl was getting close to ridiculous. He felt it should be obvious to everyone now what they were doing—the smoke screen they'd been laying to stay on the case. He felt vulnerable, exposed, and there was only one thing left. They needed an on-site look around Masters' citrus farm for hard evidence, warrant or no.

Gomez must have been reading his mind. "Why not have Public Safety try for a warrant to go after the dogs?" he suggested. "That would at least get us on the place, and we could look around unofficially."

Roberts shook his head, washing down a mouthful of food with orange juice and wiping his lips on a napkin. "They might not even get that. And if they did, it could spook them without gaining anything. It's a big place. We'd have the dogs but be nowhere near what we're really looking for—the site of the murder and the weapon." He studied Gomez closely. "I really don't see any option now, partner. You're just gonna have to put on your old clothes and start remembering how to talk Mexican. And here comes the guy who's gonna help you do it." He nodded toward the door, where Larry Preston had just come in wearing his dress-green uniform.

The Border Patrolman glanced around, spotted Roberts, and walked over, removing a stiff-brim hat to reveal a receding crew cut of rust-red hair. As Preston slid into the booth beside Roberts, the detective asked him, "You want some breakfast?"

"No, thanks—just coffee. You guys having problems with your murder case?"

"You wouldn't believe the problems," Roberts said, signaling the waitress for another pot of coffee and an extra mug. "We want to know about Dutch Masters' place and everybody on it—everything you know."

Larry Preston shrugged. "That won't take long." His long horse face wore an amiable expression. "He's been a citrus grower down in Mimbres Junction for years. His son, Jack, just won't seem to settle down and help run the place. Keeps those buildings we spotted from the air, and gambles big on the fights."

"What about their personalities?" Roberts asked him. "Jack, for instance—"

"Like I said, he's a wild hair, unpredictable. But he's just not around a lot, what with his 'dog shows.' I don't think anybody really knows him, though you might try Lupita, the barmaid at the Hanging Tree. She went with him for a while."

"If that's Lupita Morales, she's at the Watering Hole now," Roberts said. "Gomez and I talked to her, but only about the case in general and the wetback victim." He glanced at his partner. "Maybe we should talk to her again."

"Well, her new boyfriend should interest you," Preston said. "She's going with the head foreman at Masters' place now—Jesse. But hell, she's gone with everybody at one time or another. I even went with her for a week or so a few months ago. But I wouldn't mess with her now that she's Jesse's girl."

"What about him?" Roberts asked. "What's he like?"

Preston smiled. "Half Mexican, half Irish, and meaner than a junkyard dog. He's Dutch Masters' right-hand man, especially since old Dutch and Jack don't get along too well."

"And the assistant foreman—Paco Cruz?"

"A legal Mexican immigrant, and quiet as silk on satin, but nothing to mess with, either. He drinks his beer and minds his own business. You understand, Sergeant, I'm talking from a Border Patrolman's view." His homely smile showed horse teeth that matched his face, but his winsome personality overcame it all. "They all hate our guts for hassling them about their wets."

"Then they do work wets," Roberts said.

"Hell, Sergeant, they all work wets. Wetbacks are the laboring backbone of the desert Southwest."

"And Dutch—the old man himself—what's he like?"

"Mulish, crusty old buzzard, and like most growers a hard-nosed conservative. Hates any kind of government meddling except when it's handing out subsidies. Hard to deal with, and not just with us. Ask any business around town, or the agricultural agent, the Irrigation District—he gives everybody a hard time. Here—" he pulled a paper out of his jacket pocket and cleared a place on the table to unfold it. "I picked up an aerial photo of the place for you. Got it from a crop-duster friend. It's a couple of years old, but nothing's changed much from what you saw in the flyover.

"See—here's the main house and outbuildings. There's an old trash dump that's overgrown with weeds now, and this old pumphouse burned down last year. But the rest is the same. There's the big Quonset hut, and the old guest ranch on the mesa—Jack only had a few dogs then. And there, near the canal, is the maintenance shop."

"A lot of rusty old equipment strewn around the yard even then," Roberts commented.

"Here's the two-story block building attached to the shop that Dutch uses for his office. I think Jesse Peralta has an apartment upstairs. The crew pusher, Paco, commutes from Mimbres Junction. Married, with a wife and six kids."

"And the wetbacks?" Gomez asked.

Larry Preston smiled again. "Wets are where you find them, Rabbit. Sometimes here, sometimes there. Camped out along irrigation ditches, in old barns or in mesquite groves. They move around a lot." He looked at Roberts. "Well, Sergeant, I guess that's about it. Does it help?"

"Plenty," Roberts said. "I've only got one question—where's the nearest public telephone to this place?"

Preston frowned, studying the photomap. "That would be about here," he pointed, "off this map. It's a crossroads gas station with a phone booth outside." With his pen he marked an X about an inch out in the margin. "It's a good mile from Masters' front gate."

"Thanks. I think we've got what we need."

"You going in under cover?"

'He is.'' Roberts nodded at his partner. "A 'wet'—old

clothes, no ID, no gun. Naked except for his inimitable charm. Without a warrant he won't be able to gather any evidence, but at least he'll be able to see if there's any there."

Larry Preston shook his head. "Hell, Rabbit, what are you gonna do, just walk up to the front door and ask for work?"

"I guess so," Gomez said. "I don't like it either, but I don't see we've got much choice."

"Have you got a better idea?" Roberts asked the agent.

"Well," Preston seemed to be thinking, "why don't you mix him in with some real wets? There's several places we stake out when we've got the manpower, gathering points where different growers are known to pick up workers. They know they're wetbacks, but they don't ask them for papers, they just ask if they want to work. There's a place about three miles from Masters' groves." He rubbed his long tapered jaw, his eyes still on Roberts. "When were you thinking of sending him in?"

"As soon as we can set it up."

"Okay, I can draw you a rough map to the rendezvous, but let me clear it with my chief first so we can keep our agents away from it all this next week. Just have Rabbit hang out there—it's a brush-and-pasteboard camp—listen to the talk, say he's waiting for someone in particular. Or hell, Rabbit, say you're waiting for Masters' foreman—you heard he was good to work for."

"Bite your tongue, man," Gomez said, grinning.

"But for Christ's sake, be careful," Preston warned him. "Like I said, Dutch Masters' sun don't shine on any kind of government interference."

"And if you *should* get picked up by Border Patrol agents before you can get on the place, Gomez," Roberts added, "just flash that smile of yours and ask for Preston. I hope he'll get you out of the lockup before you get shipped to Vera Cruz or someplace and I have to ask Lang to pay your freight back—it's not in the budget."

Preston laughed and held out his hand to them both. "I'll be in touch as soon as I talk to my chief."

"Thanks again," Roberts told him, "and now I'll give you

something. You might want to watch a guy named Fast Freddie at the Blue Lotus out on Redondo. Ugly little guy, but a real ladies' man—and he deals in fake documents for illegals.''

When the Border Patrol agent had left, Roberts opened a briefcase and took out four sheets of paper which he laid in front of his partner. ''Here's something else I picked up this morning—rap sheets on Virgil 'Dutch' Masters, Jack Masters, Jesse Peralta, and Paco Cruz. Read 'em and weep.''

Gomez read the reports to himself. Paco was almost clean. A legal resident alien, he'd immigrated in '63 after working as a *bracero*. Arrested once for an expired license plate, one fine for DWI, and one drunk-and-disorderly charge that was dropped. Old Dutch had stayed out of trouble except for one racial incident for which he got a six-month suspended sentence.

It was the other two who caused the detective to whistle sharply. For one thing, their army records. Jesse's service had been short and in peacetime, but with a Bad Conduct discharge for striking a noncom; while Jack had served as a rifleman with the 1st Cavalry in Nam, and was brought up on charges of fragging an officer by rolling a live grenade into his hooch. ''Acquitted for lack of evidence,'' Gomez read aloud. But Jack had ended up with a BC discharge, too, for various lesser offenses. Jack had no civilian record, but Jesse had served time in the Arizona state pen for armed robbery and assault. Gomez looked over at Roberts. ''A couple of real cool cats.''

''So I've been thinking,'' Roberts said. ''Maybe I better just drive onto that place myself. I've got some business cards—one that says I'm a tractor salesman. Maybe, if I'm real polite, someone will show me around.''

''You gotta be kidding, man! All they gotta do is say, 'Okay—tell me all about your latest model John Deere or Massey-Ferguson and then where would you be?''

''Up the old creek,'' Roberts admitted resignedly. ''So I guess if we're going to look for evidence unofficially on that place, it'll have to be up to you, after all. I just don't like your going in there without a backup.''

"Don't sweat it, man," Gomez flashed his smile. "It'll be a piece of cake."

"Sure—you ever been under cover before, Rabbit?"

"Twice. Once successfully. Once I inadvertently blew it and had to get bailed out fast."

"Terrific," Roberts said. "Just remember, the nearest phone is a mile away—but try to call out every twenty-four hours, whether you've got anything or not, *sabe*?"

"Por seguro, Sergeant," Gomez smiled confidently. "So what are we waiting for? I've got my old clothes and my winning smile."

"Don't get impatient. As soon as Larry Preston gets his chief's okay—probably tonight, as soon as it's dark. Just take care, you bastard," he added affectionately. "I haven't lost a partner yet."

TWENTY-THREE

"IT's dangerous, *querido*, and it's stupid!" Anita Carrillo was pouting again. "Why should *you* be the one to do it?"

"Because I'm Spanish, *mi corazón*," Gomez answered. "You think Roberts could pass for a wetback?" Sitting on the edge of the bed, he watched her disappear into the bathroom tossing her shimmering black hair angrily, hair that extended all the way down her lanky, naked body to the sweetest, firmest, brownest cheeks he had ever squeezed and patted. *Ay, chingado,* he thought miserably, she was a constant pain in his own ass, but she was all woman.

Now she had closed the door behind her without answering, and he was glad he hadn't told her about the undercover assignment until after their lovemaking. Because he didn't feel it was either stupid or especially dangerous. It was just necessary.

He had his own ideas about the wet's killing, but it was just theory and he hadn't mentioned it even to Roberts because he didn't see how they'd ever find the guy, much less prove it. He felt now that Enrique Vasquez had probably been killed by another wetback. Possibly a trivial argument had enflamed both men, but Enrique's opponent had been heavier, more skilled, and perhaps angrier. Gomez knew it still didn't explain the excessive violence, the overkill; for Enrique had taken a lot more blows than were necessary to do the job. Whoever had done it had been one mad sonofabitch.

139

He also knew if it was a fellow wetback, he was probably long gone, and there would be no point in gathering evidence against someone who was back in Mexico where extradition was a bad joke. But Gomez was a professional; he had his orders. He would go in, and he would look objectively—for the site, and for the weapon. And for the killer, too.

"Preston fixed him up with Mexican cigarettes, a sack of tortillas, a few pesos, and a pair of tire-treaded huaraches," Roberts explained. "We cut a mark on the left sole in case we should have to track him later, and let him off a mile from the camp right after dark." He looked at his watch. "That was about four hours ago. He might even be on Masters' place by now."

"But isn't it dangerous?" Patricia asked him. "I mean for what you stand to gain? What does he hope to find?" She turned the wheel, guiding her powder-blue Granada into the drive between the two adobe columns that marked the entrance to her property, a five-acre spread exactly 22.2 miles outside the city and thirteen miles from a seventeenth-century Spanish mission ruin that was now a National Monument.

Roberts forgot the question she had asked as she parked in front of a rambling restored adobe ranch house and got out to tie up a gutsy-looking German shepherd she called Lobo. When she motioned him out of the car, he walked over to her. "What did you just ask me? I was so fascinated with this place, it didn't register."

She took his hand, guiding him under the wide ramada hung with decorative pottery, and up to the ornately carved Spanish oak door. "I asked what you expect Gomez to find on Masters' ranch—the murderer?" Taking a key from her purse, she opened the door and switched on the lights.

"Evidence," Roberts said, stepping inside behind her. "At least the site of the murder, and maybe the weapon. And yes, the killer, too." He was looking around with intense appreciation. The place was obviously old—turn of the century, but solidly built with long narrow shuttered windows set deep into thick adobe walls. High overhead, rough-hewn wooden beams braced a saguaro rib ceiling that sheltered period furnishings—heavy carved couches and chairs, and Navajo rugs. There were Western scenes by Remington and Russell on the walls, along with a mélange of De Grazia Indian figures.

"I got this place six months ago," she told him with obvious pride. "A steal at forty thousand. It was left over from an estate that needed settling fast, all that remains of an old Spanish land grant. I borrowed another twenty thousand to restore it."

"It's beautiful," Roberts said, still taking in the arched doorways and Mexican tile floor.

"The kitchen's been modernized, and the bathroom. You want coffee, or something stronger?"

"Coffee's fine." He followed her into the copper-accented kitchen and slid over a stool at the breakfast bar, where he watched her fill a fresh filter for the coffeemaker and add water. He suddenly felt drained, tired. He supposed it was that kind of case. And worse, he wasn't sure now they could really pull it off. Lang's seventy-two hours were almost up; yet he felt so close to a solution he could taste it.

When she poured a mug of coffee and set it in front of him with cream and sugar, he ignored the cream but added a spoonful of sugar. He started to add a second but caught himself in time. "I'm cutting down on sugar," he said. "Just one now and I stir twice as hard."

She smiled. "So what's bothering you, Doug? That you should lose your head over a spoonful of sugar?"

"It's getting a handle on this case. I don't know who did it, or what they used, or even why they did it. I only have a general idea of where it was done. Yet I feel so close to the answers." He shook his head. "We've got nothing, no hard evidence, unless Gomez—" He thought a moment. "I've got to talk to Lupita Morales again. She's a barmaid at the Watering Hole in Mimbres Junction. Seems like she was everyone's friend in this—including Jack Masters."

"Just so she doesn't become yours," Pat warned him. "But you don't think Jack had anything to do with this, do you? He just got back from his trip Wednesday."

"You *saw* him Wednesday," Roberts reminded her. "We don't know when he got back—yet."

"Look, why don't you relax awhile—quit fighting it. It'll all come together soon. Isn't that what most detective work is—persistence and patience?"

He smiled. "And luck. You'd be surprised how often, after all the tiring legwork, the mind-boggling deduction, the interviews and record checks and empty leads, it's just plain blind-assed luck that finally turns a case."

Bending suddenly across the bar, she kissed him; so soft and lingering he felt his face flush and his mind reel. "C'mon," she whispered, brushing his cheek with her lips, "I want to show you something else—" She led him around the bar, through a back door, and down a hallway that opened onto a patio trellised with honeysuckle and bougainvillea. "There," she said, flicking on a faint blue spotlight that illuminated a Jacuzzi, "doesn't that look like a nice place to relax?"

As they left him in a dry irrigation ditch beside the road, Rabbit Gomez had whispered, "Adios." Roberts and Preston had wished him luck. Then Gomez had melted into the moonless dark of the warm September evening and headed west, mentally following the crude map Preston had scratched in the dirt alongside the road.

Taking his bearings on the Big Dipper that shone briefly through a break in the clouds, he paused long enough to shake one of the Mexican cigarettes loose from the pack and light it. Coughing, he cursed softly. Jesus, Maria, and Joseph, but it tasted like horseshit! Besides that, his feet already hurt; and he thought about kicking off the goddamned huaraches, except the rocks and clods turning under his bare feet would be worse.

Minutes later he paused again, sweating, and drank from an irrigation ditch. He thought about eating one of the tortillas he had wrapped in wax paper, but decided to wait. He wasn't sure when he'd have a real meal again, and suspected he might get damned hungry on this assignment.

To break the monotony he put his thoughts on Anita, on her firm round bottom, her tits with their thick dark nipples, her moist red lips—until he was tramping along with an erection fit to bust his pants. Then he spotted the shadowy outline of the dense mesquite grove Preston had described, and almost simultaneously caught the scent of a campfire on the shifting breeze, a scent that was combined with the distinct aroma of coffee and beans.

An abandoned irrigation ditch bisected the grove; a broad, shallow ditch, dry and weed-grown with the years of neglect. Along one side crude shelters had been erected out of cardboard and scrap lumber. With the overhanging branches of the mesquites almost forming a tunnel, the shacks were nearly invisible, even from the air.

The shelters were empty, but as he followed the scent a few feet further along the ditch he found three Mexican males hunkered around a heap of smoky, hot coals where a coffeepot and a pan of beans were warming. One of the men was using his fingers deftly to turn three flour tortillas that lay on the glowing coals. Since they were all talking softly among themselves, they didn't hear Gomez approach until he was practically among them.

"*Buenas noches, paisanos,*" he greeted them, startling them to their feet until they saw that he appeared to be a *mojado*, like themselves, and not the dreaded Migra.

Gomez was surprised at how easy it was. Squatting down on his haunches beside them, he added one of his own tortillas to heat on the coals. One of the Mexicans, who appeared to be the eldest and whose face was heavily pockmarked in the glow of the fire, shared a battered metal cup of coffee with him and added a dab of beans to his tortilla when it was hot. "How are you called, hombre?" the pock-marked man asked.

"Juan Garcia," Gomez answered, thanking him.

"I am Jacinto Torres," the man said, smiling and showing strong white teeth under a graying mustache. "And this is Juan Velasquez, and my cousin, Jaime Valdez."

The other two nodded solemnly, watching Gomez warily, and he wondered if they suspected something. But he gave them his cover story anyway. He was from a small village in Chihuahua, and had worked in Texas for almost a year—in the Rio Grande Valley, near McAllen. Times were hard there, and after going home for a while he had decided this time to try Arizona. He had jumped the line and walked through the desert west of Nogales, Sonora.

"Times are hard everywhere," Jacinto Torres said, "but life has to be lived." And he told Gomez the three of them had crossed together east of Nogales, near an old mining town. For one of them, Jaime—a pinch-faced youth of about seventeen—it was his first time as a wetback. The other two had worked and been caught several times and thrown back across the border, but they always returned.

"Tejas is the worst," Jacinto said, adding more coffee to his cup. "The Tejanos are hard to work for."

"I like California best," Juan Velasquez said. "The pay is better. But my father died and I had to go home to Fronteras, and this was closest to return."

Gomez shared the last of his Mexican cigarettes with them, lighting his own with a twig from the fire and trying to hide his distaste. He hoped he could bum an American brand somewhere soon; these stinking things would kill him. He also hoped his feelings didn't show as he looked at Jacinto and smiled. "How long have you been camped here?"

"Two days. There should be work starting in the citrus groves around here, but no one has come and we are afraid to ask around. If no one shows up tomorrow, we will have to move on. The Migra may know of this place by now."

Gomez sighed and decided to take the plunge. "I'm looking for someone from the Masters' ranch—Dutch Masters. His head foreman is called Jesse. I heard in Nogales he's supposed to be good to work for."

Jacinto glanced at the others, but they only shook their heads and shrugged. "We don't know of such a place," Jacinto said.

TWENTY-FOUR

ARTURO VASQUEZ finished feeding and watering the dogs just after dawn. Then he returned to his room in the storage building. He shook out his blanket and was hanging it out to air when the barking dogs called his attention to the two men coming across the yard past the fighting pit.

One of them was Miguel Ramirez. Arturo didn't know the other man, but he was obviously a *campesino*, too.

"*Hola*—Arturo!" Miguel called. "*Cómo te vas?*"

It was good to see the old man again. Arturo had been told he would be working seven days a week with the dogs, so he knew he would have no time to go visiting friends. He seldom even saw Jack Masters. There was a phone on the wall which he was to use to call other parts of the ranch if there were any problems, but there had been none yet.

"This is Jorge Diaz," Miguel introduced him to the stranger, a swarthy squat little man with a nervous tic. "He knew your Uncle Enrique."

"He worked here," Jorge said, "for quite a while—up until about a week ago. Then he disappeared. He didn't get along with the foreman, Jesse. That is one bad hombre, and we're leaving, too."

"We're on our way now, Arturo," Miguel said. "To Yuma. There are lots of citrus farms there. I wanted to come by and tell you. Since your uncle isn't here, maybe you want to go with us. We can find a better place than this."

Arturo thought about it, tempted. But this was the second person who had seen his uncle on this place, and he wanted to find out more. Perhaps where he had gone.

Jorge said he didn't know any more. He hadn't seen much of Enrique since he'd worked in a different crew. He had only talked to him a few times, at night in the big metal shed where they slept and ate. And Jorge knew of Enrique's arguments with the foreman. But he was sure Enrique had gone now. No one had seen him for days.

Arturo nodded somberly, but he was still determined. "I like working here with the dogs. The *patrón* doesn't bother me, and there's no reason to leave, not so soon."

"Have you been paid anything yet?" Miguel asked him.

"No."

"From what I hear you may never be paid," the old *vaquero* told him. "Sometimes they just call in the Migra and have them take you away when they've tired of you. Jorge has seen it done."

"I will stay," Arturo insisted, "at least for a while. I may be able to find someone who knows where my uncle has gone."

He watched them leave, and then finished his work as billowing white clouds began to build along the horizon. By late afternoon the clouds had darkened and gusts of wind sent blowing dust across the mesa. When Jack Masters finally came by and told him to get in the truck, Arturo wondered if he was being taken to the Migra.

Instead, they went only as far as Mimbres Junction. Jack bought a dozen fifty-pound bags of dry dog food at the feed store, and Arturo helped him load them into the back of the truck. Jack even bought him a bag of hard candy, and joked with the storekeeper about how much his 'show' dogs ate. "Better be careful hauling that wet kid around, Jack," the storekeeper cautioned him as they left. "An Immigration van rolled by here about a half-hour ago."

"Fuck the Immigration," Jack told him. "Right, kid?" But all the same he told the boy to get in the back and stay down among the feed bags until they were out of town. He knew it had been a risk, bringing the kid at all. He could have handled the dozen bags himself and hardly worked up a sweat; but he'd be damned if he'd skulk around, hiding from the Immigration or the cops. If he couldn't work the kid like he wanted, then let 'em have him.

As it turned out they saw no sign of the Migra. But as they passed the Watering Hole on the outskirts of town, Arturo spotted a familiar truck parked across the street with the foreman, Jesse, hunched behind the wheel.

Jack evidently didn't see him as they drove on by, but Arturo's eyes met the foreman's as they passed, and the intense cruel gaze made the boy shudder. He watched the parked truck until the road turned, putting it out of sight. He thought it odd that Jesse Peralta would be just sitting there in his truck. Why hadn't he crossed the street to the bar and gone inside? Arturo wondered too at the look of pure anger in the foreman's eyes, and why it gave him such an uneasy feeling.

Jesse Peralta had been parked across the street from the Watering Hole for almost fifteen minutes, and he was furious. He had come to town intending to drink and visit with Lupita, but as he was about to park he had seen the Anglo detective go into the bar. He knew it was the detective working the Winters case because the cops weren't the only ones who could ask questions. He too had asked around, and Lupita herself had described him and his greaser partner. He wondered where the greaser was, since the Anglo had gone into the bar alone.

It didn't matter. One was bad enough. And he wouldn't have any business in that bar except with Lupita. Jesse had warned her, goddammit, he had warned her.

A twist of wind swept a flurry of dust down the street in front of him. The forerunner of a storm, it finally broke his concentration. He had been so intent he hadn't even noticed Jack's truck until it was too late to duck. But Jack hadn't seen him, either. Only the wetback kid in the back had seen him, and that would be taken care of too—later.

His hands clenched and unclenched on the steering wheel as he thought about Lupita. He had warned her not to talk to the cops again. And now this one had been in that bar for nearly twenty minutes. He thought about his .357 Mag in the box under his bed. If he had it here right now . . .

He kept thinking about it, getting angrier by the minute; then he put his truck in gear and drove off into the gathering storm. He had made his decision suddenly, impulsively. Maybe another killing would put everyone off the scent.

Lupita Morales, watching the Anglo detective leave the bar, wondered why the police were so interested in what went on out at Dutch Masters' place. But like all detectives he only asked questions, never answered any. And why couldn't the cute one have come—the Mexican with the big smile? Roberts was a big, solemn-faced gringo whose eyes bored into you like hot irons and seemed to know when you were lying.

Not that she had to lie. What did she know? Nothing. And she had told him nothing. Sure, she knew Jesse Peralta, and Paco, and Jack, too. Even Dutch himself, the lecherous old fart—he wasn't as old as he seemed. She'd taken him on a time or two and saw no reason to complain. But what could she tell a cop investigating a killing? That Jesse had a real vicious streak in him? But Jack could be mean too, and so could Dutch. Paco Cruz was the only sane one out there.

It was too early for much business, not even dark yet and a storm blowing in, so she'd had no real excuse not to talk. But she wasn't afraid of the detective. She talked because she had nothing to hide. Yet she knew she wasn't going to tell Jesse about this second visit, because Jesse was the one she *was* afraid of. She'd simply tell him she'd heard the cops were still asking about him, that's all; him and Jack and Dutch. That would be enough.

Business got brisk as the evening wore on. The sky continued threatening and the wind blew, but only dust, no rain. The bar became crowded, like any Saturday night, and she began to wonder why Jesse hadn't come in. He was usually one of the early ones on the weekend. Then it occurred to her that maybe the cops were talking to him, too.

When she got off work at 1 A.M. Jesse still hadn't come in. She helped lock up, and the boss walked her through a spattering of thick, widely spaced raindrops to her station wagon in the parking bay off the alley. She started the engine, waited while her boss pulled his jeep around, and waved as he drove on past. Then she shifted to reverse and backed her wagon out into the alley.

All she saw were the man's eyes in her rearview mirror, but it was enough. She froze, her hand still on the gearshift lever, her mind immobile with fear as the wagon jerked to a stop and the engine sputtered and died. Recognition was instant, and the intent in those eyes obvious, especially to her. She opened her mouth to scream, not even thinking of using the horn; but even that was cut off as his arm came suddenly around her throat, the pain sharp and her vision blurring.

Her fingers, reaching back, knotted desperately in his long greasy hair. It was the last thing she was conscious of besides the excruciating pain. . . .

TWENTY-FIVE

THE telephone jarred Roberts out of a deep sleep. The rain of a late-summer thunderstorm was rattling against the window, and he thought at first the thunder had awakened him. But the raucous ringing sounded again, and he fumbled the receiver against his ear as his eyes focused on the luminous digital dial of a bedside clock. It was 5:42 on Sunday morning. Gomez must be checking in.

"Yeah, Gomez—what is it?" he mumbled sleepily.

"Roberts? Lieutenant Lang. Get your head screwed on straight and listen up. A fresh stiff, and this one's ours, right in Mimbres Junction. Body found back of a bar. Female, Hispanic, age twenty-nine . . . you getting this, Roberts?"

"Yeah, I'm listening." He was sitting up on the edge of the bed, squeezing the sleep from his eyes. "I thought you were Gomez. Christ, I hope this isn't one of those grisly ones, Chief, where he's carved her twat out or something."

"Nothing like that, Roberts—clean and fast—strangled. Lab men are on their way. And she's been ID'd. Name's Lupita Morales. Barmaid at the Watering Hole."

"What? Shit, Chief, I just talked to her about this Vasquez—this Winters case; I—"

"Now look, Roberts," Lang cut him off. "This one's neat and simple—a two-bit chippy, probably done in by a jealous boyfriend. Strictly a Factor One, so don't waste a lot of time on it. Just find the boyfriend and wrap it up quick. And for

God's sake, Roberts, don't try to tie *it* in with the Winters thing. It isn't even the same M.O. The dead spic was beaten to death."

"And the banker drowned, and his girl broke her neck, Chief. You've been reading too many mystery stories. In real life a murderer doesn't always use the same M.O." Roberts was already pulling on his pants, the phone tucked under his chin. "And you've got to admit, it must be some kind of epidemic—no homicides in Mimbres Junction in over a year, then four deaths in one week."

"Okay, okay. So where *are* you with the Winters case? What the fuck drove them off the bridge like that?"

"I don't know, Chief. We're working on it."

"In a pig's ass—you're working on that dead wetback. I don't think there's any connection at all. Anyway, your seventy-two hours are up, and I want the final report on my desk by tomorrow night. I don't know why I okayed letting Gomez chase wetbacks under cover. I *know* that was a mistake. Have you heard from him?"

"No." Roberts was tucking in his shirttail, and sat down to put on his shoes.

"Well, you'll either have to get him out of there or work this one alone. I can't spare anybody else. And Roberts, you remember Trudeau, our captain? He wants to see both of us in his office."

"Shit," Roberts growled. "When?"

"It was scheduled for tomorrow morning, but we've got a reprieve until Wednesday. He's been called to a crime conference in Phoenix on Monday and Tuesday. But by Wednesday you'd better have more than one of your chickenshit reports, Roberts. You better have some solid facts!" He hung up and left the detective-sergeant with only a buzzing sound in his ear.

"Shit," Roberts repeated to himself, putting down the receiver as he finished tying his shoes. Monday morning or Wednesday, it didn't matter. The stuff would hit the fan. There was no faking it any longer. And for once Lang was probably right when he said this one had nothing to do with the others. It probably *was* a jealous boyfriend, though he was going to take a good look at the evidence before jumping to that conclusion.

In the bathroom he splashed cold water on his face and brushed his teeth. He'd have to shower and shave later. Suddenly he remembered who Lupita Morales' boyfriends were—Jesse Peralta and Jack Masters—and even Larry Preston, the Border Patrolman, had gone with her. Shit, everybody had gone with her. The question was, who had gone with her last?

"Christ, Lang," he muttered, wondering why Gomez hadn't at least checked in as he clipped his holstered snub-nose to his belt along with his handcuffs. "You can take your neat and simple cases and shove 'em where the sun don't shine!"

He drove through a violent wind- and rainstorm, with great black clouds massed clear to the eastern horizon and hiding all but a long curved saber of blood-pink dawn. The storm had finally struck sometime after midnight, but by the time he reached Mimbres Junction most of it had blown on by. As he pulled into the alley behind the Watering Hole there were only the puddles in the potholes and the smell of yesterday's garbage.

Link Johnston, the black deputy, had the area roped off, and the lab boys were already working. A police photographer took a final flash picture of the victim, and Roberts saw the TV news van and the red-headed reporter already heading his way. Brushing her off with a referral to Lt. Lang for all statements, it occurred to him that she wouldn't have Gomez to snow her on this one.

The body was still in the station wagon, fully clothed, back arched, and eyes starting grotesquely from her head. There were bruises and pressure marks on her throat, and the lab man with the impressive gap between his two front teeth was bagging her hands.

"Happened sometime between one and five this morning," the lab man said. "Ignition and lights were both still on when they found her, but the engine was cold. Everything's been dusted and vacuumed. Death was probably due to strangulation. Some other recent bruises visible too, but no other apparent injury. No apparent rape, no robbery. Her purse is there on the seat beside her, wallet still in it. Looks like a few dollars and some change.''

"Were the doors open like that when she was found?'' Roberts asked. All four doors of the wagon stood open.

"Only one back door. We figure the perpetrator was hiding on the floor of the back seat.''

"Who found her?''

"Janitor—a black guy. He's inside now. Came on at five.''

"Her boss is waiting inside, too, Sergeant,'' Link Johnston said, walking over. "He was evidently the last one to see her alive—about one o'clock this morning when they buttoned up. He's pretty shook.''

"Okay,'' Roberts said, "I'll talk to them.'' But he stood there studying the scene awhile longer. He was beginning to get an uneasy gut feeling about this one, and Lang's remark about not tying it in with the banker's case only served to intensify it. He looked up as the lab man was about to get back in his van. "Wait a minute,'' he called, hurrying over. "Ask Sam something for me when he does this one. Have him check her as closely as he did the wetback, Enrique Vasquez, and compare the results.''

The lab man's brows lifted incredulously. "You don't think the same guy did both of 'em, do you?''

"Just ask him, okay? Pretty please?'' He went through the back door of the bar with Link Johnston, and talked to the janitor first. The man swore he hadn't touched a thing, hadn't taken more than two steps out the back door before he saw that something real bad had happened. Then he went back inside and called "Mistah" Rogers.

Ted Rogers was sitting at the bar and nursing a Bromo-Seltzer. Balding, sweating, paunchy, and fortyish, Rogers had known the victim for two or three years. She'd only worked for him about a month, since he'd pirated her away from the Hanging Tree. She was a good draw for his customers, she worked hard, and she didn't drink or steal too much. Sure, she was a floozy. Sure, he'd stuffed her a time or two himself—who hadn't? But he had no idea anything like this would happen to her, or who would do it. He wanted to know if she'd been raped.

Roberts asked him which boyfriend had seen her last, and he had a ready answer for that one. "Jack," he said. "Jack Masters. He was in just the other evening, early. Wednesday it was. No, Thursday—that's the day I get my beer deliveries. They talked quite awhile."

"Any argument?"

"Not so's you'd notice. Just talk."

"Anybody else see her—say yesterday? Anybody special?"

"Not since you was in and talked to her, Sergeant. The regular Saturday night crowd, nothing unusual. A quiet night, not even any fights. Hell, man, you don't think Jack Masters done it, do you?"

"I'm not paid to think, Mr. Rogers. I just gather facts." He walked outside with Link Johnston. "Jack Masters," he said. "That name keeps popping up everywhere I turn these days. You know much about him?"

Link shook his head. "Don't even see much of him around here. He's away a lot."

"What about her?"

"Lupita?" Link shrugged. "Just like Rogers said, she slept around. I popped her once myself. You think it was somebody she knew killed her, right? Not a stranger?"

"No robbery," Roberts said. "Evidently no rape. So why? Some personal motive?"

"Isn't it usually a jealous husband or boyfriend?"

Roberts smiled. "Usually. We'll see what the lab turns up." But he still had this gut feeling that even if it was a boyfriend, it could lead straight to Dutch Masters' ranch. Christ, he wondered if Gomez had even gotten on the place yet.

TWENTY-SIX

BOUNCING around in the back of the pickup as it roared down the rutted dirt road between the rows of lemon trees, Rabbit Gomez tried his best to brace himself and to grin and bear it.

Four other wetbacks rode with him, all of them holding tightly to the sides of the truck while the suffocating dust boiled up around them in the late-afternoon heat. This was the second group of illegals Gomez had joined. The first had grown impatient and wary. By seven on Sunday morning, after weathering a violent wind- and rainstorm, they had decided to move on.

The detective had remained in the dampened camp alone, knowing no Migra would be coming, wondering if anyone else would. Until about 10 A.M. when this group had come trudging silently through the mesquite grove. They too had shared their food with Gomez and accepted him as one of them. They were willing to wait with him, hoping it would be an employer who showed up and not the Migra.

Gomez had told them his name was Juan Garcia, and one of them had asked him how long he'd been waiting. "Only a day," he had answered, and told them his cover story, and of the others who had tired of waiting.

"Sometimes it takes several days," another one said, "or even a week. But if you are patient, someone always comes."

And someone did. Late in the afternoon they heard a

pickup, and Gomez eased back in the brush with the others until the truck appeared in the clearing, battered and scarred and faded, with a big, black-bearded man behind the wheel.

While the others asked for work and then climbed into the back of the truck, Gomez stood to one side, hesitant. He wasn't sure what he should do, but finally called to the driver in Spanish, "What ranch is this that offers work?"

The driver stared at him with hard gray eyes and scowled. "What do you care? It's work."

"I'm looking for Señor Masters' place," Gomez persisted. " 'Dutch' Masters—he's supposed to have a lot of work."

The bearded driver continued to study him, his eyes curiously hostile, as if not quite sure what to make of this one. For a moment Gomez thought he had somehow given himself away. "Get in," the man ordered finally, "you've found Masters' place. I'm his foreman."

Now the pickup turned sharply, fishtailing as it straightened into a clearing and pulled up in front of a large barnlike hut of corrugated steel. "Everybody out!" the driver yelled back at them. Then he got out himself and propped a notebook on the hood of the truck while he ordered them into a line and began writing down their names.

"Juan Garcia," Gomez told him when it was his turn.

"We deduct for Social Security and taxes here," the foreman said. "You're in the U.S.A. now."

"If you're deducting for that, don't you need Social Security numbers?" Gomez asked almost without thinking, and flinched at the sudden savage look in the man's gray eyes—a look that left the detective feeling like a man of glass. But the foreman only sneered and said nothing as he printed Juan Garcia on a clean page of the book and the date beneath it.

When he had everybody's name, he told them all to go inside the big Quonset and get settled. He would pick them up at sunrise.

"When do we get paid?" someone asked him.

"When you have done enough work, *mojado*," the foreman answered, glaring around at the rest of them. "Any more questions?"

"What do we call you, *patrón?*" Gomez asked innocently enough. As their eyes met again, the detective promised all the saints in Heaven if he just got away with it this one last time, he would stop calling attention to himself.

"My name is Jesse," the foreman said, staring at him with a gaze that could break bones. "But you called it right, hombre. I *am* your *patrón.*"

Inside the metal Quonset were a dozen more Mexican laborers. Two of them were cooking tortillas and a pot of beans and macaroni on a wood-burning stove made out of a fifty-gallon oil drum. Dirty mattresses lined the bare cement floor under both the curving walls of the hut, and the big double doors at either end were open to admit the occasional cooling breeze.

Cardboard boxes and wooden crates of personal belongings were stacked beside some of the mattresses, and a few pinups clipped from girlie magazines had been stuck to the walls. A washtub was half full of sudsy water, and a stack of metal plates rested on one end of a trestle table that also held bags of dried beans and macaroni and flour, along with a sack of onions and several large cans of tomatoes.

Someone told him the *patrón* furnished the food and they took turns cooking. Gomez picked up a plate, dished out a generous helping of macaroni and beans, and laid a smoking tortilla on top of it. Finding an empty mattress, he sat down cross-legged, balancing his plate on his lap. By the time he was finished, it was getting dark.

One of the men lit a kerosene lantern and hung it from a wire dangling from the curved ceiling. Another picked a guitar from his box of clothes and began strumming softly and singing a sad Mexican love song. While several others dragged a mattress under the lantern and started a card game, Gomez wandered through the hut to see what he could find out.

In the next hour he struck up several conversations, but it was always the same. No one knew of any such boy as Gomez described, nor of anyone named Enrique Vasquez.

Then, when he was about to give up, the detective found his lead.

Jesus Martinez was ageless. He could have been forty-five or seventy-five; he seemed frozen in time. Stringy as a raw-hide rope, he had a smooth brown face and streaks of gray in his thick black hair and mustache, and he limped. But he had been on the Masters ranch for about three months, working for a while as an irrigator and then at the maintenance shop. It too was deep in the groves, near the canal, he said. The Señor Masters had an office in a block building there, and the foreman, Jesse, lived in an apartment upstairs. Jesus Martinez was paid every month—one hundred fifty dollars.

But only last week he had damaged some equipment, and Jesse had knocked him around and then put him back in the groves to pick. But what was really important, he had known a man named Enrique Vasquez who also helped with the equipment around the shop—greasing tractors and changing oil in the trucks. Then Enrique had disappeared—a week or so ago. Jesus didn't consider this unusual—it happened often among *mojados*. And he had not seen any boy named Vasquez, only the man.

Gomez spent a restless night tossing on the dirty mattress while mosquitoes whined in his ear. At dawn everyone was up and breakfasting on warmed-over tortillas and beans and macaroni. The detective settled for two mugs of strong black coffee. And as the first rays of sunlight stole down the dusty road into the clearing, they brought with them a big stake-side truck with Jesse Peralta behind the wheel.

Climbing in the back, where several others had already loaded long ladders, clippers, gloves, and picking bags, they set off for the groves. And the first day just about killed off Gomez.

The longest day of his life, it was one of mindless, endless toil. Climbing up and down the twenty-foot ladder with a sixty-pound bag of lemons slung on his shoulder, and using the unfamiliar clippers to free the fruit from among dense branches and inch-long thorns, he moved the heavy ladder from tree to tree as he filled the bag, climbed down to dump it in a common bin, then climbed to fill it again. All while the incessant nuisance of gnats swarmed around his eyes and ears, and the heat hung like a living menace among the dark green foliage. Soon he was fighting dizziness and nausea and fatigue as the hours dragged by like years. At noon they rested for a quick half-hour, and the second foreman, Paco, brought out their lunches—thin baloney sandwiches on stale bread, to be washed down with tepid strawberry Kool-Aid.

That night in the Quonset, his legs trembling, Gomez was too tired to eat the beans and macaroni. He chewed listlessly on a tortilla, then flopped down on his mattress and slept until dawn. Stiff and sore, he got up and ate a breakfast of beans and an onion wrapped in a tortilla, washed down with hot coffee, and wondered how he was going to face another day of this. How anybody faced the days and weeks and months of grinding labor in the fields—unless it was all they knew. And he thanked the Blessed Virgin that his own mother had raised him to be a policeman and not a tiller of the soil.

He dreaded the sound of the approaching truck that would haul them once more into the breach. He had always considered himself a survivor. But what was Roberts thinking of, sending him into this? How was he going to get any evidence this way? What more could he possibly get besides sore muscles and an aching ass? Or an eye poked out by thorns?

But the vehicle that came was not a truck, and to Gomez it seemed heaven-sent. It was a jeep, and the man who came to the door of the Quonset was a stranger. When he asked if anyone had any *carpintero* experience—"Anybody good with a hammer and nails? Nothing fancy, I'm just putting fresh tarpaper on some doghouses—" the detective almost broke his neck getting to the front to volunteer.

TWENTY-SEVEN

"I'M Jack," the driver said. "Jack Masters—you speak English?"

Bingo, Gomez thought. First Jesse Peralta and now Jack Masters. "Doghouses" had been the key word, though he'd have gone just about anywhere with anybody to get out of another day in the hot, gnat-filled groves. "I speak good English," he answered, "and I'll work hard."

He was sitting alongside Masters in the jeep now as the road curved away, out of the trees, and headed up onto the flat open mesa. He studied the young rancher in the reflection of the windshield. Jack was well-muscled with dark, wavy hair; a good-looking guy who could probably handle himself in any situation that got physical.

"Where'd you learn English?" Masters wanted to know.

"L.A.," Gomez said, holding onto his straw hat and raising his voice above the grumbling engine. He was making this part up as he went along. "I worked for two years in the brickyards and in a bakery. I've been in Texas this past year and then went home for a couple of months. I just got back."

Jack Masters glanced at him. "Where'd you do carpentry work?"

"At home—in Chihuahua." Gomez gave the rancher the rest of his cover story. The detective wasn't sure he could even nail a sheepskin to a barn door. "These dogs," he asked to get on another subject, "they for hunting?"

"Naw." Jack gave Gomez a sidelong glance now, as if wondering how far he could trust him. "You ever been to an organized dog-fight?"

"A fight? Like in a ring? No—" he grinned. "Cockfights, sure, and a bullfight once, but no dogs."

"Well, these are fighting dogs—pit bulls. It's against the law so I call 'em show dogs. But I haul 'em around to fights all over the country, even in Mexico."

"They bite?" Gomez asked uncertainly. "People, I mean."

"Naw—just each other. Tear hell out of another dog, but they're friendly with people, easy to handle. I got a kid taking care of 'em now."

"A kid?" Gomez felt his pulse quicken.

"Thirteen, fourteen—don't worry, he's wet, too."

Gomez let out his breath slowly and wondered if he dared ask. He decided to risk it. "What's the kid's name?"

"What?"

"The kid. What's his name?"

Jack Masters laughed. "Christ, I've forgotten—Valdez, Ortez, something like that—I just call him kid." He looked over at Gomez. "Hell, I don't even know *your* name."

"It's Juan," the detective answered, "Juan Garcia."

With the jeep parked in the shade of a salt cedar, and the dogs raising a ruckus all over the place, Jack Masters walked Gomez over to one of the stone buildings used for storage and gave him a carpenter's apron, a hammer, and a sack of roofing nails. Then he handed him a pair of heavy shears and pointed to a roll of black tarpaper. "Bring that and I'll show you where to start."

Gomez, tying on the apron and tools and shouldering the heavy roll, studied the rest of the place while following Masters. The stone buildings were in worse shape than they'd looked from the air: windows broken out, doors hanging askew, all apparently abandoned. But it was secure enough. The gate they had come through was chain-locked, and the entire area fenced with eight-foot chain-link and hung with NO HUNTING—NO TRESPASSING signs, and a couple of BEWARE THE DOGS.

The animals themselves, still barking furiously more in excitement than in anger, were chained individually in front of each doghouse, and the houses were scattered among all the stone buildings. They passed the old swimming pool that had been converted into a fighting pit, but he didn't see any sign of a kid. He decided not to push his luck by asking. He had probably been too nosy already for a wetback.

"Start with this one," Jack Masters said, walking up and quieting the dog, which was trying to lick his hand. "Several of them leaked in that rain Saturday night, but all the roofs are old and rotted by the sun, so might as well do all of 'em while we're at it. Just tear off the old stuff and nail on the new—got it? We'll tar 'em later."

Gomez nodded and almost said, "It sure as hell beats picking fruit," but he bit his tongue.

Working all day, he tarpapered six doghouses. He counted twenty-one scattered around the area that he could see, but only twenty dogs. He figured one had probably been killed and not replaced yet. He tried to work slowly enough to make the job last, yet not so slow that Jack would take him back and get somebody else. And surprisingly, the dogs *were* friendly. They even seemed glad for a little human company. Although they were well fed and watered and apparently healthy, they were battered and scarred up bad. Anybody who would mistake these poor devils for show dogs would have to have shit for brains.

He didn't see the boy until late in the day. Jack Masters came driving through the gate in his jeep, and he had a young Mexican on the seat beside him. Gomez watched as he let the boy out; then he watched the boy disappear behind one of the buildings while Masters drove on over and examined the work he'd done on the doghouses. Masters didn't say much, but he seemed satisfied. "Okay, I'll take you back to camp and bring you out again tomorrow—unless you'd rather go back to picking fruit?"

"No thanks," Gomez said, "but I'm going to need some more tarpaper. And maybe the boy could help," he suggested hesitantly. "I see he's back."

Jack Masters shrugged. "Sure—why not?"

*   *   *

Around 10 o'clock that night Gomez slipped quietly out of the Quonset. A mile away, he climbed a fence and crossed the road to a gas station. The station was closed and dark, but the phone booth just outside was lighted. He had a dollar bill folded and pinned in his shirt pocket, and another one in his pants. And he had six quarters in change. Roberts had said if he hadn't gotten enough info out with six phone calls, he might as well forget it.

Entering the booth, he skipped the office number and dialed Roberts' apartment. He let it ring six times and then hung up. The quarter tinkled down the return slot and he inserted it again, concentrating, trying to remember the other number Roberts had given him; it was unlisted. He dialed it and got an answer on the second ring, a woman's voice.

"Mrs. Lane? This is Gomez—can you take a message for the sergeant?"

"Wait a minute—he's here."

Pause. "Gomez? Where in hell you been?"

"I'm finally on the place, man, and it's bitchin'."

"But have you found anything? Any evidence?"

"Not yet. But I met Jesse Peralta, the foreman—big and mean, a real asshole. Also Jack Masters—big too, but doesn't seem as bad. I also met all twenty of his dogs. That's where the kid is."

"Arturo?"

"No name yet, and I haven't met him, but could be him. I saw him from a distance, and he's the right age."

"Good. Now get to him—talk to him. Maybe *he's* found out something."

"I'll try tomorrow. Oh, I also found a man who knew Enrique Vasquez. Says Enrique worked as a lube man and mechanic's helper at the maintenance shop, but he disappeared and nobody's seen him in over a week, or knows what happened to him. That's the best I've got so far."

"You're doing great, kid. Talk to the boy, and see if you can get to that shop—tell 'em you're a hell of a mechanic."

"*Jesucristo*, hombre, I already had to lie about being a carpenter to get to the dogs. But I sure as hell don't want another day in the groves—you ever pick fruit, man? The thorns alone'll kill you! And I thought lemons were yellow. These are green. It's hard to even find them among the leaves.''

"They're always green when they start the harvest," Roberts said, "they'll turn later, or they'll shoot 'em with something. Everything's phony nowadays. So stick it out, Gomez, a real day's work'll do you good. But be careful. We've had another killing in Mimbres Junction." And he told him about Lupita Morales.

"Shit, Sergeant, you think somebody here did that one, too?"

"She's gone with Jack and Jesse both, and everybody else, but we'll see what the lab turns up. You bore in from that end. I'm still trying to get a warrant. Try for a look around that shop without getting burned. But if they even suspect you're not a wet, get the hell out. And remember, any evidence you find is still illegal. So don't touch anything, just look, and at least we'll know what's there."

"Christ, man, your encouragement is only exceeded by your pessimism. Call you later."

Hanging up the bedside phone, Roberts rolled over next to Patricia's naked warmth.

"Is he all right?" she whispered in the darkness.

"He's on Masters' ranch, working as a wetback. He's met the foreman, Jesse, and he's met Jack. And he thinks he's found Arturo Vasquez and a man who knew Enrique."

"My God—that's great." She snuggled closer. "What happens now?" All they had over them was a sheet, and the air conditioner was purring softly.

"We wait," Roberts said. "He's going to try and get to the maintenance yard. That's where any evidence should be, because it's probably where he was killed."

"You don't really think Jack did it, do you? Killed both of them?"

"Anybody can kill, Pat," Roberts said thoughtfully. "Killing goes back farther than loving. It's an atavistic instinct modern man has tried to overcome with a thin veneer of civilization. He hasn't been very successful. Why else are we still perfecting newer and bigger and better weapons—more efficient killing tools, *mass* killing tools?"

"It's depressing," she whispered.

"So is individual murder. But *that* I can at least do something about. Though I still don't know quite what to think about this one—these two. I try not to let myself think too much about it yet. I just keep digging. And anyway, that's not what's worrying me the most. What's really worrying me is what I'm going to tell Captain Trudeau when I face him in the morning. Because there isn't a chance in hell that he'll keep us on this case.'"

TWENTY-EIGHT

"THIS is it? This is your report, Roberts?" Lt. Lang threw the paper back on his desk like it had something nasty on it.

"It's abbreviated, Chief. I didn't have much time to flesh it out. We've been busy."

Lang couldn't say any more. Grinding out his cigar, he turned his back to Roberts and stared out the window, obviously trying to get hold of his self-control. "And that's what you want to take in to the captain?" he asked without turning around, his words clipped like he was biting bullets. Little beads of sweat glistened on the back of his bald dome in spite of the refrigerated room. "That's all you've got to say about a case you've strung out for a week and a half! It should have been wrapped up in four days, the important part!" He whirled around suddenly and eyed the sergeant through his ever-present shades. "Shit, Roberts, you can't hang a wash job like this on me. You think I'm some kind of fucking virgin?"

"Only in your left ear, Chief," Roberts cracked without so much as a smile. "And it's all I've got—honest injun."

"Goddammit, Roberts, you don't have a connection! The banker and his girl are dead, the fucking wetback is dead, but what's the fucking connection except that his body was found with theirs. So why would he be hauling a dead wetback around in his trunk—answer me that!"

"Maybe he was planning to adopt him. How the hell

166

should I know, Chief. Maybe the body was planted there to embarrass him or maybe the banker killed him in some kind of self-righteous sanctimonious fit. I just don't know. It's a confusing mess, and there's no solid evidence. That's why it's taking so long to solve!"

"And why did I ever let you send Gomez undercover on that goddam ranch? What's he looking for? Exactly."

"Hard evidence, Chief. The weapon, dried blood, anything. He's already got a couple of leads—"

"Leads, my aching ass," Lang scoffed. "He's in there without a warrant because I couldn't get one on the shit you've got. It'll take more than a couple of leads to square this with the captain. C'mon, dammit, we might as well get it over with." He led the way out of his office and up the stairs to the third floor, deeper into the hallowed halls of law enforcement to a door with gold letters on its frosted glass: CAPT. HAROLD H. TRUDEAU—CHIEF OF DETECTIVES.

In the outer office they had to wait while Trudeau's shapely blond secretary announced them. The captain was a stickler about protocol and all the prudish bullshit that went with it, when everybody in the building knew he was banging the secretary on weekends at a no-tell motel.

When they were finally admitted to the inner sanctum, Lt. Lang already wore the hangdog look of a man with a paper asshole. His hat would have been in his hand if he'd had one. Roberts was surprised he didn't walk up to the captain's desk on his knees.

The office itself was well suited to a chief of detectives with political clout and high ambition, from the sturdy leather furniture to the polished walnut desk and the lined red drapes that shut out the sun behind it. But Trudeau wasn't at his desk. He was standing in front of a large wall map of Mimbres County, staring at it.

The map was scattered with tiny pins of varying colors, and Roberts knew the red and white pins were homicides— homicides with an unofficial kill factor of five or better. White pins designated which of these homicides were already solved this fiscal year; red pins were those still unsolved. Roberts always referred to the map as an example of pinhead mentality, and at the moment he was staring himself at the two red pins sticking squarely into Mimbres Junction: Edwin Winters and Kathy Cole's pins. Vasquez and Morales didn't rate pins.

It was these same two pins that seemed to be rankling the captain as he turned around, immaculately dressed as usual in a suit and vest and tie. After all, Roberts reflected, he never went out in the noonday sun anymore, except to have lunch at the country club with the county attorney or the mayor or some other high-class dignitary.

He was tall, but Roberts didn't think he was handsome. His face was too long-jawed, long-nosed, and his long thinning hair had been slicked over and pasted to his skull to hide a bald spot. He had that lean and hungry look in spite of some twenty extra pounds that spilled over a Texas-size belt buckle, a result of too much desk time and baked Alaska for dessert. It was a look Roberts attributed to excessive ambition, and there were rumors the county attorney had better keep a tight asshole.

Trudeau also had those piercing dark eyes you read about, and he was piercing Roberts with them now, ignoring the fawning lieutenant beside him as he flicked a monogrammed lighter and sucked fire into a big briar pipe. "All right, Sergeant," he said, seeming to choose his words carefully, "what the hell are you and that greaser up to?" He snapped the lighter shut, dropped it in his pocket, and loosed a cloud of blue smoke toward the ceiling.

Roberts bristled. "You mean Detective Gomez, Captain?"

"You know who I mean, Roberts." If Trudeau's eyes had been knives, Roberts knew he would be bleeding, but he kept his cool.

"Okay if I sit down first, Captain?" He motioned to the heavy leather chair in front of the desk.

"Sit," Trudeau said.

"Okay if I take one of these?" He opened the box of panatellas the captain kept at the front edge of his desk. "My partner likes 'em." He could almost feel Lang flinching behind him.

"You're cruising dangerously close to insubordination, Sergeant," the captain warned him.

Roberts tucked the cigar in his shirt pocket and sat down with deliberate ease. He looked up at the chief of detectives in all innocence. "I assume you're referring to the Winters case, Captain. If so, I can only say it's been a real ball-buster for all concerned."

Trudeau threw a frustrated, angry glance at Lang as he took two steps and snatched the latest report out of the chief of homicide's hand. "I don't even have to read this crap to know it's just more bullshit!"

"Under the circumstances, Captain, it's the best—"

"Shut up, Roberts—just shut the fuck up." He threw the report on his desk. "Now listen for a change. You too, Lieutenant. You're supposed to stay on top of these clowns." He took his pipe from his mouth and tapped it nervously on a big brass ashtray. "Okay, Roberts, you've got a Factor Eight or Nine here with the banker and his little friend. But for reasons known only to yourself and your partner, your reports are mostly about the death of a wetback, a Factor One. You're poking around in the damned barrio. You've got Gomez under cover on a citrus ranch, looking for evidence without a warrant for God's sake—and," he turned his glare on Lang again, "you authorized it. Why?"

"There seems to be some connection, sir—" Lang started a feeble excuse but Trudeau cut him off, holding the floor.

"Connection my mother's virgin ass." He looked again at Roberts. "What's the connection, Sergeant? Specifically."

"So far only that he was there when the car was brought up, was killed about the same time, and went into the water about the same time. We're looking in the barrio and on the ranch because that's where the trail leads, the only trail we've got that might turn up hard evidence."

"Evidence of what?" Trudeau persisted.

"Of where exactly the wetback was murdered, and by whom—and that the murder somehow involved the banker and his girl."

"But you haven't found out any real connection between them—have you, Sergeant?"

"Not yet. But when you read that report you'll see a mention of another homicide in Mimbres Junction early Sunday morning, a week after the first one."

Lt. Lang groaned audibly as Trudeau glanced involuntarily at the report on his desk, then back to Roberts. "You're talking about the barmaid at the Watering Hole? Lang already briefed me on it. Are you claiming *that* one is tied in with the banker and the wetback, too?"

"I'm waiting for the lab report," Roberts answered, sensing suddenly that he still had a chance. "I've got a gut feeling—"

"Fuck your gut feelings, Roberts. I don't give one goddam diddly-shit about your gut feelings. I'm getting pressure from upstairs. They want the Winters thing closed. Closed meaning solved—a positive termination, two white pins on the map, Roberts. They don't care about a wetback and a barfly whose deaths are unfortunate but also unimportant. We're over budget, Roberts—way over budget. It's just that simple."

"Okay, Captain," Doug Roberts got to his feet with a sigh, deciding to go for broke. "Just give me another seventy-two hours; hang tight with me on this for three more days, and I'll lay it all out for you on a silver platter."

Trudeau exchanged heavy glances again with Lang, then looked at the map. At the white pins, many of them the result of Roberts' unorthodox ways. At the few red pins, including the two now stuck in Mimbres Junction. And he thought of the future—his future. The only reason the Department put up with a bastard like Roberts was because it paid off. In spite of everything it paid off in white pins on his map and points in high places. Roberts was an administrative hemorrhoid, but a political asset for anyone on his way to the top.

He looked back at the detective and picked up his cold pipe. Sucking it thoughtfully, he nodded. "All right, Sergeant," he said reluctantly, "but only forty-eight hours, not seventy-two. And I'll even get you your warrant—but only because the judge owes me, not because you've got any probable cause."

THE KILL FACTOR · 171

Then he took the big briar from his mouth and pointed it at Roberts like a Colt .45, and his eyes were painfully piercing again. "And I'll tell you what I want in exchange, Mr. Smart-ass. I want results! You read me loud and clear? In two days I want one more goddamned report on this Winters case—the final one."

TWENTY-NINE

WHEN the Señor Masters told him he was to help repair the roofs of the doghouses, Arturo was pleased. He was even more pleased when he met the young Mexican known as Juan Garcia.

They worked well together, tearing off the old tarpaper from the roofs, cutting and fitting the new sheets and nailing them down. Garcia was talkative, friendly, and sympathetic to Arturo's attempts to find his uncle, though he claimed he hadn't been working here long enough to know him.

The work went fast. At noon, while they sat in the shade of a salt cedar eating the usual baloney sandwiches and drinking the tepid Kool-Aid Jack had brought them, Juan Garcia grew serious and seemed deeply troubled about something.

"I'm going to tell you something in confidence, Arturo," he said somberly, watching the sky where dark clouds were building to another storm. "If you betray me, we will both be in danger."

Arturo stared at him, puzzled.

"My name isn't Garcia, it's Gomez. Inocencio Gomez. And I'm not a *mojado*. I'm a Mexican-American policeman— not a Migra, a detective—and I know what happened to your Uncle Enrique."

Arturo's jaw dropped; his eyes grew wide. "A policeman? *Madre de Dios,* my uncle's in jail?"

"No, Arturo—worse. Your uncle is dead." He crossed

172

himself. "His body is at the county morgue. He was identified through the Border Patrol by his fingerprints. He was murdered—beaten to death. I'm sorry, Arturo. I'm looking for the one who did it."

Arturo's expression collapsed in sadness, but he didn't cry. "Who would kill my uncle?" he asked. "He was a good man. He never hurt anyone."

"We think he was killed on this farm. A week ago Sunday. I'm looking for evidence of exactly where he was killed and who killed him. Will you help me?"

"Of course, *por seguro*. But how can I help?"

"You wrote him that you were coming to replace him, so you knew he was here, right?"

"Not here exactly. I wrote to a box number in Mimbres Junction. I had to look for this place myself. And now I will have to go home." He looked suddenly thoughtful, confused. "I'll be needed at home. My father is sick. But I'll need to earn some money, too."

"Arturo," Gomez said, trying to hold the boy's attention, "in your uncle's letters to your family, didn't he ever mention what kind of work he was doing, or anyone he was having trouble with?"

The boy frowned in thought. "No. I read all the letters to my mother, and he only said he was working on a citrus ranch near Mimbres Junction, and he sent some money when he could. There is one thing, though—"

"What?"

"A girl—here. She's a maid for the big boss of this place."

"Dutch Masters?"

Arturo nodded. "I talked to her once up at the main house. She knew my uncle. She said he worked at the maintenance shop for Jesse, the foreman." And he told the detective what Juana had said about last seeing Enrique driving off with Jack Masters late that Sunday afternoon when he disappeared.

"You're sure it was Jack, not Jesse?"

"She said it was the Señor Jack," Arturo insisted. "She said he'd just returned from a trip, and gave my uncle a ride down to the shop."

"And this shop is the one near the canal?"

"Yes. I was there once too with the Señor Jack. I can draw you a map if you wish to go there."

"That'll help," Gomez said. "I flew over this place once, and studied an aerial photo, but I'm kind of turned around now and I need a look at that shop." He was glancing over the boy's shoulder and saw a pickup barrel up to the gate in a cloud of dust, and he knew their little talk was about over. "Here—" he handed Arturo a stick, "show me—draw me a quick map of this place." It would not only test the boy's memory and observation, but verify what they had seen in the flyover and his own memory of the photo.

While the pickup approached across the mesa, Gomez watched the boy make a hasty sketch of the kennels, the main house, the big Quonset, and the maintenance yard. A few inches behind the maintenance yard he drew a long curvy line. "What's that?" the detective asked him. "A fence?"

"No, that's the main irrigation canal."

"Beautiful, *chamaco*," Gomez breathed. "Now how far is that from the maintenance yard?"

"About a fourth of a mile. It leads—"

"I know where it leads—to the highway bridge where your uncle's body was found." He was watching the pickup halt in front of the stone storage house where the boy slept. "You've been a big help, Arturo," he said. "Now just keep your eyes open and your mouth shut, because we're going to have company."

Jesse Peralta had stepped out of the truck and was arguing vehemently and waving his arms at Jack Masters, who had come out of the stone house to meet him. Gomez couldn't catch the drift of the argument, but he gripped the boy's arm hard as the two men turned and started toward them. "Remember, I am Juan Garcia, and I'm just another *mojado* on this place. Understood?" He was busy rubbing out the ground sketch with his foot.

Arturo, suddenly so frightened he couldn't speak, just nodded dumbly.

Gomez and the boy were both standing as the two bosses moved into the shade under the salt cedar. Jesse's face was flushed with anger. He was clenching and unclenching his fists. Even Jack Masters was cursing softly. "Only four fucking houses to go, and you've got to have him back in the groves!"

"I need every man I can get in the picking crews," Jesse told him. "You've got the boy to fix your doghouses. The man is mine. I hired him."

"Goddammit, Jesse, they can finish by this afternoon—then you can have him back in the morning."

Gomez was standing there, fascinated, wondering who would win this test of wills; who was dominant on this place, Dutch's son or his foreman, when Jesse suddenly turned his hard gray eyes on him. "Get in the truck, hombre, you're going back to the groves."

Gomez glanced hesitantly at Jack, and then flinched as Jesse yelled at him, "Get in the goddam truck, *cabrón*! *Ahorita—ándale!*"

Gomez thought he was going to hit him, and he moved quickly away toward the truck, glancing only once at Arturo, whose expression was almost inscrutable. It gave away nothing, except that he was terrified. Behind him, Jack Masters didn't say another word.

Climbing into the back of the pickup, Gomez crouched on the spare tire in the corner and braced himself as Jesse started it up. At the gate, Gomez got out and held it open while the foreman drove through, then closed it behind them and climbed back in the truck.

Huddled on the spare tire again, he felt the wind stand his hair on end as they barreled down the road. He gazed back toward the kennels, where the boy was still standing beside Jack. Working with him all morning, the detective had been impressed by Arturo's self-assurance. He seemed mature for his age, and he was smart. And he had taken the news of his uncle's death with a quiet reserve of inner strength. Now that he knew what was going on, he ought to be able to stay clear of any trouble—at least for a little while.

So why was he nagged by the feeling he should have gotten the kid out of there while he had the chance, even if it meant tipping his hand? There was a lot of potential violence in both these men; especially Jesse. But at least Jesse was with him, so if Arturo just didn't panic . . .

The truck lurched as it turned sharply through the open main gate of the ranch, and Gomez cursed softly. It was his own ass he should be worrying about. He was convinced now that even though Jack had evidently been the last one seen with Enrique alive, it was Jesse they were probably after. All they needed was proof.

But to get that, he still had to get to the maintenance yard. And instead, they were heading back to the goddam groves!

THIRTY

THE second storm hit again an hour later, rolling across the valley as if the long summer was determined to end violently. The rain flew before the gusting wind and dust and lashed the fruit-laden trees. The day's picking was interrupted under the darkening sky, and the afternoon temperature dropped ten degrees, like a sudden taste of winter.

Jesse hauled them all back to the Quonset in the open stake-side, so they were soaked by the time they tumbled from the truck and ran inside. But for Gomez it was the chance he needed. He had to check in with Roberts.

Moving back to the open front of the Quonset, he flinched at the sudden crash of a thunderclap as sheet lightning flashed across the gray-black sky. He saw the stake-side still parked in the yard outside. The foreman was hunched behind the wheel, his arms folded across it, his face a blur behind the rain beating against the windshield. Shit, thought Gomez miserably.

Behind him, the others were trying to dry off with scraps of clothing and dirty towels. Two were warming coffee on the old cookstove as Gomez turned and made his way through the length of the Quonset to the open rear door. He glanced back once, then darted out and crossed the clearing to disappear among the trees.

He ran most of the way to the phone booth, but even so the brief rainstorm was over by the time he got there. Still, he felt he had to make contact. He had to tell Roberts what he had, or at least leave a message.

The switchboard at the Sheriff's Department put him through to the squad room, and one of the detectives he hadn't met yet answered. Gomez told him who he was and who he wanted.

"Who—his partner? Just a second—I saw him around a minute ago."

Gomez waited anxiously in the booth, the water still dripping off the edge of its roof outside as he wondered if he should just hang up and get back. The sky was clearing and Jesse would be wanting everybody back in the field sure as coyotes crap in the desert. But if he hung up now and Roberts came to the phone . . .

"Gomez?" Roberts' voice was suddenly there. He sounded worried. "You okay?"

"Yeah, man, I'm fine—if soaked clean through and worked down to a stub is fine—but I'm getting there." And he told Roberts about his conversation with the boy, and what he'd found out about Dutch's maid, who had known Enrique and seen him the day he was killed, and about the argument between Jesse and Jack Masters over his services.

"And Jack was the one who was driving him back to the shop?" Roberts asked.

"Yeah, but Jesse is the hard-ass. He hauled me back to the groves and Arturo stayed with Jack."

"So Jack *was* back Sunday, and out at the ranch." Roberts was worried about Gomez leaving the boy, but he didn't say anything. "Things are starting to fall into place, Gomez," he said instead, "and I think you're right in the middle of it. I've been at the lab with Sam all morning. He got a match on the bodies of Lupita Morales and Enrique Vasquez. The girl was strangled—bruises deep under the skin and her hyoid bone crushed."

"*Jesucristo*—they were killed by the same person?"

"Not that good a match, yet. And she wasn't killed the same place as Enrique. But the point is she had *been* at the same place he had, and recently. And she had been with the same person. Grease, fertilizer, citrus residue all matched—same lint under her nails as under Enrique's, and the same hair cream—on her hands, not in her hair.''

"Then it had to be the same guy killed 'em both, man!''

"It's possible. Sam found the same strands of dark human scalp hair and khaki fibers not belonging to either victim, but matching each other, on both victims.''

"But why——?'' Gomez decided he'd already been gone too long and cut it off. "Look, I've got to get back or I'll be missed. It's stopped raining and the foreman is a bear and a half.''

"Storm must be heading west—we haven't had a drop here,'' Roberts said. "Okay, get on back and see if anyone saw the Morales woman on the place. And find a way to get to that maintenance shop. That's where they both must have been. Then you'd better get the kid Arturo and come on out, especially since he knows about you. He might let it slip.''

"He's too smart for that, but I'll get him. Anything else?''

"Only that we've got another deadline.'' And he told him about the morning meeting with Trudeau.

"Two days? How can we wrap this up in two days, man?''

"Only forty-three hours now. But we're that close—I can feel it. And Trudeau is getting us a warrant.''

"How's he gonna do that?''

"He's gonna shit one. Now get into that shop and find some physical evidence. Don't sample it yet—just see if it's there. I'll put what we've got in the warrant and be on the ranch myself by tomorrow morning, if not sooner. At that point anything you find should be legal. It may be ruled invalid later, but we'll have to chance it.

"Try to call me one more time, at the Mimbres Junction substation. I'm meeting Preston and somebody from Public Safety. They're getting warrants to do their thing too, and coming with me for backup and a diversion. So if I'm not there when you call, we'll be on our way in.''

"Right, Sergeant. See you soon.''

"Stay loose, Rabbit. We're almost there.''

Running most of the mile back to the Quonset, Gomez found his fears were justified. The big metal building was empty. He ran through it and out the double front doors. The stake-side was gone too. But surprisingly, Jesse Peralta's pickup was parked nearby, and the foreman was standing by the front fender, one booted foot on the bumper while he shelled some peanuts and popped them one at a time into his mouth. He was staring at Gomez.

"Where *you* been, *cabrón?* We missed you."

"I was taking a crap," Gomez answered almost too quickly. "I had the runs."

Jesse Peralta smiled, but only with his mouth. His gunmetal eyes were smoldering with anger. "Get in the truck, *cabrón*," he said. "I've got a job for you."

THIRTY-ONE

"TELL me everything you know about Jack Masters," Roberts said.

"My God, Doug, you don't really think—"

"My mind's still open, Pat, but I have to know."

"It's not possible—" She stared at him. "What about his being on the road, traveling? He didn't even get back until Wednesday, and Enrique Vasquez was killed Sunday night."

"You mean you didn't see him until Wednesday," Roberts corrected her. "Gomez has found someone who saw him on the ranch late Sunday afternoon—with Enrique. Jack just didn't come into town to see you until Wednesday. He also is known to have dated the second victim, Lupita Morales, and was seen talking to her a couple of nights before she was killed."

Patricia Lane excused herself and went into her kitchen. "I'm fixing coffee—you want some?"

"Got anything stronger?" he called.

"Scotch or bourbon?"

"Scotch on the rocks." He felt uneasy, restless. Getting up, he paced across the living room in front of the wide picture window. He wasn't used to having a partner under cover, especially without a backup handy. But at least they had a warrant now.

Outside, the storm was raging far across the valley. The late-afternoon sun was only a bloody gash in the dark clouds

as lightning played around their edges. "You've got a magnificent view," he said, turning. He got a whiff of her
perfume as she handed him his drink.

"You really want to know about Jack?" she asked.

"No—not really. But I have to—you understand?"

"Yes. So—" She returned to the sofa, sat down, and
crossed her legs. She had met Jack Masters about four months
ago, at a party, and then again at a dance. He had come on a
little strong, but she had liked him at the time and she'd
managed to settle him down. They'd begun dating—casually
at first; then it began to get serious.

"Like with us—now," Roberts said, pacing the room again
and scowling. "And you brought him here?"

"Not like us. Please, Doug, don't be jealous. I didn't even
know you then."

"Go on." Roberts gulped his Scotch. Somehow he was
going to have to keep his emotions from overriding his
judgment.

"Well, he never really talked much about what he did. I
got the idea he's had money from his mother's side of the
family, and he's led a rather wild life. He was in the army in
Vietnam, but he never talked about it much, either. He was
also an amateur boxer in college, and turned pro later on."

Roberts' ears perked up. "He was a professional fighter?"

"He said he had only a few fights and lost most of them.
He was smart enough to quit."

"Then his hands could be lethal weapons," Roberts mused.

"That was years ago, Doug, before his army service."

"What else has he done?"

"He's tried a lot of things. I know he raced cars for a
while, and worked as an extra in a couple of movies filmed in
Tucson. He even sold real estate at one time. I think he's still
got a license. And he's always helped his father off and on at
the ranch."

"But he's never really been interested in the citrus business?"

"That's evidently been the main hassle between them. And
lately all he's had on his mind are these fighting dogs, and the
gambling that goes with it. It's become almost an obsession."

Roberts looked at her for a moment without speaking. Then

he asked softly, "Did you know he was seeing the Morales woman again?"

"No. But I wouldn't have cared, if that's what you're getting at. I think he saw several other women while he was dating me. And when he was off on those trips, I'm sure he didn't have many lonely nights. Maybe it didn't really bother me because I wasn't in love with him. I can't even imagine being in love with him now. Does that make you feel better, Sergeant?"

"A little," Doug Roberts admitted sheepishly, then he gestured futilely. "Dammit, Pat, if he *did* kill them—Enrique and Lupita—he could have killed you, too."

She shook her head adamantly. "I don't believe it. He has a temper, and a cruel streak that shows at times. And he trains dogs to fight to the death. There's a lot of violence in his life-style, but I wouldn't think him capable of killing another human being."

"Anyone is capable of killing—remember? And he got a Bad Conduct discharge from the army, did you know that?"

"No."

"He was even charged once with murder while in Vietnam, but it was dropped for lack of evidence. Christ, Pat, any human being, given a specific set of circumstances peculiar to him alone, is capable of killing." He stood up, staring out the window a moment, then turned. "By the way, what kind of hair conditioner does Jack use?"

"Hair conditioner? I don't really know—some kind of cream, I think. Why? Is that important?"

"It may be."

"Oh God, Doug, I don't know what to think." She got up and went into the kitchen again. "*I* need a drink now," she called. "You want another one?"

"No, thanks." He finished off his Scotch and followed her into the kitchen. "I've got to go."

"So soon? It's not even—"

He took her hands to pull her to him and kissed her gently. "I'm already late. I've got to meet Preston and a Public Safety man in Mimbres Junction. They've got warrants for dogs and wets both now, so we can make it a coordinated effort. Tonight's the night, or tomorrow morning at the latest. We'll dazzle 'em with distractions until I can stick a murder warrant under someone's nose.''

"And the boy—the young wetback?''

"We've got to get him out of there, and Gomez, too, after he finds some evidence.''

"You're so sure it's there. What if it isn't?''

"Then we're back to square one—except that Trudeau will cancel the game. So if we don't score now we'll probably never get the killer of a Mexican and a barmaid. It'll go unsolved—until he kills again, and maybe next time someone with a little higher status.''

"It's disgusting,'' she said, "that unofficial kill factor you told me about.''

"It's life in the fast lane, Pat.'' And he kissed her good-bye.

She walked him to the door. As he was approaching his car she called, "What about the other two—the banker and his girl? Was that really an accident?''

"Right. A little bizarre, but an accident. I'll tell you about it sometime—when I know you better,'' he teased.

Driving the few miles on into Mimbres Junction, Roberts crossed the bridge where they'd found the bodies. The open gap in the rail was still unrepaired. As he considered that Gomez might even now be looking at the hard evidence they needed, he was momentarily tempted to go straight onto Masters' ranch. But he managed to control the urge, and instead he drove on by the big main gate and into the town itself, to the old courthouse and sheriff's substation where he hoped at least to get one more call from his partner.

Then they would go. Because now that they had warrants, everybody was to get something: Public Safety the dogs, the Border Patrol some wets, and he hoped in the confusion that he and Gomez would catch the brass ring—a killer. If not, he knew their careers would be up for grabs, and a murderer would be free to kill again.

Parking out front, beside a Border Patrol jeep and a Public Safety van, he climbed the stone steps and went in through the double doors and down the dusty hallway to the lighted office. Larry Preston and Link Johnston and another black man he assumed was from Public Safety were all drinking coffee together. Preston introduced him to Sergeant Dell Warren, a beefy bear of about fifty with graying, kinky hair and matching muttonchop whiskers. "Meet Sargeant Doug Roberts, Homicide."

Warren's grip was as strong as his ready smile was wide. "Sergeant, I hear we all get a little piece of this action. But I don't see much sense in my part of it. We never go after these dog lovers. It won't never stick in court."

"Don't feel bad," Larry Preston said. "A lot of the wets we'll bag will be back across the border before the next shift ends. But Roberts has the real warrant. He hopes to find evidence of murder, and maybe even the killer—right, Doug?"

"If not, my ass is creamed cheese," Roberts answered, pouring himself a cup of coffee. "You guys got your papers?"

"All typed out neat and legal," Preston said. "A little search-and-seizure is said to be good for the soul."

"Except that nowadays it's hard to tell what a court is going to accept or throw out," Dell Warren said, "even with murder. It's all becoming a legal hodgepodge of everybody's rights."

"Except the victim's," Roberts added. He had perched on the edge of a desk and was looking at Link Johnston over his coffee rim. "No word from Gomez?"

The deputy shook his head. "Everything's been quiet today."

"So how you want to work this, Sergeant?" Preston asked, laying out the aerial photo of the ranch on a table. "I've got a spotter plane available to do a flyover, but it'll have to be before dark or after dawn."

"Everything will have to be before dark," Roberts said. "Whether I get one more call from Gomez or not, I've decided I don't want to leave him and the youngster in there another night alone."

"Okay. I'll have a dozen men, and Sgt. Warren will have a dozen. We can use a walkie-talkie for contact with the plane."

Roberts was studying the aerial photo. "Unless I hear something different from Gomez, the maintenance yard is my main target," he said. "It's been the most likely place for evidence all along. But we'd better let the whole thing ride as a dog raid and search for wetbacks at first. If the killer knows it's murder evidence we're after, he might destroy something before we get there. So I'll spring the murder warrant later, as a kind of bonus. Meanwhile, I'll find Gomez and the boy and get them out of harm's way while your people round up wets and dogs."

"We'll have to find somebody to serve the warrants on," Dell Warren said.

"With luck, Jack Masters should be at the kennels—he and the boy." The detective looked up from the photo. "So we'll go in there. There's also old Dutch and the head foreman, Jesse, and another foreman named Paco. No telling where we'll find them. But we'll have to play everything by ear anyway until I can find Gomez, especially if he doesn't call."

"You know, this bunch is not known for its sweetness and light," Preston reminded him. "Dutch and Jack, and that head foreman, Jesse, are not going to welcome any of us with open arms on that place. In fact, the old man is likely to tell us just where we can stick our warrants, and Jack and Jesse will help us put 'em there."

"Well, boys," Roberts said, "if we have to knock some heads, we'll knock some heads." But his bravado had a false note and he knew it. Something was wrong. He couldn't put a finger on it, but he sensed it. They were moving too fast, but there was no time for further deliberation. He would just feel a hell of a lot better about the whole deal if he could hear from Gomez again first.

THIRTY-TWO

CROUCHED in the rear of the pickup again, Gomez braced himself as the vehicle lurched and jolted over the rutted road, finally emerging in a clearing that held a two-story cinder-block building, with an open garage and stalls attached—the maintenance shop. Gomez couldn't believe it. Jesse had brought him right where he wanted to be.

Old pieces of equipment lay rusting around various parts of the yard, and stacked bags of fertilizer covered with a tarp were piled six feet high along one side, with some wooden pallets stacked beside them.

Parking the truck near the fertilizer stacks, Jesse got out and pointed to the fifty-pound bags. "Load 'em," he ordered. "Twenty bags—*veinte, sabe?*"

Gomez nodded and climbed out. The sonofabitch could have made it easier by backing up to the stack and lowering the tailgate. It was harder to heave the bags over the side, but at least it would take longer and give him time to survey the yard and shop, however superficially. Gomez knew damn well the foreman didn't plan to help.

But surprisingly, Jesse didn't just stand around and watch, either. He crossed the yard and went up some side stairs to what was evidently his apartment on the second floor. Gomez, soon sweating and breathing heavily with the unaccustomed labor, managed to study the layout of the garage as he carried the bags to the truck and dumped them in.

A tractor stood over a grease pit, and all kinds of tools were scattered around what was a very messy shop. But he knew he would have to get a closer look to discover anything specific. He was nearly finished loading, and was taking a breather when Jesse came back down the stairs. The foreman started into the shop, then noticed Gomez wasn't working and walked over to the truck. "What's the matter—you sick or something?"

"No, *patrón*—just resting. I'll—"

Jesse hit him then, his closed fist coming so unexpectedly that it caught the detective solidly in the solar plexus. He found himself on his knees, his breath gone, his head ringing, and Jesse's harsh voice still somewhere above him, "—I say when you work and when you rest, *cabrón*. Now you've rested, so finish getting these bags loaded—*ándale pues!*"

With great effort, Gomez got to his feet, pulling himself up by the tailgate. He'd never wanted to respond to aggression so much in his life. But he held back. Still getting his breath, he met Jesse's steel-gray eyes and saw the challenge there, the curiosity and suspicion—the outright dare. Everything now depended on how he reacted to the foreman's use of forceful discipline. If he challenged it . . .

Forcing himself to lower his eyes, he whispered, "I'm sorry, *patrón*," and walked a little unsteadily back to the bags. The bastard had a punch like a pile-driver—his gut would ache for a week. But he ground his teeth, hefted another bag to his shoulder, and carried it to the truck.

A minute later he saw Jesse disappear into the cinder-block office. Five minutes later, when he had finished loading the last of the bags, the foreman still had not come out. Pushing his hat back, Gomez wiped his face with a bandanna and licked his dry lips thirstily as he glanced again toward the shop. He needed a closer look. He knew he could slip back later, but he wondered if he dared risk a look now, while it was light. He was sure this was the place for any evidence—it had to be. Yet he couldn't just wander over there. He needed some excuse—and then he spotted the water spigot at the corner where the stairs climbed the end of the building, and without further hesitation he walked on over.

Squatting beside the faucet, he turned it on and soaked his bandanna. Then he removed his hat and began mopping his face and hair and holding the cool cloth to the back of his neck while he surveyed the shadowed interior of the shop.

Sangre de Cristo, he thought, the closer he got the better it looked. Everything was here—an old trailer parked beside the tractor had undoubtedly hauled fertilizer bags and bins of citrus. Now it had a jack under one hub where a wheel was missing. And the lubrication grease was everywhere. The shop looked like it hadn't been cleaned in years. But what would the weapon have been, he wondered—rusty, and something like a pipe, but not a pipe? Maybe there was something among the twisted rusted wreckage of farm implements in the yard outside. He was about to look away when he paused long enough to lower his mouth to the water spigot to drink, and there it was right under his nose.

"Jesus, Maria, and Joseph," he breathed. Not two feet away, lying on a pile of burlap in the corner of the shop, as if tossed carelessly aside, was a heavy length of rusty chain, the rusted links spattered with brown spots that certainly looked like dried blood. Whether it was human blood, and of a type that matched Enrique's, would have to wait for testing in a lab.

Inside the office, Jesse Peralta was still talking to Dutch Masters on the phone. "There's something wrong with this new guy, Dutch. I don't know what, but he's not like any wet I ever dealt with before."

"What's the matter with him—won't he work?"

"It's not that. He's willing enough, but he's not used to hard labor, I can tell that. And he's an insolent bastard."

"Now, Jesse, what's he said to you?"

"Nothing, Dutch. It's just his actions, his manner. I had to hit him, and just for an instant he looked at me like he was going to explode. Then a quick funny kind of look, a kind of silent contempt shit before he apologized and got back to work. I'm either going to have to put the blocks to him and straighten him out, or get rid of him."

"Jesse, listen to me. No more bodies. That's over. There's

just too much heat on this last one. We made a mistake and they came too close—''

"If you'd of let me bury him like the others—''

"Just shut up and listen, Jesse. If he's trouble, get rid of him—by firing him.''

"Yeah, I guess. But we need workers, Dutch. The harvest's just starting.''

"New workers are coming all the time, don't worry about that. We just can't have any more trouble right now. No more beatings, Jesse, that's final. The cops are still working on the Vasquez thing, and I don't want 'em nosing around here.''

"You think this guy might be a cop?''

"A cop? No, of course not, but get rid of him anyway if he's trouble. And the Vasquez kid, too. Don't hurt 'em, just pay 'em off and put 'em on the road. Tell 'em there's plenty of work in the groves up around Mesa.''

"You don't think he might be a ringer, do you, Dutch?''

"A what?''

"A ringer—somebody the social workers or unions send in just to see what's going on. I've heard of it.''

"Christ, Jesse, I don't know. But what can they do if you just fire him? Send him away?''

"Maybe he ought to join the others, Dutch—in the grove this time, him and the kid—deep in the grove.''

"Goddammit, no! I told you, no more of that!''

"Okay, okay, I hear you. I'll take care of it.'' He hung up the phone and stood there a moment, thinking. If the guy was a ringer—or a fucking cop . . .

He opened the office door and looked out. The bags were loaded on the truck but the wet was nowhere to be seen. Then he saw him, squatting down by the water spigot at the corner of the building, drinking. Jesse stared at him a moment longer, still wondering. Then he shouted, "Let's *vamos, cabrón*. Into the truck!'' And he watched him slap on his hat and hurry obediently across the yard to climb into the back.

Driving directly to the front gate of the ranch, Jesse stopped the truck. He'd decided to get rid of this one now. He could get one of the others to unload the fertilizer. "Out!'' he yelled back at his passenger, and watched him in the side mirror as he climbed from the truck bed and stood there, looking puzzled and wary.

"You're fired," Jesse said, "take off."

"What's wrong, *patrón*? What did I do?"

"I can't use you—you're too soft. Try up around Mesa. Maybe they'll hire you—or Yuma. They've got a lot of citrus picking over around Yuma."

"But what about my pay, *patrón*? I want to see the Señor Masters."

Jesse Peralta's eyes narrowed dangerously. "You want to see the *chinga* Migra, *cabrón*? Or more of this?" He held up his big balled fist.

Gomez stepped back a pace, trying to look suitably chastised and fearful, which he found wasn't too difficult. "No, *patrón*."

"I didn't think so," Jesse growled, and putting his truck in gear he drove off. He would find the Vasquez kid now and get rid of him too, one way or the other. And having made his decisions, he felt a sudden surge of animal well-being. He was still in control of things; still king-of-the-hill.

Gomez, watching him drive away, wondered if the sonofabitch had suspected he was a fake. It was getting late in the day. He was hungry and tired but still excited with his find. And then he thought about the long walk to a phone booth to call Roberts. He knew that was what he should do first—report in. He had seen some of the evidence, he was sure of it, there in that shop—the grease, the fertilizer, probably the weapon. He was also certain Jesse Peralta was their man. But had he seen enough?

And since he couldn't do everything, he decided to forget the call. That was out. The question simply was whether to get Arturo out of there now and go with what they had, or try to find the rest of the evidence—evidence that would tie Jesse directly to the killing; evidence he was sure he could find if he had a few minutes in that upstairs apartment.

Torn two ways, he groaned aloud in frustration as he considered Arturo's safety against the evidence to stop a killer. The kid was responsible, mature, resourceful, and he wasn't in immediate danger—no one knew that he knew about any of it. But the evidence could disappear or be destroyed at any time. So Gomez made his decision, however reluctantly.

Turning, he ran back down the drive toward the groves, heading again for the maintenance yard. He tried not to think about what might happen if he were caught.

THIRTY-THREE

AFTER leaving Gomez, Jesse Peralta dropped the pickup off with Paco to be unloaded. Since he had exchanged it for the old stake-side with dual rear wheels, he decided to take a shortcut through a sandy, little-used trace that led up onto the mesa road and the kennels.

The maintenance yard was closer, and he had thought about just going to the shop and calling first to be sure the kid was still there. But Jack might answer and he didn't want to argue about it on the phone. He'd just go directly to the kennels, the most likely place, and then maybe the main ranch house. The kid had to be someplace.

But a hundred yards down the rutted, weed-grown trace through the groves the left front tire on the truck blew out. Cursing, Jesse stopped the lurching vehicle, dragged the jack and lug wrench from behind the seat, and set to work. It was after five now, and though the last storm had passed on by, the sky was still overcast and black, like his mood. He pulled off the flat and heaved it into the back, then got the spare out from underneath the bed.

Finished, he was lowering the jack when he found himself staring at two faint depressions in the ground between the rows of trees. He realized where he was. It was where he had buried the two wetbacks he had killed before Vasquez—where he should have buried Vasquez, too, instead of listening to Dutch. He wouldn't have had to kill Lupita Morales then.

But it was done now, and since there would probably be more, there was no sense in brooding over that mistake. Tossing the jack and wrench back in the cab, he paused again and looked around. Nothing appeared disturbed here. They lay deep beneath the sandy loam. Not even Dutch knew where the bodies were buried. And he had got away clean after killing Lupita. So there was really only this damn Enrique Vasquez business to worry about—and the boy.

Climbing back in the truck, he started it up and headed on along the trace toward the mesa road. Even if the sonofabitch he had fired *was* a cop, he reasoned, he sure hadn't found anything incriminating. What was there to find except the bodies? And what could connect him to either the Vasquez death or Lupita's? There had been no witnesses to either. There was only the boy that afternoon before he killed her. When he had waited in his pickup parked across from the bar, Arturo Vasquez had been in Jack's truck when it went by. Jack hadn't noticed him, but the boy's eyes had locked on his own in recognition.

Well, Jesse thought sourly, it would just be another disappearance. And this time, Dutch wouldn't have to know.

In the small stone building on the mesa, Arturo was packing his few belongings into his striped fiber bolsa. He had folded away half a dozen tortillas which he had cooked, and then dampered the stove. He had fed and watered the dogs one last time too, and found he really regretted leaving. He liked working for the Señor Masters, but the fact and manner of his uncle's death had shaken him.

And the worse part was that the murderer was probably still here, somewhere on this place. He had no doubt that what the detective had told him was true. He did not trust the police in his own country—no one did—and he was afraid of the Migra. But this Garcia or Gomez had been kind, and he had no reason to lie.

Arturo also regretted leaving because he needed the work. But with Enrique's death he was needed at home. And to make his decision even harder, he was remembering the girl, Juana, who worked for the old *patrón*. She was practically a prisoner here. He could not leave this place without at least offering to take her and her child with him.

He glanced around the gloomy room to make sure he had everything that was his. He decided he would go to the main house first and talk to Juana. Then, with or without her, he would take the back road that led through the maintenance yard to the canal. The canal would lead eventually to a road, and he could decide then what to do. Maybe the girl could even help him decide. She was older, and she had been here longer.

The dogs barked and leaped against their chains, frantically wagging their tails as he left. He followed a path that took him past the old water tower. Ten minutes later it had led him to the outbuildings behind the ranch owner's sprawling brick home. He was wondering where in that huge structure he might find the girl, or at least get her attention without being seen, when he saw her come out of a side door carrying a basket of clothes.

The rainstorm had blown on through, but the sky was still filled with scudding clouds, and lightning flickered menacingly all along the horizon. There was a low rumble of distant thunder as he watched her carry the clothes under the clothesline and into a big garage. Running across the yard to the side of the building, he peered in through a dusty window in time to see her set the clothes down and begin to string a clothesline from the rafters.

He tapped lightly on the window. She looked up, startled. He waved and then came around the corner to the door and stepped inside.

She looked frightened. "What is it? What are you doing here?" Nervously, she kept on working.

"I'm leaving," Arturo explained, holding his bulging bolsa tightly in front of him. "I found out my uncle is dead. Someone killed him—here, on this place. I thought you might want to leave too, you and your baby." He didn't tell her that the man who told him was an undercover policeman; he didn't want to frighten her any worse. But he thought she should leave too, and he told her so. "I will take you wherever you want to go, Juana. We might even find work someplace together, but I couldn't stay long. Without me or my uncle, my family has no man to care for them while my father is sick.''

She stared at him, a clothespin in her mouth and a damp shirt hanging from her hand. Her expression was hesitant, confused. He sensed that she was deeply afraid of the old *patrón*. ''I don't know, Arturo,'' she whispered, as if afraid even of being overheard. ''I want to leave, too—'' She kept glancing toward the door like she expected someone might come in on them at any moment. ''The old *pendejo* is inside, talking to his son, so maybe we *could* get away.''

Arturo drew himself up a little taller. ''Don't be afraid, Juana. I will protect you.''

She smiled, still hesitant. He was only a boy, but he was determined. Impulsively, she decided to chance it. ''All right,'' she said, tossing the shirt back in the basket along with the clothespin, ''I'll go with you. I just need to get the baby and a box of my things.''

She got as far as the door and stopped, drawing back inside. Arturo ran to the window and looked out. A truck had pulled into the yard outside, and a man was getting out. ''Don't worry,'' Arturo whispered, ''it's not your old *pendejo*. It's only the *mayordomo*—Jesse.''

THIRTY-FOUR

"WAIT here," Arturo told her softly. "I'll go see what he wants." But before he could reach the door, he heard other voices outside. He withdrew quickly back to the window as Dutch Masters himself came out from between the washhouse and the garage, with his son Jack beside him.

"Now what's all this shit you're giving me about Jesse?" Old Dutch was carrying a cigar in one hand and a glass of whisky in the other.

"He's here now," Jack Masters said, pointing at the stakeside truck as the foreman turned away from the garage and walked toward them. "And I still say he's got to go. He's trying to take over this place—giving *me* orders now!"

"Somebody's got to take over," Dutch said sarcastically. "You're sure as hell never around. But what's he doing here now? He's supposed to be out with the crew."

"I'm telling you, Pop, if you're smart you'll fire him—now."

Dutch took a sip of his whisky and stared arrogantly at his son, then deliberately raised his voice to be sure Jesse would hear. "You want me to fire the best goddamned foreman I ever had? Why can't you just get along with him?"

Jesse walked up to them and stopped, scowling at Jack. "Who's out there now with your fucking dogs? That Vasquez kid sure as hell ain't—where is he?"

"What do you want with him?" Jack shot back defiantly. "You already took the other one."

"I need him, too," Jesse answered. "I want him." He ignored Jack's furious glare and turned to the old man as if he had explained enough. "It's time the kid joined the others, Dutch," he added meaningfully.

Jack Masters looked at his father. "What's he talking about?"

Dutch waved him off with his cigar, his own suddenly angry gaze turned on his foreman. "You crazy bastard—shut up. I told you just to fire 'em—put 'em on the road. Vasquez is only a kid. What does he know?"

"It won't work, Dutch," Jesse insisted. "I sent the other one away, but the kid's got to join the others in the groves."

"The fucking hell he does!" Dutch suddenly exploded, hurling his whisky glass and shattering it against the side of the garage. "I'm still the boss around here, goddammit, Jesse! *I* still say what goes on!"

Still standing by the window of the garage, Arturo had heard enough. He grabbed Juana's hand and they fled together out the back door of the garage. Circling around to the other side of the main house, he boosted her through an unlocked window and waited while she got the baby and her box.

The time he waited was only minutes but it seemed interminable. He felt suddenly like a hunted animal, and it was all he could do to keep from running away without her. But she came back at last and handed him the baby and then her box. "Where are we going?" she whispered as she climbed out and took back the child, tucking a pacifier into its mouth.

"To the canal," Arturo answered, hefting the box to his shoulder and picking up his own bolsa as he led her into the citrus grove. "Then we'll follow it till we come to a road."

"But the canal is so far!" she protested.

"Not this way. We're taking a shortcut through the maintenance yard; the canal is just beyond it."

*   *   *

Back at the garage, Dutch Masters was still arguing with his foreman, and he was beginning to see what Jack meant. Maybe his son was right—Jesse was getting out of hand. "Forget about the goddamned kid," he ordered finally. "Leave him alone. Go pack your own gear, Jesse—you're the one who's leaving. I've had enough of your shit!"

Jesse Peralta wasn't sure he'd heard it straight. His hard gray eyes fixed on Dutch Masters', his fists still at his side but beginning to clench and unclench with nervous tension.

Jack and Dutch moved instinctively together, side by side; father and son suddenly closing ranks.

"You can't fire me," Jesse warned them evenly, his voice so low and full of venom they could barely hear him. "Not now, at the beginning of harvest—"

"Pack up and clear out of that apartment, Jesse," Dutch said. "Now. Paco can take over the harvest—and Jack." He turned on his son. "You want him out, goddammit, Jack, you take his place! That's the way it's gonna be!" He looked back at Jesse. "I'll follow you down to the office and write you a check for wages. I'll even give you a bonus. But you're through here, Jesse. You're too damn much of a risk anymore."

Together they watched the big foreman turn and stride angrily back to his truck. Dutch thought for a moment he was going to reach for some kind of weapon under the seat, but he only climbed inside and ground the gears as he drove away.

"I'll be back later, when he's paid off," the old man said, and started for the garage to get his own truck.

"I'd better go with you," Jack offered.

Dutch shook his head. "No, you stay here—he'll cool down. I'll take my rifle to make sure."

"Okay," Jack muttered softly, letting out a long slow breath, "but that half-breed sonofabitch is dangerous."

Virgil "Dutch" Masters grunted, grinding out the stub of his cigar against the frame of the garage door. "You don't know the fucking half of it," he said.

THIRTY-FIVE

MINUTES before, Gomez had arrived back at the maintenance yard and shop, his lungs heaving until he was forced to
slow down by a painful stitch in his side. It was still daylight.
There was plenty of time to search Jesse's apartment before
the work was over for the day, and then find Arturo.

Pausing at the edge of the trees surrounding the silent yard,
he looked for some sign of Jesse or Dutch Masters. All the
trucks were gone, but to make sure he ran over to the office
window and peered inside. The place was empty. Circling
behind the tractor shed, he rounded the corner and came up to
the stairs leading to the apartment.

Sure now that the evidence in the shed fixed the site of
Enrique's death, he had only to tie Jesse himself to the scene
and to the victim—maybe to both victims. And that evidence,
if it existed, had to be upstairs. Roberts had said no killer
ever left the scene without leaving something of himself
behind and taking something of his crime with him. They had
dog hairs and human hairs and hair cream and cloth fibers,
but without something to match them against, they had zip.

Gomez mounted the stairs two at a time. It was only
seconds before he had picked the cheap door lock with his
penknife and he was inside, closing the door behind him. The
apartment, tightly closed and with the window air conditioner
off, was stifling and filled with a miasma of stale odors.
Nothing moved except a fly, caught in a web and buzzing

angrily against a window as the detective tried to take it all in at a glance and relate everything to its occupant. From the unmade single bed by the window, to the open closet door and dining table cluttered with miscellaneous junk that left no room for eating.

In the kitchen alcove the sink was piled with unwashed dishes. Everything was in careless disarray, as if Jesse Peralta never really lived here; he just existed physically, like an animal in its den. In fact the whole place had about it the feel of its occupant—a smallness, a meanness that reflected a shambles of a life; an inherent brutality and petty distaste for anything clean and orderly. There was a lot of hate and bitterness in the room, and he really didn't know where to start to hunt systematically for specific evidence of murder. But time was pressing him—the light was already getting bad. So he started working from left to right, eyeballing mainly personal items and clothing.

Ten minutes later he had spotted most of it—a khaki shirt with a scattering of faint brown spots that could be blood-stains in a box of dirty laundry, a hairbrush on the cluttered dresser with strands of long dark hair tangled in the bristles, and beside it a half-squeezed-out tube of Brylcreem. Christ, he thought, could we be that lucky?

Moving to the open closet, he pushed the hanging clothes aside and looked in the back, under the shoes, on the over-head rack. Nothing. He checked hurriedly through the kitchen cupboards, and then glanced quickly into the tiny filthy bathroom.

Maybe he'd found enough. He glanced anxiously around, his skin prickling with the heat and tension. It would all have to be sampled and marked later, when Roberts got on the place with the goddamned warrant. Right now he still had to find Arturo.

He was passing the dining table on his way out when he saw the crumpled sheet of paper that had missed the over-flowing garbage pail under the sink. Curious as to what Jesse might be throwing away, he picked it up and smoothed it out on the sink, squinting in the fading sunlight that shone through the kitchen window.

It was a page torn from a ledger. At the top was the name Enrique Vasquez, and below it three columns of dates and figures. Gomez noticed the last column had totaled out at 42, and something clicked. The date at the top of the last column was two days before he was killed, and the number 42 was the same total as on the cash-register receipt they'd found on his body. Only Gomez realized now it wasn't a cash receipt. It was an adding-machine tape, and if it could be matched to the machine he had just seen through the office window downstairs, and the handwriting in the ledger was Jesse's . . .

He had seen enough. Crumpling the ledger page, he placed it carefully back on the floor beside the garbage pail. He was starting for the door again when he paused to glance under the rumpled bed and found something completely unexpected—a handgun.

Lying in its open box along with the cleaning gear and a box of shells, it was a man-stopper—a .357 Mag. Gomez crouched there, stunned by his find, staring at the weapon nested amid its cleaning paraphernalia as sudden doubts held him immobile.

Suddenly everything they had seemed circumstantial. Their killer hadn't used a gun. He was a man who used his hands, who beat his victims or strangled them. Yet Jesse Peralta owned a Magnum, and kept it loaded—he could see the lead tips of the bullets in their chambers.

He was still considering what it all might mean when he heard the squeal of brakes in the yard outside. Running to the window, he could see the back corner of a truck that had just stopped—Jesse's stake-side. But what was worse, Arturo Vasquez had just emerged from the trees across the yard at the edge of the grove. He had someone with him—a girl with a baby in her arms!

Then he froze as he heard the truck door slam and footsteps pounding up the stairs.

THIRTY-SIX

THE sun had just slipped beneath the clouds on the horizon, but there was still plenty of daylight as Larry Preston, in his pale green carryall with its round blue Border Patrol logo on the door and a reinforced front end, crashed through the padlocked chain and wire mesh of the gate to the Masters place. He was followed closely by Doug Roberts in a county car.

Behind them was a van full of Border Patrolmen, and behind it a Department of Public Safety station wagon carrying DPS agents and dragging a trailer full of metal cages.

As the vehicles all braked amid swirling dust and the raucous, discordant barking of the dogs, a Piper Cub banked low overhead and then flew straight across the treetops wagging its wings. A Border Patrolman with a walkie-talkie to his ear nodded toward Preston and called, "Contact—loud and clear!"

Dell Warren, the Public Safety sergeant, ran over to where Roberts had joined Preston beside his carryall. "Looks like the dogs are all we're going to find around here, gents," he said. "There's no one at home over there in that travel trailer, no one around at all."

"Spread out and search all the buildings!" Preston shouted to his agents, then turned to the one with the walkie-talkie. "Any movement sighted by the plane?"

"Negative. Any wets probably took shelter from that storm,

or they're back in the groves but hiding in the trees. He can't spot any camps, but he's going to keep circling. He says there looks like a little-used road behind that old water tower leads to the main house.''

Roberts was unrolling the aerial photo and spreading it out on the hood of the carryall. They studied it a moment as Preston said, ''Obviously nobody's here, Sergeant. No vehicles around, no Jack Masters and no Arturo Vasquez.''

''But the dogs' water dishes are full,'' Roberts answered, rerolling the photo. He walked over to the nearest building, stepped through the open doorway, and checked inside.

Preston joined him a moment later. ''A wet's been living here,'' he said, ''I can still smell him.''

''Yeah, the cookstove's still warm,'' Roberts said, deftly touching the metal and feeling a keen sense of alarm. The mattress on the bunk had been rolled up, and no personal belongings were about. He looked at the Border Patrolman. ''Gomez said Arturo was here with the dogs.''

''Well, he must have just left,'' Preston answered, ''and we'd better go, too. Let's find somebody to serve these warrants on while Warren's people are rounding up the mutts, and then let's find Gomez and the kid. How about heading for the maintenance yard?''

Roberts thought a moment, then shook his head. ''Let's try that back road to the main house first. It's closer.''

After watching Dutch leave, following Jesse, Jack Masters had started back to the house to get his own gun. The more he thought about letting old Dutch go down to the maintenance yard alone, the more—he turned at the sound of an approaching vehicle, thinking for an instant that either his father or Jesse had returned. Instead he saw a green Immigration carryall careening into the yard, with an unmarked sedan following close behind it.

Cursing and full of righteous indignation at their trespassing on private land, he turned to face the uniformed Border Patrolman who got out of the carryall and the heavier man in plainclothes who had emerged from the car. Both were walking swiftly toward him. "You Jack Masters?" the border agent asked.

"You're goddamned right I'm Masters, and—"

Larry Preston handed him two warrants, one at a time. "This one's to search for illegal aliens, Mr. Masters, and this one's for keeping fighting dogs. DPS officers are rounding up the animals now, and my agents are hunting for your alien camps."

"And this one's a little more serious," Doug Roberts said, stepping up beside Preston. "It's a murder warrant for the death of one Enrique Vasquez. You're under arrest." And he read him his rights.

would think of a storage hide inside small apartment the door had been 'open' and Jesse. People stood on the threshold...

THIRTY-SEVEN

DUTCH MASTERS, with his deer rifle mounted on the rack behind his head, hunched over the wheel as he neared the maintenance yard. He was so close behind Jesse that the dust raised by the stake-side was still settling in the ruts.

He had driven off after his foreman with a lot of reluctance and not a little foreboding, knowing the whole damn thing should never have gone this far. Now, he had to be sure that Jesse got clear of the place, for good.

He pulled up in the yard beside Jesse's truck, which was parked at the foot of the stairs, got out, and was immediately aware of the violent sounds of destruction coming from the apartment above. "What the fuck—" he muttered, grabbing his rifle and starting up the stairs.

Huffing and puffing by the time he reached the landing, he had just touched the doorknob when the door itself splintered with a roaring sound. Something hit him a solid blow just under the heart, hurling his heavy body backward against the railing, which shattered, too.

When Gomez heard the truck stop in the yard outside, and saw Jesse there and the two kids standing at the edge of the trees, he knew it was too late to run.

With the footsteps pounding on the outside stairs, the only other possible exits were the two closed windows, the nearest one partially blocked by the air-conditioning unit. Before he could think of a place to hide in the small apartment the door had burst open and Jesse Peralta stood on the threshold, staring at him with openmouthed anger and surprise.

For an instant Gomez thought of going for the gun in its box beneath the bed, knowing this moment of shocked incomprehension was all the advantage he was going to have. But the gun was reversed in its box and half covered with the cleaning rag, and he knew instinctively he'd never make it. Instead, he grabbed the rumpled blanket from the bed with both hands, and turning, hurled it into Jesse's face as the foreman roared, "You gut-eating spic bastard! I'll kill you, too!"

Rushing past him to the door while Jesse was still caught in the entangling folds of the blanket, the detective had it open and one hand already on the door frame when Jesse, still howling his rage, got his own hands and face clear and caught him by his shirttail, hurling him back inside the apartment and slamming the door.

"*Ladrón!*" he hissed. "Thief! *Chingado mojado cabrón!*" He rushed the detective with both massive hands balled into fists.

Gomez ducked the first wild swing and kicked the foreman in the shin to slow him down. He tried to knee him in the balls but missed, and caught a glancing blow alongside his head that momentarily dazed him. The bastard was a maniac. He had called him a thieving wetback, and the thought flashed through the detective's mind that it couldn't be worse to tell him the truth, that he was a cop. Just then a third blow caught him squarely in the belly and doubled him up.

His knees buckled and he saw stars. He thought he would never suck in another breath and wondered if he would suffocate before he was beaten to death like Vasquez as he rolled onto the floor and beneath the bed.

As the room came into focus again and he found he could breathe, he could see the gun nested cozily in its box right under his nose. Jesse was dragging on his legs, grunting and cursing. In desperation Gomez grabbed for the revolver with both hands, then threw his shoulders against the underside of the bedsprings, kicked free, and rose violently, surging upright and tumbling the bed against the wall.

But Jesse was quick, too. He kicked the detective's legs from under him so that he crashed down again, and the Magnum was jarred loose as he hit the floor. He was barely able to roll out of the way as the other boot aimed a blow at his head. Scrambling to his feet, he made once again for the door, with the maddening knowledge that Jesse must by now have the gun. He grabbed the knob and pulled just as the gun's explosion filled the room with sound and cordite.

The heavy-caliber slug shattered the inch-thick panel of the door just above his shoulder. Then he had it open and was lunging through, expecting the roar again and the hammer blow against his back as he dove onto the landing and tumbled down the stairway. He was barely aware that someone else had just gone through the railing and hit the ground below with a thud.

Landing jarringly at the foot of the stairs himself, Gomez caught one leg in the rail and heard the snap of a bone. It flashed through his mind that after all this he at least deserved a clean break and not a compound fracture. Then the pain hit, and the blast of the Magnum sounded again, splintering the rail beside his head, and he knew only that he did not want to die. But when he tried to drag himself around the corner of the maintenance shed out of Jesse's sight, the pain shot clear up to his hip and he almost blacked out. His leg was still caught in the damn rail and he couldn't move.

Then he saw a worse horror—Arturo and the girl with the baby were still there. No longer at the edge of the trees, they had moved up to crouch beside a stack of wooden pallets, squarely in the line of Jesse's fire. They seemed petrified with fear. Gomez tried to shout a warning just as a car roared into the yard and braked in a cloud of dust. He knew a heartfelt surge of relief as he recognized Doug Roberts behind the wheel with Jack Masters on the seat beside him.

But as the detective-sergeant stepped out of the driver's side, Jack emerged from the other—wearing handcuffs. Gomez's relief turned to savage torment. He cried out hoarsely as he heard again the heavy bark of the Magnum above him. "Shit, man—it's not Jack! It's Jesse! And he's got a fucking cannon!"

but Jesse was quicker. The .357 Magnum blasted him from under him, so that he twisted down again, and the Magnum was jarred loose as he hit the floor. He was bent over, the ...

THIRTY-EIGHT

DOUG ROBERTS realized his mistake as he drove into the yard. He had the wrong man. And the knowledge hit him like one of Jesse's slugs, the third one now slamming through the radiator and into the engine block of the county car as the foreman shifted his aim to this new menace. God, Roberts thought, why hadn't he seen it! Now it was all happening so fast; yet at the same time everything seemed to be moving in slow motion.

A part of him was aware of Dutch's body lying prone and unmoving on the ground below the stairs, and of Jack Masters stumbling at a crouch across the yard toward it, handcuffs and all. But mainly he saw Jesse Peralta on the top landing with the big revolver in his hand—all this in the instant it took him to draw his own snub-nosed .38 from its belted holster and kneel behind the front fender of the car. It would provide scant protection from the heavy caliber Jesse was using, but at least it obstructed his view.

And then Roberts saw that Gomez wasn't moving away. Crumpled unarmed and apparently helpless at the foot of the stairs, he was right in the line of Jesse's sight. And to complicate matters, a blur in his peripheral vision became the boy, Arturo, as he left the shelter of a stack of wooden pallets and ran across the yard intent on helping Gomez, who was frantically waving him back, while up on the landing Jesse was bringing his gun to bear on them both.

Roberts acted on instinct. "Peralta!" he yelled, leaping out into the open to distract him. He crouched with his own revolver leveled and braced at the wrist with his left hand. "Police! Drop the gun—now!" Fear and tension constricted his breathing as it always did when he had to use his weapon. At the sound and sight of the detective crouching now in full view, Jesse shifted his aim and fired again. Roberts dropped to one knee and felt the slug literally part his hair and heard it smash into a stack of wooden bins behind him. He squeezed off his own shot, then thumbed back the hammer and squeezed off another, knowing it was over.

His first shot took Jesse in the throat and the second hit him full in the chest. The gun tumbled from Jesse's hand, and his body came crashing down the stairs to land heavily in the dust beside Gomez and the boy.

With the noise of the shots still ringing in his ears, Roberts knew only the thin coppery taste of fear, and regret, and immense relief. They were safe. They were all safe, he thought sadly, until next time. . . .

EPILOGUE

INOCENCIO Gomez lay in a bright and sterile hospital ward, with his leg in a cast and strung up in traction. Besides a compound fracture, he had numerous bruises, cuts, and abrasions, and a magnificent black eye, all of which unaccountably failed to distract from his flashing smile. "Well, man, that was a fine mess I got us into. You gonna kick my tail back to Robbery?"

Doug Roberts handed him a box of his favorite slim, dark cigarillos. "Smoke 'em in good health, Rabbit. At least you were after the right guy." He glanced at Patricia Lane, who was sitting in the chair beside the bed. "I was so jealous of Jack Masters, I went after him like a blind dog in a slaughterhouse."

Patricia reached out and took his hand. "I'm sorry," she said. "That was my fault."

"No, I broke the first rule of police work—I let emotions get in the way of facts. I'm lucky he isn't suing me for false arrest."

"What about the evidence, man, did it match up?"

Roberts nodded, smiling. "Enough—and with both victims. The chain *was* the weapon with Enrique Vasquez. And Jesse's khaki shirt, the dirty one—the spots were human blood, all right, same type as Enrique, not the same as Jesse's. Bloodstains on the chain weren't enough to type, but bits of rust matched those imbedded in Enrique's face. And the hairs and hair cream on both victims matched with Jesse's. He must have killed Lupita Morales simply because she had talked to us—afraid she'd told us something or would tell us something.''

"Yeah, and I heard the old man died."

"Dead before the ambulance got there. He lived long enough to tell about some other wetbacks Jesse had killed and buried in the groves. He didn't say where or how many. Maybe he didn't know. But we'll find 'em—hopefully without digging up the whole place. The ground should be depressed over any old graves."

Gomez shook his head. "Christ, man, if he hadn't made the mistake of dumping this last one in the canal, it could have gone on and on. But why? Why would he do it? We never did establish a motive."

"Sometimes there isn't one. Oh, there always is to the killer, I guess. He's always got a reason of some kind that at least makes sense to him."

"And what about Arturo and that little maid?" Gomez asked. "What'll happen to them?"

"Preston's got 'em in custody, along with fifteen or twenty others. They'll have to go back to Mexico."

"Shit, man, the country's crawling with wetbacks—there's millions of them—what's a couple more? Larry said himself the Border Patrol is just a token force. There's no real control until they start zapping employers for hiring them. Why doesn't he just let these two go?"

"So they can get in more of the same kind of trouble?" Roberts shook his head. "Immigration's in a bigger mess than Homicide. But the girl's baby was born here. She can get it a baptismal certificate. And with her baby a citizen it'll be easier for her to come back legally and have some protection. Arturo doesn't want to come back. He's had enough of the gringo North. We took up a collection—Jack Masters even kicked in the kid's wages and yours, and I added fifty bucks, so he won't go home empty-handed. And the Justice Department is sending Enrique's body home."

"So what happens now, man, with us?"

"With us? Hell, I don't know if there still *is* an 'us.' I've still got a shooting report to make out and all the red tape that goes with it. And the chief wants to see me about the report I already turned in, closing the Winters case as an accident. He also wasn't exactly ecstatic about my turning in a county car with a cracked block—it's not in the budget. So my day is just starting. You take it easy."

"Jesus, man—" Gomez grinned and gripped his outstretched hand. "I never did thank you—you saved my Chicano ass."

"Just Departmental policy, Gomez," Roberts said, smiling. "Partners look out for each other. See you."

"Fuck you, Roberts," Lt. Lang said.

"Whatever happened to congratulations, Chief?"

"For what—a blow job? For Christ's sake, it took you over a week to determine it was a fucking accident which you think was caused by"— he glanced back again at the report on his desk and quoted—" 'by the girl committing an act of fellatio on the driver, thereby causing him to lose control— '?" He glared at the detective through his shades.

"I guess I'm not very good at my job, Chief. Maybe I'm getting old, slowing down. I should have seen it right away."

"Shit, Roberts." Lt. Lang chewed neurotically on his cold cigar.

"Well, at least we got the wetback and barmaid killings all tidied up. And they're looking for the other bodies now."

"Shit, Roberts," Lang repeated, "a fucking Factor One— all of 'em! But that's what you were working on all along, wasn't it? You slick sonofabitch, you knew the banker thing was accidental. You figured that out right away. You withheld evidence in your fucking reports!"

"It was in the reports, Lieutenant. You just didn't read 'em close enough. Is that my fault?" Roberts was tired, but he felt he was at least holding his own.

"Shit, Roberts. You know what the captain's gonna say about all this? You know what he's gonna *do*?"

"I never claimed to walk on water, Chief. I too am human, imperfect, vulnerable—"

"Sarcastic and cynical—Jesus, Roberts, *I'm* the one that

gets burned in something like this. *I'm* the one has to put my balls in a vise and let Trudeau turn the goddamned crank.''

"But you do it so well, Chief,'' Roberts smiled bravely.

Lang's expression suddenly softened momentarily. He took off his shades and stared at his subordinate with an apparently honest yet uncharacteristic uncertainty as to just where the sarcasm ended and the man began. "You okay, Roberts?'' he asked seriously. "The shooting, I mean.''

"Yeah, sure. I'm okay, Chief. It was close, but I'm okay, honest. Thanks for asking.''

"Shit, they're all close the way you work, Roberts. You're gonna shave it a hair too close one day. Anyway, Peralta was worthless—you took out another of the world's slimeballs. You saved the state the cost of a trial. Look at it that way.''

"Right, Chief, he was just another Factor One. Can I go now, before we both break into tears? There's that shooting report—''

"Hell yes, you can go.'' He had put on his shades and returned to his old gruff and irritable self, a man Roberts felt a lot more comfortable with. "But the shooting report can wait. Here—'' He shoved a paper into the detective's hand. "We got an attempted homicide in the desert off Highway 19 last night. Victim is a local socialite—crawled out of a shallow grave and reported it herself. She's at Good Samaritan Hospital, and the doctor says she can' talk. See if you can check that out without getting your tail in a crack.''

"You're all heart, Chief,'' Doug Roberts said. "And what about Gomez? He's already pinching the nurses and throwing bedpans. Can I give him any good news?''

"You'll have to do without a partner again, Roberts—until Gomez mends. Then if you still want him, he's yours. But don't look for any commendations for either of you—you could still get a suspension.''

"Right, Chief,'' Roberts answered. "See you.'' He glanced at his watch as he went out the door. It was just like in the fairy tales—things were never quite as bad as they seemed. Why, if this interview at Good Sam just went off without a hitch, he might even catch the last half of the Steeler-Raider game on TV.